Pirate's Queen
Shades Of The Sea
Book 1

Riley West

Copyright © 2023 by Riley West

All rights reserved.

No part of this book may be reproduced in any form or by any electronic or mechanical means, including information storage and retrieval systems, without written permission from the author, except for the use of brief quotations in a book review.

Jacket Art: *Monna Vanna* by Dante Gabriel Rossetti, 1866, oil on canvas. Original artwork provided by Shelby Standage. Interior illustrations from depositphotos.com

❀ Created with Vellum

To everyone who has watched a ship under sail, and wondered. And to the Grey One, I think this is finally something you would have been at least amused about.

Contents

Introduction	vii
Chapter 1	1
Chapter 2	26
Chapter 3	51
Chapter 4	66
Chapter 5	84
Chapter 6	97
Chapter 7	116
Chapter 8	133
Chapter 9	159
Chapter 10	188
Chapter 11	213
Chapter 12	236
Chapter 13	246
Chapter 14	275
Chapter 15	290
Chapter 16	312
Chapter 17	336
Chapter 18	364
Epilogue	381
About the Author	383
Also by Riley West	385

Introduction

I have chosen to use the Atkinson Hyperlegible typeface as well as enhance readability by using a ragged-right alignment as well as spacing instead of indentation to delineate paragraphs. This was done with thought and purpose as a Dyslexic and Autistic person. The hope is that it makes the book a more enjoyable read. Thank you to Vellum for providing the option

1

LUCIA

Lucia huffed in irritation as the comely woman beneath her moaned again, the noise echoing against the tiled ceiling of the royal bedchamber. She was used to sycophants and their flattery, but the girl's yowling was a bit much. Lucia's skills might be legendary, but that was when she cared. At the moment, all she felt was boredom as she rolled off.

"Oh, for God's sake," Lucia scolded. "Enough. I can barely hear myself think about how bored I am."

The scullery maid, or at least Lucia thought that's where the girl had come from, looked up at her in terror. Lucia rolled her eyes.

"Just go. Now." Her voice was tired as she spoke —jaded.

In a brutal moment of self-introspection, Lucia realized that was exactly what she was—jaded. At the ripe old age of twenty-eight, it felt as though she'd seen and done everything and everyone. There were perks to being queen, but there was also a crushing banality she could not escape.

The girl did as she was told, dressing quickly and scurrying from the room, while Lucia tied a silk robe around her shapely form, aware that it accentuated her oft-remarked upon hourglass figure. Sighing, she pulled the length of her thick silver-blonde hair from the robe's collar and lamented upon the state of her existence as she poured a glass of wine. The statecraft necessary to rule her kingdom left her very little time to indulge in her true pleasures, and lately, her bouts of ennui were becoming more frequent.

There was a knock on her door. It was late. *Only important business then.*

"Enter," she called, unsurprised to see her chief advisor, Lord Valeri, shuffle in. He was bent with old age, and barely a wisp of white hair clung to his speckled head, but his mind had remained sharp as ever. Lucia was grateful for his council, most of the time.

"Your Majesty." He bowed deeply before her, unfazed by her state of undress. It was hardly the first time they'd conversed in such a way. Lucia wasn't known for her modesty, nor did she enjoy the same level of privacy afforded to her subjects.

Lucia drank deeply from the glass in her hand before turning her attention to the man in front of her. "Grave news to bring you to my bedchamber at this hour, Valeri," she said, her tone serious as she accepted the unsealed letter from his trembling hand.

"Your Majesty, word has come from Vetreon. Your cousin has ascended to the throne. He sends his love, along with a proposal of marriage."

Lucia's heart stopped for a moment. She knew this day would come eventually, but she had hoped to avoid it somehow. Her refusal would mean war. Acceptance would be the death of her. There were no good choices.

Lucia had risen to greet Valeri, but sank back into her chair, groaning. It was an expected marriage—a match her father made the day her younger cousin's birth was announced. Upon his eighteenth birthday, Ramir, she was sure at the insistence of her uncle, sent her a dozen jeweled eggs and a poem professing his love. Being a queen in her own right had given her the leeway to put the prince off for a time. Yet, with his newly anointed crown, the young king meant to claim what he thought was his.

Moranth and Vetreon will be united as they once were, he wrote.

Lucia understood her duty where the line of succession was concerned. It was imperative for her to have an heir. Upon her father's death and her subsequent crowning, Lucia knew she would never marry a man. She would never bear children. For years it had been presumed that her younger cousin, Sebastian, would be her heir, but Lucia had yet to make it official. Naming the boy would have been a dangerous signal to Vetreon that she had no intention of marrying Ramir.

Not once had she desired a man's company in her bed—even if she had, Ramir would not be her choice. He was known to be abusive toward women, and men, for that matter. There were even rumors one of his mistresses was found drowned in a canal. Choosing marriage to Ramir would be to sign her own death warrant.

War or marriage. The messenger must surely be awaiting my answer.

She saw worry and fear in Valeri's eyes. The old man was as close to a father as she had in the world, but it could not be his decision. It must be hers alone.

"Myself or my people?" she spoke softly.

"Your Majesty," Valeri's eyes were fixed on a spot just before her feet, "if only it were that simple, I've no doubt of your answer."

Lucia's eyes brimmed with tears as they locked with his. Valeri had never looked at her with fear. She'd never once felt she scared him, as she did so many others. Lucia was grateful for that. She hoped that when he looked at her, he saw Lucia, not the tyrant her father had been.

"Even if I sacrifice myself in marriage, we both know what Ramir is. Moranth will tear itself apart if forced beneath such a ruler again."

Smiling, Valeri straightened. "It's to be war, then?"

Breathing deeply, Lucia shut her eyes for a moment before answering. "War."

"Very well. I'll let the messenger know. Will it be a simple no, or shall I grab my pen and paper?"

Lucia chuckled. "Why do I feel as though you've been looking forward to this moment?"

"Your Majesty, if you'll allow me?" he asked. She nodded. "You are quite aware of my feelings toward your late father and that those feelings extended to your uncle, the late king of Vetreon." A smirk pulled at a corner of her full lips. "And," Lord Valeri went on, eyes narrowing, indignation tensing his body, "I've no love lost for that pompous little snot who now thinks he can threaten you!"

The old man's words brought a broad grin to her face.

"We'll have to call the council tomorrow," she said, shaking her head in exhaustion, knowing she wouldn't get any sleep. "Little snot or no, Ramir is now king, and he means to take my land."

The weight of her position settled around her as she sunk further into her chair. The wheels of her mind were already turning, trying to find a solution that would keep her kingdom intact. Keep her people safe. She noted her counselor's eyes softened as they met again. She guessed he did not envy the decisions set before her. Though her lords and ladies would meet in the morning, the final decision rested with their queen.

Valeri's hand landed on her shoulder. Lucia realized with a start that his touch was the only non-sexual contact she'd had with another human in months. Not since Sebastian hugged her goodbye as he left for a much-needed adventure outside the city. A court was no place for a still half-wild fourteen-year-old, as she well remembered. Lucia missed the lad terribly, and without his gregarious enthusiasm, her palace was far too quiet. He was the only family she had worth having, becoming a mother to him when his own was killed.

Resting her hand atop Valeri's in thanks, she gave it a pat. "Go, try to sleep. I need time to think. I know the messenger is waiting. Tell him to eat and rest. He will have his answer after our council has convened."

Valeri smiled down at her in what she imagined was a warm, fatherly look. Her own father had never gazed upon her so kindly. "You sleep too, Your Majesty. The next few days and weeks will tax us all. None more so than yourself."

"Will you see someone you trust is sent after Sebastian? His safety is of the utmost importance to me."

Valeri bowed. "Of course. Till the morning, Your Majesty."

"The morning, Valeri."

———

A dull ache had bloomed at the base of Lucia's skull. Catching a glimpse of herself in the mirror, she winced. It had been well past midnight before she managed a fitful sleep. Her skin felt too tight over her bones, her eyes were sunken hollows, and her body creaked with every movement as if it couldn't settle correctly. She had dressed in an elaborate red velvet gown, hoping the color would do something to hide her pallor and the dark circles under her eyes.

An old nightmare stalked her sleep and was much to blame for her appearance. Her mother's screams echoed through Lucia's memory. Last night, though, the dream had been different. She was no longer a child hiding in the shadows, but the queen. A man's hands were wrapped around her throat, and the black fringed eyes full of hate staring back at her were Ramir's.

The image stuck with her as the palace guards opened the doors to the council chamber. She took a shallow breath, willing the ghost of her mother to leave her in peace for the time being.

The council chamber was an ugly room. Like most of the palace, it was made of limestone with high, thin, arched windows, but where the rest of the palace's interior was made with a creamy color, the council room was grey. Even the shafts of mid-morning light filtering through the thick glass took on the muted quality of the room. It was not a place for frivolity.

"Your Majesty," Valeri greeted her.

He looked a decade older than he had the night before. *As do I, I'm sure.* For him, she could manage a tight smile.

She glanced about the room. "Where's Blanxart?"

"Here, Your Majesty," a man said, sweeping into the room. "Forgive me."

Lucia gave him a curt nod. That was all members of the council accounted for.

"Valeri," she began after all were settled into their seats; she remained standing at the head of the table, "will you relate the contents of my cousin's letter for my lords and ladies?"

The old man bobbed his head. "Without preamble, Ramir has begun his reign in full, as we all knew he must. And he has proposed a marriage between himself and our fair queen."

Blanxart cursed under his breath as people sighed and heads shook around the table.

"Its been a long time coming," Lucia said, stating the obvious. "Both his crowing and the proposal. I've not wished to discuss the topic before, given the instability within Vetreon."

"Would have been too easy if someone had killed the bastard for us," Blanxart interjected, immediately turning red.

Lucia smirked. "Now," she said, "we can no longer ignore Ramir. We must give him an answer."

Her back already ached at the thought of the coming hours spent in her carved chair as she took her seat and let her council speak.

Her eight lords and ladies began talking all at once as they sat around the long, dark table. It was an ancient thing, nearly as old as the castle's foundations, made of long, cracked planks that often left splinters in council members' hands.

Her father had done away with the traditional council when he became king, but Lucia had reinstated the tradition upon taking the throne. There were a few amongst them she genuinely liked, but she respected them all. The men and women before her had been appointed not for their titles but for their good sense, of which she was in need.

Valeri was on her right. Lord Blanxart, who would lead her army should a land war come, at her left. Blanxart, unlike the others at the table, in their fine court silks, was dressed for a hunt. A leather jacket opened to show his linen shirt and high leather boots, the look topped by his mop of sandy-colored hair. He cut a rakish figure and always caused a stir among the court ladies when he was in residence. Lady Esnault was further down the table. Silver hair swept back from her sharp-jawed, aristocratic face, intelligent brown eyes cast downward as she listened, ear cocked while Valeri spoke of the dangers of not standing up to Vetreon and their new king. She was nodding in agreement, but Lucia knew of the Esnault family connection to Vetreon.

Lucia's eyes scanned her council, fixing on her friend Lord Royce Aldana. If anyone were able to get the room to come to a consensus, it would be Royce. It wasn't that any of them truly thought she should marry Ramir, but it was how to avoid a war that was causing turmoil among them.

After nearly two hours of heated discussion, the group was still no closer to a decision than they had been at the start, and Lucia finally had enough.

"My lords, my ladies, simply put, Vetreon has a finer navy than Moranth." Lucia's voice echoed in the chamber, silencing the squabbling nobles. "Yes, if we could coax them into a land battle, then perhaps we would have the upper hand," Blanxart nodded in agreement, "but that is a hope, an unlikely one at that."

Slamming her hand on the table, Lucia stood. "Ramir is young, but he's no fool. He knows the power of his navy. He knows my father neglected ours after banishing most of his captains and officers. Although we've made improvements, we have a long way to go." She shook her head in resignation. "No, I don't see a way out of this without war, nor have I heard anything to the contrary from you today," she finished, taking her seat.

"Your Majesty, if I may?" It was Lord Blanxart. He was one of the men present who Lucia both liked and admired. Like most of the council, he was plainspoken, and she knew he would not mince his words. Being a decade or so older than herself, he had spent his formative years in exile thanks to her father, as had many of the nobility of that age.

She nodded. "Of course, Blanxart."

"My queen, I may be speaking only for myself, but I hope I do so for most, if not all of my esteemed colleagues when I say that we would rather fight and die for Moranth and her people than live under the yoke of another tyrant."

Lucia leaned forward, steepling her fingers. "Then I shall consider myself lucky that you do not think of me as one, my lord." She watched Blanxart's face go pale before he caught her jibe for what it was.

Lucia was glad the man felt he could speak so freely. She never wanted any of her people to think they couldn't. She was not her father, and it cheered her to see her councilors nod, murmuring in support of Blanxart's words.

Lucia went on. "We'll have to be smarter than Vetreon. Use our resources to our greatest advantage. What we have is trade. Vetreon may have the greater navy, but they rely far too much on our exports. We need to play the long game. My uncle wasn't quite the man my father was, but he wasn't far behind. The people of Vetreon will be at the same tipping point we saw when I ascended to the throne. Surely Ramir is smart enough to recognize that."

"Just as you did, Your Majesty." Valeri tipped his head toward her, and Lucia felt her cheeks flare. She'd done well as queen, it was true. She couldn't help but be proud of the progress made to right her father's wrongs, but the attention being queen garnered still made her uncomfortable at times.

"Thank you, my lord." Smiling at him, Lucia took a deep breath before making her pronouncement. "I intend to send my cousin my condolences, as well as good wishes for his reign. I will also make it clear that I do not intend to marry him. His response will show us what kind of king he intends to be." There was a moment of uncomfortable shifting amongst the group. "I'll speak to the head of the trade guild. It won't be pleasant, but should Ramir make rumblings of war, as I suspect he will, trade between our two kingdoms must cease."

Lucia turned to her Lord High Treasurer, Royce Aldana. "My lord, I believe we've recovered enough from my father's misuse of the royal purse to put our plans on naval expansion into place?"

"We have." Aldana inclined his head in agreement, the waves of his black and silver hair shining in the afternoon light. He wasn't one to wax poetically.

Lucia gave him a fond grin as his dark brows drew together in consternation.

Lord Royce Aldana was known as a frugal man, a noble that grew up without the insurance of a wealthy family—it was his frugality that recommended him for the job. He and Lucia were of similar age and grew up within the confines of the palace together. He was as close to a sibling as she had. Lucia knew Royce didn't want to expand the navy or spend money where it wasn't absolutely necessary. However, with war looming and the recent increase in piracy, he could no longer avoid the expense.

"It could take years to be ready, my queen." His sky-blue eyes met hers with genuine concern. Lucia could tell that Royce was worried he had waited too long, been too conservative with the royal purse. She could see it was eating away at him.

Lucia stood, and her council followed suit. "There is nothing more we can do now but prepare ourselves. I doubt Ramir will take long with his answer." She gave a slight bow of her head in dismissal. "My lords and ladies."

Watching them file out, she caught Lord Aldana's sleeve. "You and I should speak, Royce."

The man raised a brow but nodded. They waited patiently for the others to leave.

With a loud creak, a page closed the heavy wooden doors, and they were alone.

Royce paced the length of the cramped chamber, waiting for Lucia to speak. There was a time when he longed for moments alone with his queen, but he had come to terms with the fact that Lucia could never love or want him that way years ago. In fact, she hadn't called him *Royce* since the day he proposed.

They'd been sitting in the same room, awaiting the signal to enter for her coronation. Only eight years had passed, but it seemed like a lifetime ago.

Lucia looked resplendent in her cloth of gold gown, the sea lion of her family arms embroidered throughout in silver thread. The length of her thick, ashen hair hung loosely around her shoulders, and the small emerald ring he had given her on her birthday the year before was on the little finger of her right hand.

Beyond the doors, courtiers and priests waited in the great hall, and outside the palace, commoners anxious to catch a glimpse of their new queen had packed the royal grounds. Lucia had given Royce the honor of carrying the coronation swords before her, so just for one moment, they had been alone.

While Lucia's father lived, Royce never presumed that a marriage between himself and his dearest friend could ever take place. Like so many other nobles, his family was out of favor at court, hated even. It was why he'd been a hostage within the palace walls nearly all his life as had many other children. He reconciled himself to the role of friend and protector of the princess. He couldn't help loving her, but he could steel himself against the dream of being her husband. With her father gone, with the freedom Lucia would gain as queen, Royce dared.

He knew Lucia enjoyed women as lovers, but he thought it a passing thing, a way to indulge her lusty nature without risking the kingdom's future with an accidental pregnancy. If she would have him, he would spend the rest of his days a contented man.

Music sounded from the other side of the closed doors, the signal for him and Lucia to ready themselves for the long walk up the aisle toward her throne.

He watched her take a deep breath, forcibly blow out the air, then straighten her shoulders. "Are you *ready?"* she asked. Her voice was hesitant in the quiet of the room.

Royce reached for her hand, holding it tenderly as he never had before. The words he so wanted to say nearly stuck in his throat as she looked at him quizzically. "Will you marry me, Lucia?" A flash of what he thought was regret came across her beautiful features, but then it was gone.

Her hand slid from his as she pulled it gently away. "I can't," she answered. Her voice turned cold, the voice of a ruler. "Don't ask me again."

When the doors of the chamber opened, the raised voices of the choir washed over them, and Lucia stepped forward, but Royce plucked at her sleeve. His hopes were dashed, but there was still work to be done. "I believe I proceed you, Your Majesty." He gave her a tight smile, an attempt at masking his wounded heart.

She jerked her chin toward the door. "Best get to it, Lord Aldana."

Outside of court affairs, it was almost a year after his proposal before Lucia spoke to him again. Their friendship took longer to repair, but repair it, they did. It wasn't the same, but it was there.

Standing alone once more in an empty council chamber with her, Royce wondered at how they'd changed in the intervening years. Perhaps not Lucia so much, but he certainly had. Married for five years, he had three wonderful children, but much of his time was taken up with his responsibility as Lord High Treasurer and having to look after Sebastian. It was meant to be an honor, a position of great trust, but getting the kingdom back in order had caused him more than a few sleepless nights, something his head full of grey hair could attest to.

Royce's chest tightened as he watched Lucia sitting before him, her head dropped in her hands. He still thought her to be the most beautiful woman he had ever laid eyes on, but his once all-encompassing lust for her cooled over the years as he grew to love and adore his wife. There were moments, of course, when he dreamed of Lucia in his arms, but he no longer held illusions of its possibility. When he looked at her, he saw his queen, and the queen looked exhausted.

"I know what they're all thinking," she murmured, not lifting her head to look at him.

"And what's that?"

"That I should have married you when I took the throne."

Scoffing, Royce made a dismissive gesture. "Then Ramir would have come up with some other excuse to attack. This is just the laziest one."

Lucia glanced up, her brow raised. "Are you saying it isn't just me he's after?" There was more than a hint of sarcasm in her rich voice.

Royce tipped his chair back with the heel of his boot, rocking slightly in the off-balanced seat. "While your charms are unparalleled, I don't think Ramir is that foolish. Though I suppose wars have been fought over lesser things than a man's hard-on."

Sighing, Royce wished that he and Lucia still enjoyed the close friendship they had as children. She was in need of a friend—that much was clear. "I don't think that's what everyone was thinking, by the way. Perhaps a few, but for most," he shrugged, "your plan for succession has been clear from the start. Bastian is a good lad, quick, kind, even. He'll make a good king when the time comes."

Lucia breathed heavily, and Royce knew why. It was an unpleasant truth of ruling, having everyone constantly thinking about what would happen once you were dead, but planning for such an event was necessary.

There was something else he wished to speak with her about, an awkward topic to broach, but Royce thought it as good a time as he was likely to get. "I do think," he began, hoping not to rile the queen's famous wrath, "that it would be good for you to have someone, though. Name a royal consort. Have a bit of domestic bliss in your life. Sebastian is nearly grown. He'll be off gallivanting across the land before too long."

Her jaw tensed. "He better not be. You just said what a good lad he was."

Royce chuckled. "We were good, and you remember the trouble we got into. Anyway, it's not him I'm worried about. When was the last time you saw Uridice?"

Lucia cut her eyes to the side, her cheeks flaring red. "You speak to her often enough, don't you?"

"I do." In fact, he'd been to see the brothel owner the night before on state business.

She crossed her arms, eyes narrowing. "Then I'm sure you know I haven't seen her in years."

Royce let his chair down with a thump against the stone floor. "She's good counsel, and you know it. She wouldn't have her position if she weren't." A snort of laughter broke from Lucia, and he couldn't help but follow suit. "Poor word choice, perhaps, but you and her, you were..." His voice trailed off as he caught the dark expression on his queen's face. He knew there was no one she could choose to be at her side, especially not Uridice. *How can there be when she is surrounded by flattering, scheming courtiers?* She couldn't even leave her palace without a disguise. Lucia's subjects were loyal, even fond of their queen, but her father had made many enemies during his reign, and there was more than one threat to her life.

A wave of sadness washed over Royce as he realized she didn't even fully trust him, but he knew he was right about Uridice. There was no good reason for Lucia to have abandoned such an ally.

She thought of dismissing Royce for a moment, not wanting to delve too deeply into her own wants, but she needed to speak to him as her advisor. Too much was at stake for her to let her temper get in the way. She cleared her mind of any thoughts of her former lover, of the release she offered, and focused instead on the problem at hand.

"I need you to find a way to finance the building of new ships. We can't ignore the state of our navy any longer."

Royce clearly took the hint that Uridice was still a touchy subject, and his tone returned to that of a council member. "No, we can't, but building takes time, which we may not have. Earlier this year, when the Treathen ambassador was at court, I spoke with him on the matter. They've been making great use of their privateers."

"Bloody pirates!" Lucia tsked. "And don't get me started on the remnants of the Empire. I'm not about to be pulled into someone else's war. Tell the Ambassador *that* if he comes looking for an alliance."

Royce raised his hands in defense. "It would give our pirates something better to do than go after our ships. It may also buy us the time we need. Our friend in Vetreon still needs a push."

Lucia's pulse quickened. "I won't beg her, and I'm not yet ready to pay her price. Sebastian is too young."

She worried at her thumbnail—a mannerism never indulged in front of anyone else. It was something she did when she allowed herself to drop into the deep recesses of her mind. She could never be so at ease before her other courtiers. It had been too long since she'd even allowed herself such an open discussion with Royce. The loneliness she'd felt the night before came creeping back in, and she stilled as her mind followed that thread through to her childhood, to the hours spent alone in the woods, to her mother, then back to Ramir and the looming war.

Royce standing caught her eye. He'd known her since childhood, so he knew the conversation was over without her having to say a word.

"Your Majesty." He bowed, and only when she dipped her head in acknowledgment, her eyes briefly focused on him, did he retreat, leaving her to her thoughts.

Later, ensconced once more in the comforts of her chambers, Lucia sipped at her wine while studying the charts and maps the ancient Admiral Girona provided her. Pain pulsed behind her right eye as she pinched the bridge of her nose in irritation. *I need a break, but then what? If I'm not handling the situation, then who else will? Still, a good fuck might inspire me.* Arching her back, her dressing gown pulling tight over her hardened nipples, Lucia ran through the list of her various consorts before settling on a blonde kitchen wench who'd proven more than willing last time.

The girl arrived less than an hour later, a pink flush on her round cheeks and an excited smile on her lips. Lucia was waiting for her, clad only in a green silk robe tied loosely at her hips, her hair in a tousled plait, and a glass of wine in her hand.

"You look lovely," Lucia said, offering the glass to the woman. She didn't look as nervous as the last time, perhaps even more eager. *That's good.*

The maid bobbed her head. "Thank you, Your Majesty. As do you."

There were plenty of benefits that came with being the queen's favorite. For instance, after a night in Lucia's bed, she would be allowed to sleep late, and one of the other girls handled her morning chores. Lucia didn't want that to be the reason the maid was looking at her with that smile, though. A reluctant lover was never something she was after. Of course, the power of her position was not lost on Lucia and only made it much harder to discern the truth of another's feelings. It was imperative that she never forced anyone, like what Ramir wished to do to her.

Lucia's gut suddenly twisted even as the woman sipped at her wine, slinking toward the bed where Lucia sat, waiting. She remembered the maid's mouth on her skin, her own tongue thrusting inside the girl, her breathless screams of delight. Taking the wine and setting it aside, Lucia's hands beckoned the other woman closer, their fingers entwining.

ALMONT

The king's secretary was silent as he watched Ramir from the doorway. Almont knew that the view from the king's balcony made the might of his navy clear. Masts of Vetreon's battleships swayed with the languorous current—a floating black forest against the night sky. Twenty warships lay at anchor in the bay or safe within their berths, while another fifteen were at sea.

He cleared his throat to let Ramir know he was there. "Majesty?"

Ramir spun around in surprise, his hand gripping the hilt of his ever-present dagger. A sardonic smile graced his deceptively inviting lips.

"I nearly killed you." The king laughed, clapping Almont on his back.

He gave his young sovereign a nervous grin.

"Is it done?" Ramir asked, guiding Almont to a chair.

Almont licked his lips. He wasn't a man known for such anxiety, but the king made his blood run cold. He'd been in the royal service for nearly twenty years. Ramir's father had been bad enough, but the son sought to bring back glory to the ancient kingdom, and he didn't care what he had to do to get it. It left the royal secretary in a precarious position.

With raised brows, Almont nodded his head toward the royal bed. A young woman was there, tears brimming, the sheets pulled up to her chin, and a newly darkening black eye marring her pretty features.

Glancing up, Ramir caught sight of the girl and smirked. "I'd forgotten she was there. You," he snapped his fingers at her, "get out of here."

Still naked, she ran from the room, clutching her clothes to her chest. Almont couldn't meet her gaze as she fled. He didn't blame her haste, but she was one of the lucky ones. She was still alive.

The king's dark eyes turned to Almont. "I can have her brought back if you want. Though I must warn you, she did not impress me. Not much of a fighter."

Almont was sweating as he worked to calm himself. His king fed on fear. Swallowing, he answered cooly, "That won't be necessary, Your Majesty. My task is complete. All I desire now is a stiff drink and a warm bed." *And a great deal of distance from you.*

"Then it is done."

Ramir was clearly excited as he poured two glasses of wine, offering one to Almont. He didn't dare refuse a drink from his king. Although, if Ramir were as cunning as he liked to think he was, it would be the perfect time to kill the one man who knew every detail of his plan, and well Almont knew it.

Almont took the proffered glass, sniffing as if admiring the vintage. "Done, Your Majesty. The messenger bird just arrived. My man sent it the moment the palace alarm was raised in Moranth. According to his message, that was three days ago."

Ramir tapped his fingers on the table. "Three days by bird. Roughly two weeks by sea." He smiled.

"I've no doubt Lucia will make a lovely bride," Almont ventured. It was not in him to harm a woman, but he had a wife and children of his own. What Ramir was capable of terrified him. He would do what was necessary to keep them safe.

"No doubt, indeed, no matter how unwilling. I warrant she'll put up a far better fight than that last little bitch." Ramir glanced down at him. "You're not drinking." The king snickered, quaffing his own glass of wine. "There's still far too much to be done to kill you. Drink the wine, man."

Almont wanted to vomit, but instead, he gulped the wine, then hurriedly took his leave.

2

ALESSANDRA

The captain had been dead for less than an hour.

Alessandra stared down at her father's corpse. One minute, he'd been standing at the helm, his eyes fixed on the horizon; the next, dead on the deck of his ship. Pascal D'Allyon was a dried husk of a man in death. His skin, once tan and weathered like an old tree, was pale, his strong bearing gone.

The Medusa had been skirting off the coast of the kingdom of Moranth for days. There was little fear of detection, for the pirates knew the state of the Moranthese navy, as well as each and every secret cove along the way. These were the home waters of their late captain, making it easy to slip in and out undetected by the royal navy. The haul from their last raid, silks, oils, and the most costly and rare porcelain, lay in the cargo hold. It was a fine load, too fine to be taken and sold in the markets of Silver Cove, where they could safely offload in the pirate-friendly port. Instead, they were heading for a secret little islet close to Calan, the capital city of Moranth. From there, they could make their way into the town of Marshport and then on to the city to sell their stolen goods. It was dangerous, but without their take, there would be no money for more supplies.

"We should bury him before we make port," Alessandra said, turning to her first mate. "It's what he would've wanted. Especially with us going into Moranthese territory."

Cyril's face twisted as he turned his head and spat at the kingdom's name. "Aye. I'll see to it that the lads take care of him. Why don't you get some air? He's starting to stink." the man blurted out before bumbling an apology.

He was right. The day was unusually warm for such waters—the cabin was stifling. They'd be in the cooler climes of the capital soon, but until then, they were still under a hot sun, and the captain's berth smelled of death. Jerking her chin in approval, she squashed her hat back on her head, gave Cyril's shoulder a pat, then stepped out onto the deck, grateful to be breathing the fresh air.

With their captain dead, the crew looked to her, his daughter. The men had voted, all one-hundred and forty-seven of them, and agreed the great warship was hers to command. The Medusa wasn't the prettiest ship on the seas, but she was slung low and had enough guns to make her a threat to any ship she crossed. She had been an aging vessel in the royal fleet when Captain Pascal D'Allyon was a young man with a new commission.

Alessandra took a moment to stare out to sea, steadying herself for the role ahead, the thick braid of her ruby red hair falling heavily over her breast. She needed to get off the ship; needed the space to mourn her father's passing. She couldn't grieve onboard, with her men always watching. She couldn't let them see weakness. Most were good lads, but that didn't mean she fully trusted them.

Alessandra wouldn't be going into the city with the others—she never did. It would be up to Cyril to reap what profit they could from their plunder. It would give her the time to pull herself together. She was also desperate for a good tumble. They'd be in the derelict harbor of Marshport in two days, and she hoped that the plump, blonde barmaid at the only serviceable tavern in town was still there, lusty as ever.

"You're thinking about Celeste, aren't you?"

Alessandra nearly jumped out of her skin as Rafe, her closest friend, shimmied down a rope, landing gracefully at her feet.

Alessandra shot him a confused stare. "Who's Celeste?"

Rafe laughed. His teeth dazzled against his light brown skin as he tossed back his mop of black curls, the gold hoop in his ear shining as the sun lit his large hazel eyes. "Marshport tavern, blonde, enormous—" He cupped his hands to his chest.

"Right." Alessandra chuckled, thankful for the dose of levity. "Never can remember her name."

"You're the kind of pirate that gives us a terrible reputation," Rafe teased. "How am I supposed to convince a lass my intentions are honorable with you around?"

Alessandra tilted her head. "Are they?"

"Not yet," Rafe answered.

His countenance turned serious. "What's next, Captain? After Moranth?"

Alessandra groaned. "Don't know if I'll get used to that title anytime soon." She didn't want the responsibility of the ship, the men. She thought she had years ahead to decide what her life would look like, but with her father dead, her only option was to continue on the course he had set.

"I don't know, Rafe." Her father's plan, as always, was to harry vessels when they could be found, scuttle the ships, take the gold or wares, and continue on until death. It had never been much of a plan, but then, she had a suspicion her father never expected to live as long as he did.

Maybe they would go back to Silver Cove. Most of the crew's family lived to the south on the island. It would be winter in a few months, and they always lay anchor in the deep waters of the pirate port while the seas remained too dangerous to sail. It would be early for them to turn up, but they'd be welcome.

After *The Purge of Moranth*, the survivors settled in Silver Cove. When the refugees landed, it was a small place, mostly hovels and dens of iniquity. Since then, the exiles had transformed the island into a bustling seaside town and port of call to trade ships and pirates alike. It was a place where they felt safe, where she felt safe.

Alessandra and her father had a home there, a squat stone cottage, but it was theirs. She also knew where her father's hoard of buried treasure was. That, along with her take in The Medusa's hold, could set her up for life if that's what she wanted, what she wanted being the key question.

Rafe rubbed at the dark scruff on his chin, leaning in conspiratorially. "Alex." His voice was low in warning. "Now, you know I don't mind dying in a fight, but I have no intention of taking a knife while sleeping in my rack."

She turned from the sea, her gaze raking over her crew, hard at work, wondering which one of them would be capable of betrayal. *Aren't we all?*

Rafe followed suit, palms against the warm wood railing, elbows bent as he took in the scene. "Take what time you need when we reach port, but don't speak like that around the rest of the men. Everyone here knows the sailor you are, the captain you could be, but that doesn't mean some won't see your father's death as an opportunity. It's not wise for a captain to be indecisive."

Her hand found his, grasping it for just a moment. "I know. Thank you."

The pirate flashed her another brilliant smile before pushing away from the rail to go about his business, leaving Alessandra to ponder her new position.

Her father never liked being this close to the capital. 'Too many memories,' he'd always say. He would soon rest beneath those waters forever.

Alessandra watched, unshed tears in her eyes, as her father's wrapped body tipped over the ship's side, plunging into the depths below.

"I hope you find her," she whispered, staring at the spot where his body slid beneath the surface.

After a moment's silence, she set her hat on her head and turned back to her crew. "Set sail," she called out, watching the men scurry to their tasks.

A steadying hand pressed into her shoulder as Cyril's eyes met hers. She knew he was hurting too, already missing his old friend.

"He's with your mother now," he said, his eyes swimming with emotion.

Alessandra sighed. "I'm not sure I believe that."

"Not sure I do either, lass, but I like to think it just the same."

"Thank you, Cyril. I know you'll miss him as well."

"Aye, I will. Not too many of us left from the time before."

The time before was how the exiles of Moranth spoke of their lives before The Purge. Alessandra had been so young, she only remembered snippets of her old life, but mainly it was that one night when everything changed, the night her mother was killed. The fires burning, the people running, splashing into the dark surf. Her mother didn't scream, but her grandfather had as he watched his daughter's life drain in a river of red before he too, was silenced.

The whole of The Medusa's crew had once been Moranthese. All royal navy men, they were sentenced to a life of wandering simply for being assigned to a ship captained by a wanted man. Only a handful of those original crew still lived.

Her father was a pirate for twenty years. *And for what?* After the first few years, Pascal D'Allyon possessed a large enough fortune to take his daughter and disappear forever. Perhaps it was her mother's death or his hatred for the crown, but something more than necessity or greed drove the former navy captain. What that was, Alessandra never knew.

The sun began its descent, clouds lighting pink and gold around them, as she leaned her elbows on the ship's railing, finding a measure of comfort in Cyril's presence.

"I don't suppose you're going to the city with us?" he asked. "No one would know you there. You could have a proper meal—"

Alessandra fixed him with a hard stare. "There's nothing for me there."

The stout man folded his arms over his paunch, staring right back. "Not much for you in Marshport either."

Alessandra disagreed. She knew what she needed—solitude, drink, and women. She admitted to herself that 'solitude' wasn't exactly the right term, 'distance from her crew' was more appropriate.

"I want you and the lads to enjoy yourselves. I'll not be fit company for anyone." She gave the butt of the pistol in her sash a pat. "Besides, don't think I'd be able to stop myself from drawing down on anyone making a toast to that queen of theirs, and I plan on being too drunk to defend myself."

Cyril snickered. "Devil, take all those royal bastards." He grunted. "If it's all the same to you, I'd like to have Jacques and Kier with you. You're the captain now. Can't have anything happening to you."

Alessandra's anger began to rise. She wasn't a child. "I don't need looking after," she retorted, catching the petulance in her tone.

Cyril must've caught it too, hearing it for the hurt it was. "When I lost my boy," his voice dropped low, "I lost three days." The pain he'd felt all those years ago was etched into his face. "Your father could've had me flogged or court-martialed, even hung for desertion, but instead, he disobeyed the admiral's orders." Alessandra's eyes widened in surprise—this was a new story. "It took him another two days to find me in the corner of some back alley, sleeping in my own piss and vomit. He got me back on the ship and took the punishment himself." Cyril sighed. "Your father was the best young captain in the fleet. He could have been admiral one day but for that disciplinary charge. I'll tell you something else. Not a single man aboard said one word of my behavior, not one." He gave Alessandra's arm a squeeze. "We all have to grieve, Captain."

Alessandra gave him the hint of a smile. "Wise words from an old sea dog."

"I don't have many." He grinned, which brought a bark of laughter from her as she well knew the intelligence of the man before her.

"Make sure Jacques and Kier get an extra ration of rum and let them know they have their captain's appreciation," she said.

"Just so, Captain." Cyril nodded in approval as he stepped away, leaving Alessandra to contemplate her path.

———

The Medusa sailed into the town of Marshport on the evening tide two days later. The village was known for its fishing and proximity to the capital, which made it an ideal port of call for smugglers and pirates. The painted homes sat jumbled, one atop the other, along the grey, pebbled beach and into the low hills beyond. The houses were once brightly colored, but the sun had bleached them all to dull shades of rust and lemon.

Fog rolled in with their ship, blanketing the town in an eerie quiet. The vessel was too large to bring into the small harbor, forcing the crew to load up all four dinghies and make numerous trips to offload both men and booty. It was near midnight by the time their task was complete.

Alessandra and Cyril were the first ashore to meet with their contact, securing transportation for their treasures. Their man in town, a one-eyed codger by the name of Quint, set them up with two horses and two carts. One for the men and one for the treasure.

Those not fortunate enough to find a place in the cart would walk the seven miles into Calan—worth it for the three days they expected to be gone.

Alessandra knew the men would come back with amusing stories and painful hangovers. She sent them off with waves, good wishes, and a warning to keep their purses close. Then she watched impatiently, her hands shoved into the pockets of her coat, foot and back braced against a dock piling, as Cyril gave Jacques and Kier a talking to. It was ridiculous that Cyril thought she needed security—she'd spent a good deal of her life in dockside taverns and gambling halls—but she welcomed it for the kind gesture it was.

When told of their duty in guarding their captain, the lads did their best to hide their disappointment by boasting that they were the finest, bravest sailors aboard The Medusa—the only ones that could see to her safety. Alessandra didn't miss the ring of genuine pride in their voices, knowing they'd soon be placated with rum in their bellies as the extra coin Cyril was giving them jangled in their pockets. Kier and Jacques nudged each other excitedly, no doubt already planning how to lose it, when Cyril lumbered over to Alessandra.

"More like you'll be watching over these two fools than the other way around," he said, jerking his thumb at the sailors. "You sure you don't want Rafe to stay?"

Alessandra hooked an arm over her first mate's shoulders as they strode from the dock, stopping outside the tavern's painted blue door. "The only thing I'm in trouble of here," she pointed over her shoulder at the door, "is being overcharged by the girls, and honestly, it's been a long trip. I'm going to get blind drunk, and if those lasses take every bit of coin I have on me, it'll be well spent."

Kier slapped Cyril on the back. "Don't worry, man. We'll look after the captain." Cyril shook his head, muttering an oath under his breath before leaving them to their debauchery.

Of course, their good intentions were soon tested as the three entered The Careless Goose, Marshport's finest drinking establishment. Such a description wasn't saying much. It was still a small inn in the middle of a backwater town, with its backhanders and shady deals, but the alcohol was strong, and the beds were soft. Alessandra spotted Celeste as they entered the cramped, dimly lit room. She was pouring wine while flirting with another table of half-inebriated men. Their eyes met for half a second, and the blonde's smile broadened into something real.

The moment was interrupted when the innkeeper recognized Alessandra and immediately shooed his near-unconscious patrons from their seats, offering them to the pirates. "Please," he sputtered, setting wine and ale before her, wiping sweat from his brow.

Alessandra knew they, like all pirates, had a reputation and was sure the man was nervous, but they were frequent enough visitors for him to remember she tipped well and mostly kept her men in check.

"You have any dinner left?" Alessandra asked the squat innkeeper, kicking her boots up on the table.

"There's a bit, and I'm thinking you'll be needing rooms?"

Alessandra flipped a gold piece to the man. "One for me and one for these two." She gestured toward Jacques and Kier. It would be a treat for them to have a room for the night instead of sleeping in the common area, as they usually did.

The innkeeper bobbed his head, retreating to the kitchen.

Kier nudged Alessandra, jerking his chin at the luscious blonde making her way to their table. "There's a fine lassie."

"Aye." Alessandra smirked, opening her arms in greeting.

Celeste gave her a wink before settling into her embrace. "I've missed you," the barmaid crooned, her soft bottom warm against Alessandra's thighs.

"Missed you too, Celeste." Alessandra's hand brushed up her back, tangling in the mess of coarse locks.

Celeste whistled. "Look at you, remembering my name this time. Must be love." She laughed.

Alessandra threw back a pint of ale, licking her lips. "Must be."

———

Three days later, her head nodded as if to the rhythm of the sea. Her fingers had a loose grip on what could have been her tenth or twentieth shot of rum. She had lost count, along with feeling in much of her body, hours, maybe days ago. She was safe; she could grieve. Her men wouldn't let a soul near her. She wondered briefly where the pretty wench—*Callie? Katie?*—had run off to, but the thought was short-lived as she tried to keep her seat.

"Captain?"

Alessandra's bleary eyes turned toward the voice, trying to bring the face into focus. The best she could do was squint with one eye closed, which still wasn't doing the trick as she saw doubles of her first mate. The blustery little fellow wouldn't be talking to her if it weren't of some importance. She had known Cyril all her life. He knew just what losing her father cost her and her intent when he left her at Marshport. She hadn't even allowed herself to cry on board for fear her tears would become the racking sobs of her true pain, pain that she was dulling with drink.

Cyril drew closer, putting a friendly hand on her arm as if to rouse her. "Alessandra?" he whispered. He would never have called her anything but 'Captain' in front of the others.

"Don't know about this," he called over his shoulder.

While Cyril and whoever he was talking to continued their conversation, Alessandra tried to decide whether she wanted to vomit or pass out.

"Speak," she finally managed.

"Um," Cyril began, keeping his voice low, "got a proposition for you."

"Does it involve making money?"

"It does. A queen's ransom."

She let out a loud belch before wiping her mouth. "Is the crew in agreement?"

He waved a hand in front of his face to clear the air. "They are."

Alessandra had just enough presence of mind to wonder why his voice sounded questioning, going higher at the end as if he wasn't all too certain of himself. Alessandra had just enough presence of mind to wonder why, but Cyril was a second father to her—he would never harm her.

He had been an officer in the king's navy, happy in his position as first mate aboard The Medusa when her father was a young captain. Shrewd and fair, the finest sailor in the royal navy, was how Cyril always described him. It had been Margthe, Cyril's wife, pregnant with their third child, who had seen to Alessandra's safety on that terrible night long ago. When the king decided his nobles had too much power.

People like him and Margthe were of no consequence to King Teodor, but Cyril's place at her father's side made him a wanted man. Margthe had been right to flee when she did, ensuring Pascal's small daughter was at her side.

Alessandra knew all that and more, had grown up at Margthe's hearth, raised on stories of Cyril and her father's adventures. *I trust him with my life*.

Alessandra vomited onto the sawdust strewn across the tavern floor before looking up at Cyril, who looked on in disgust.

"Get the captain to her quarters," he said to Kier and Jacques. "I'll see she's paid up."

She was barely conscious but saw the tavern keeper raise his hands, smiling. "No need, sailor. Your captain has been very generous." Her mouth twitched with amusement as Cyril laughed, giving the man another coin for good measure.

At least I had a good time, Alessandra thought as steady hands grasped her and hauled her back aboard her ship. Safe in her bunk, about to finally give into oblivion, she could've sworn she heard a shout and felt the ship rock as if the sails had suddenly snapped tight, but that couldn't be. She was the captain and had given no order to set sail.

The creak of the ship's rigging woke her. Alessandra coughed, then wished she hadn't as the action reverberated through her skull. "Oh, God."

Her eyes felt like they were glued shut. She opened one, testing her surroundings. She was in a large, beautifully appointed room with lush rugs and fine hangings, a heavy desk, and a large, ornately carved bed. It was the captain's cabin—*her* cabin. A paltry light filtered through the leaded windows.

The ship swayed with the open sea beneath her, making her stomach turn. She rolled to the edge of the bed and vomited into a chamber pot. Her nose wrinkled. She reeked of sweat and drink, still in her clothes from the night before. With the sour taste in her mouth, bile threatened once again. *What happened? How long have I been in a drunken stupor?* It wasn't her way to drink like that, to lose herself so completely, but her father was dead, her purpose, place, or whatever she wanted to call it, along with him. *I'm alive, though. That is something.*

She ground her palms against her eyes, taking a last moment for herself before she donned the mantle of *captain*. The ship, *her* ship, was under sail without her order.

Alessandra clutched at the bedpost for support. It took a minute, foggy and unsteady as she was, to find her feet, then she located a washbasin with clean enough looking water. It was the best she was going to get onboard. Stripping off her soiled shirt and underclothes, not caring to glance at her appearance in the mirror—her imaginings were bad enough—she gave herself a quick scrub, knowing it would do very little.

Someone, she thought it must have been Cyril, had laid out clean clothes for her on the desk, for which she was grateful, unsure she could expend the brain power it would take to find anything else.

After nearly throwing up again, Alessandra finished redressing when a knock sounded on her door. "I'll be out in a moment," she called.

"Aye, Captain," came Cyril's gruff voice. "The sooner, the better, I'd say."

Alessandra paused in rolling the cuffs of a fresh shirt. Her first mate sounded nervous, an unusual state for the man. She hurriedly finished buttoning her breeches and threw on her greatcoat. Drawing her hat down low over her eyes, she opened the door to her sweaty, red-faced first mate.

"What's wrong? Why are we under sail? We were to stay in Marshport for another day, at least."

Cyril wiped at his face with his hand. She thought they were in the Northern Sea; he shouldn't be sweating, but the stout man was, profusely. Alessandra realized she was too. If they were still close to Marshport, then this was rare, unseasonable weather.

"God, it's hot." She shrugged out of her coat, threw it back into her cabin, then eased the door shut, not wishing to hear it slam while in her present state.

Cyril blinked, then chuckled as if she had been making a joke. "Well, first off, Captain, you've been near unconscious for three days from what that tavern keeper said." Alessandra scanned the deck, noting the men's averted eyes. Cyril shifted his feet as sweat continued to pour down his florid countenance. "The other thing is—Well, we couldn't stay in port once we kidnapped the queen."

"Oh, fuck!"

Alessandra swallowed hard as her stomach dropped. She vaguely remembered Cyril mentioning a job worth a queen's ransom. Pushing the man aside, she hurried on deck, grabbed hold of the rigging, and scanned the horizon for the familiar coast of Moranth, but it wasn't there. They were just a speck on the vast open sea.

Cyril joined her at the railing. "You're acting like you don't remember our conversation the other night."

Alessandra's gold eyes narrowed, her fists clenched, her knuckles white. "I believe you left out some key points. I think you know I would never have agreed to such idiocy, sober. I should keelhaul you!" she shouted.

Every movement on deck ceased as Cyril's skin paled. Keelhauling was the worst punishment that could be meted out to a sailor, some saying a quick death was a more desirable fate. Alessandra knew he'd only seen it once during his long life as a sailor because he'd spoken of it. A lad had stolen from the captain on his first post. The boy, no more than fifteen or so, had been stripped, tied to a rope, and secured to the ship's hull. The process and punishment were quick but brutal, and after less than a minute in the sea, the sailor was hauled, unconscious, back aboard. The barnacles on the ship had torn every inch of his skin, leaving him a blood-soaked mess. Infection set in soon thereafter, and the boy died, having never regained consciousness.

"We have that kind of misunderstanding again, and I won't care that you're a second father to me. It'll be the plank," she seethed through gritted teeth.

"Understood, Captain. Uh—we still have a kidnapped queen on board, and the only way we get paid is if we deliver her."

Alessandra pulled the hat from her head and wiped a hand down her face in frustration. The ship had been her home from the time she was five, and Cyril predated her arrival by a good decade. He was family; she loved him, but she would kill him if it came to it, or so she told herself.

"Where is she? I'm assuming it's Lucia." Her arms crossed over her chest as she thought of the queen.

Alessandra had been to court only once as a child, shortly before The Purge. The princess had been a lovely creature, a few years older than herself, but the two children never spoke, were never introduced. Alessandra used to imagine what Lucia's life was like growing up in the palace, having everything she wanted. As Alessandra grew into womanhood, she heard the stories told in taverns of the beautiful, untamed princess. When Lucia took the throne, Alessandra had harbored the smallest hope that, as queen, the girl she had once seen could fix all that had gone so wrong.

Her father would drink, sometimes too much, and curse them all. Wanting to please him, Alessandra hid her fascination over the very girl who had grown into a woman captive on her ship.

"In the hold. Yes, it's Lucia."

"Where are we meant to take her?"

"Vetreon."

Alessandra made a disgusted face, shaking her head in irritation. "You know Vetreon wants Moranth. This is an act of war." She'd heard stories about Vetreon's new king, too.

"Usually is when royalty's involved. Were you hoping for a jealous suitor we could double cross? She's a blasted queen."

Alessandra glared, lowering her voice as the crew pretended to work around them. "We can't be involved in this."

Cyril backed into the shadows beneath the quarterdeck, dropping his voice to match hers. "We're pirates, lass."

For just a moment, Alessandra wondered about her life—the life that could have been. She was from aristocratic stock and should have been a fine lady with a line of suitors and marriage proposals, not a pirate or a thief, but there was no helping it. She was their captain and had accepted her place in life. It was past time she came to terms with it.

Cyril's eyes softened as they had when she was a little girl and had climbed onto his lap to pull at his whiskers. "We've kept your name clear thus far. Your face isn't on any placards. I doubt the crown even knows you're still alive. It wouldn't be a thing for us to let you off at the next port, taking what you're due. You could be whoever you wanted."

Alessandra knew that he was trying to be kind. She also knew that no ordinary life would have ever suited her. She might have only been a child at the time of her mother's death, but she had already been chafing at the society bridle.

Sighing, she gave Cyril's arm a pat. "You know I would never abandon you lot, but I need the story from the start. I need to know how we got into this mess."

"Not much to it." Cyril shrugged his broad shoulders. "Me and the lads were drinking and wenching in the capital, a little place I like down by the docks. We were just sitting there when a sly looking fellow approached, asking if we were from The Medusa."

"How did this *fellow* even know we were in town?"

"Captain, it's not any great secret when a ship like ours comes in, not amongst certain people. Besides, we'd already offloaded the plunder. Any one of half-a-dozen folks could have talked. Anyway, this man sat down, and as it was obvious he wasn't working for the crown, least, not hers—"

Alessandra stopped him. "How was it obvious?"

"I've been at this a very long time. You can practically smell it on them." Cyril grinned.

Alessandra shut her eyes, sighed, then motioned with her hand for him to continue. No doubt her first mate was correct.

He went on. "Once he'd ascertained who we were, he plopped down a purse full of gold and asked if we'd like never to have to step foot on a ship again. Not quite how I would have put it to lifetime sailors, but we understood his meaning. Then he told us that if we could get Lucia from Moranth to Vetreon, Ramir would fill The Medusa so full of gold she'd barely float. I had to take a proposition like that to the crew."

"At any point, did you think it might not be a fine idea to have the entire Moranthese Navy looking for us and *us* alone?"

"It may not have been the most circumspect moment of my life, I can see that now, but it's done, and we've got to make for Vetreon quick as we can. That's why I didn't wait for you to give the order to sail. You were ..." He looked embarrassed. "Well, let's just say tales of your feats at The Careless Goose may become the stuff of myth."

Alessandra's cheeks flared hot. "That bad?"

"Best to not dwell on it, lass." He nudged her with his elbow, smirking. "Although, I don't think any wench there will have to work for the next six months. The innkeeper said you showed them quite a time and tipped very well."

Alessandra groaned while massaging the back of her neck. Her eyes narrowed at a vague image of the blonde's head between her thighs while another woman straddled her. The two were so hazy in the fog of her memories that it was hard to tell one from the other.

"Guess I should introduce myself to our guest."

Cyril grabbed at her arm in warning. "She's a right hellcat, Captain."

Alessandra shoved him off. "I can handle one over-indulged royal." She scoffed, making her way to the hold.

3

LUCIA

Lucia fumed. She was bound tight. Pain pricked at her hands and feet as the rough ropes bit into her soft flesh. She knew her way around knots and had understood very quickly that so did the men who took her. There were individual knots at each ankle and wrist, and more rope and knots connected her ankles to wrists, all coming together at her waist. Exhausted and restrained, she deeply regretted the all-night session of fuckery with the kitchen maid the previous evening. She could have at least been kidnapped following a good night's rest.

Lucia squirmed against her ropes for the hundredth time, knowing it was useless, but it made her feel better. Her ribs ached on her right side, where she had been thrown over a kidnapper's shoulder as they raced from the palace. Every breath she took hurt. At least the brigands removed her hood before leaving her below. Still, it was dark beneath the deck of the ship, dark and rank. The hold reeked of spoiling food, spices, and mildew. Shafts of daylight filtered through the cracked planks, illuminating her prison. Crates were lashed to the sides, supplies no doubt, bolts of silks were piled in a corner, and two chests sat squat before her. She was unimpressed. It was hardly a fabled pirate's hoard. She had been expecting piles of gold coins, jewels by the buckets full, perhaps even a crown or two.

Fascinating as her surroundings were, Lucia's mind turned to who she had to thank for her circumstances. *Ramir, it has to be.* She had been planning on her cousin's betrayal for years, but she had been preparing for war, not this. *A kidnapping? The sheer hubris of the bastard. Hubris and cunning.* If Ramir's plan worked, she would be forced to marry him, to bed him. Moranth would be in his control as her husband, and she would no doubt spend her days locked in a tower. Lucia was sure that was how her horrid cousin foresaw his plan. She would have laughed had she not still been gagged. Ramir thought so little of her to think she would ever let it come to such a thing. Lucia steeled herself. *I will die before it comes to that.*

The little boy with beautiful black eyes always had a mean streak. Lucia had never been one to hold a stubborn character against anyone except herself, but Ramir went beyond that. He was eight years her junior, enough of a gap for her to recognize his childish behavior for what it would become, enough to hear and understand the fervor of his words. Lucia took note when Ramir spoke of regaining the kingdom of his mother's people. Moranth and Vetreon had once been ruled together, and the boy that had been Ramir thought no woman had the right to a kingdom he believed his. Much less a princess with a lowborn mother.

A stream of light burst through the darkness, followed by thudding footsteps down the stairs. Someone was coming for her. A form shifted against the brightness. Lucia couldn't move, couldn't speak. She tried anyway, but her bonds held fast, the ropes biting further into her wrists, and an angry snarl was all she could produce behind her gag. The dark figure took shape and bent before the queen, tipping a hat back to meet her gaze. *A woman.* Lucia's eyes widened for a moment. Her body stilled. She tried to speak again, another litany of incomprehensible curses.

The woman produced a blade, and Lucia flinched, nearly falling over to get away, but the pirate caught at the ropes binding her wrists. "You're on a ship in the middle of an ocean," the redhead said. "I'm going to get that gag out of your mouth, and you're not going to scream. Understand?"

Lucia nodded. Her shock at seeing another woman onboard shifted to hope. *Perhaps the woman will be useful? Who is she?* Lucia was not overly familiar with naval protocols, but she did know it was unusual for a woman to be on a pirate ship. Whoever she was, she was clearly not a captive.

The woman's dagger easily cut through the fabric, and Lucia coughed before taking in great lungfuls of air. She didn't scream. Instead, she chose to glare.

"I assume," Lucia rasped, "you know who I am."

There was uncertainty in the woman's eyes as she slipped her blade back into its sheath. "You wouldn't be my guest if you were anyone else, Your Majesty."

Lucia's eyes narrowed as she appraised the woman before her. She had intelligent eyes, but beyond that, she was a grimy mess dressed in a loose man's shirt and breeches, a saber and pistol at her side. Although dirty, she possessed a commanding presence. This was a woman who didn't take orders. She gave them.

"Are you the captain of this vessel?"

"Alessandra D'Allyon." She bowed elegantly. "Welcome aboard The Medusa."

Lucia couldn't help but swallow hard. The ship was infamous.

She thought back to what she knew of the man who had made off with The Medusa so long ago. A noble naval officer turned pirate. His wife was murdered by her father. *Had there been a daughter?*

"Your father is Pascal D'Allyon?" Lucia chanced, thinking the woman was too young to be his wife. She was shocked at the break in the pirate's voice.

"Was. At least he left this world a free man, never seeing the inside of your dungeon."

Lucia raised her chin, tried to straighten her back, and flared her nostrils, acting as if Alessandra and her father barely warranted a thought from her. The effect was severely hampered by the ropes binding her. "Your father was a pirate. He deserved death."

Lucia continued her vain struggle as Alessandra lounged back against a post. "What my father did or did not deserve is of no consequence now. You're the one tied up in my hold. Can you guess where you're bound for?"

Lucia turned her head and growled. "Vetreon."

"That's right," Alessandra said. "Now, to be honest, my crew took it upon themselves to find us a nice fat purse for the trouble of kidnapping and delivering you, alive, to your cousin." She clicked her tongue. "I was rather displeased by this turn of events. It's not for me to get involved in the squabbles of families, but here we are."

"Are you asking me to beg for my life? Tell you I'll pay you more to take me home?" The bravado of her words did not match the panic roiling her stomach. If she ended up in Ramir's hands, he would marry her against her will, rape her until she'd given him enough heirs to please him, then kill her to ensure there were no uprisings in her name. She couldn't let that happen. Her fate lay in the hands of a pirate.

Alessandra sighed. "All returning you to Moranth would earn me is the hangman's noose. No, we're taking you to Vetreon, Your Majesty."

"Ramir will kill you as sure as I will, or worse." Her eyes raked over her captor's female form. It was hard to tell if she was a beauty beneath the oversized shirt and tricorn hat. However, Lucia was a connoisseur of beautiful women, and from the smokiness of Alessandra's voice alone, she was willing to bet on it. "You'd be better off giving yourself to the sea than letting my cousin get his hands on you."

The pirate finally reacted, her face blanching, though she quickly recovered her poise. "You've got two weeks aboard this ship, Your Majesty. I can keep you nicely fettered down here, sleeping in your mess, or you can behave, follow my rules, and breathe the clean air above. Your choice."

"I could jump," she threatened, but Alessandra's gaze held hers.

"You won't. Not yet, at least."

"You aren't so foolish as to trust me," Lucia said, trying to work out the pirate's motivation. The captain didn't seem cruel, perhaps even felt a tad sorry for her.

"You're right, I don't trust you at all, but I also don't want to waste a man's time down here, constantly checking on you. Easier to keep you on deck, where I can watch you."

Lucia huffed but knew it was the best offer she was going to get. She could always try to take the captain unawares if there was an opportunity for escape. Her eyes wandered over the captain's figure once more. Seducing her would not be an unpleasant adventure either, and might be her best chance.

"Fine," Lucia said, resigned for the time being. "Get me out of here."

Alessandra nodded, then bent to the task of cutting her loose.

Once free, Lucia stood and stretched, her arms curving over her head as she arched her back. Her silk robe parted, and her spectacular nude form was on full display. She watched as Alessandra's brows rose. Her breasts were high and full, her waist tapered. Her wide hips and sculpted rear completed a fine, lush hourglass figure. She was beautiful and well aware of the effect.

Lucia winked over her shoulder. "Perhaps there's another bargain we can make?"

Alessandra's eye twitched. "I'll find you something to wear," she grumbled. "Stay here, and don't mess with anything."

ALESSANDRA

Cyril was waiting for her at the top of the stairs, obviously pretending he hadn't been straining to hear every word exchanged between the two women. "Didn't hear any screaming," he said. "Impressive. She nearly took one of Smith's eyes out with those claws of hers. Even with a hood on, Rafe had a time getting her tied up."

Alessandra brushed past the man on the way to her old cabin, where the majority of her clothing remained. Her former room was located with the other 'officers' cabins' directly below the captain's. She was going to have to let the men move her things soon. Cyril had more than a right to her old cabin. It was his before her father brought her on board all those years ago. The man before her thought it unseemly for a little girl, a lady, to be expected to share the rough bunks of the crew, or even one of the smaller cabins of the lower officers, so he gave her his own. It was a kindness she always wished to repay. He followed as she wound through the swinging canvas bunks in the crew cabin, nodding as she went to the few sailors off-duty.

Alessandra's body was strung taut with unwanted desire. When she'd descended those stairs into the hold of her ship, the last thing she expected was the most beautiful woman she'd ever seen. Lucia, light falling on her long, ashen locks, the green silk of her robe, those angry grey eyes. Lucia, sweaty, dirty, and bound.

"You didn't think to clothe her before you tied her up?"

Cyril laughed. "You've seen the walls of her castle. You think I'm the one who did the climbing? It was Smith, Rafe, and Ben," he told her. It made sense. They were her three strongest and quickest men.

She sighed as they reached topside. "I'm going to let her on deck."

Cyril guffawed as he puffed after her. "But Captain!"

A balmy breeze tugged at the collar of her shirt as Alessandra took a moment to breathe the sea air while they strode over the deck. She turned on her first mate. "Worried she'll distract the men? Seduce them or me?"

Cyril blustered. "Well, you've seen her. All of her by the sound of it. She's—Well, she's distracting."

Alessandra wasn't even going to try to argue that point. She placed a reassuring hand on Cyril's shoulder. "I'm sure you and the men can maintain control over yourselves, and I've never had any problems on board. I'll find her some clothes, and it will be fine." She knew the statement wasn't entirely true. Rafe had turned her head when he joined the crew two years prior.

He was gorgeous and flirtatious, and though Alessandra had never been with a man, he was pretty enough to make her wonder what it would be like, but being pregnant on a pirate ship was one of the worst scenarios she could think of. Not to mention the fact her father would've killed any man who touched her. Her father hadn't much cared for her dalliances with women either, but he tolerated them. The mutual attraction between her and Rafe was acknowledged, then quickly put aside. There was no room for it. Once that understanding became clear, they formed a strong friendship, and for once, she hadn't felt so alone on the mighty ship.

They descended another set of stairs that led through the cook's chamber and another down to the gunroom and what was once the junior officer's quarters but had become a second gunroom, then through to her snug cabin. It was a rabbit's warren beneath the deck, but it was home. She was light on her feet as she set a brisk pace, navigating her ship's circuitous inner workings. The same could not be said of her first mate. Sweat poured down Cyril's face as he attempted to keep up with her, dipping low to miss a swinging lantern as they finally reached her cabin's door.

"If you'll permit me," Cyril asked. Alessandra answered with a grunt. "You're as fine a lass as any, but you were the captain's daughter. You know it's not the same. It's not you and Rafe making eyes at each other across the deck." Cyril lowered his voice. "From what I hear of the state they found a serving girl in, in Her Majesty's chamber, it's you I'm worried about."

Alessandra laughed, but her stomach flipped as her imagination took hold. *Exactly how did they find Lucia's servant?* She made a mental note to ask Rafe about it later. "I don't see the appeal," she lied. Lucia was exactly what she liked, at least physically, with her middling height, that wasp waist, and full, soft curves. Alessandra ground her teeth against the mounting desire that came with her memory of the queen's naked body.

Cyril raised a bushy grey brow. "Woman like that, it's hard to miss."

Alessandra shook her head and thumped him on the back. "Well, I shall try to steel myself against her charms." Her first mate shot her an unbelieving look but said nothing. "Get back topside while I handle this." She jerked her chin. "Make sure Smith doesn't wreck my ship. You know how he can be."

"Aye, Captain," Cyril grumbled before hauling himself back on deck.

Once he was gone, Alessandra put her hand on the battered door of her childhood room, resting her forehead on the cool wood for a moment. It had been her sanctuary amongst the bustle and ceaseless noise, but even as she took quiet, deep breaths, she knew it was no longer.

The door opened with a creak. Stepping forward, her heart heavy, she stood alone in the little room that had been hers for the last twenty years. The cabin was far sparser than her father's—than *hers*. Sunlight streamed through a bank of leaded glass windows, warming the little bed that was pushed up against them. At its foot was a costly rug, thick cream shag with undulating lines of red and blue throughout. She had liberated it from a merchant ship's hold in her first raid—she'd been twelve. She'd make sure it reached her new quarters, preferring its plush softness to the more tightly woven rugs residing there.

The bed was rumpled in a way that would not have been acceptable had her father still been living. Alessandra twinged at the disarray she had allowed to accumulate over the last few days, but it spoke more to her natural state than the buttoned-up naval tidiness her father had demanded.

Two trunks filled with clothing her father stole or bought for her, most too precious to be worn on the hot, salt-sprayed deck of the ship, were open, clothing strewn about the room. She didn't even remember what she had been looking for. She figured something in there should be appropriate for their guest. Though a gown wouldn't do for ship life, her father had always wanted her to have the clothing he thought she deserved, the sorts she would have had as a lady. They rarely, if ever, saw the light of day, but it meant the world to her that he had thought her worthy of such costly things.

Alessandra rummaged through the fine dresses meant for courts and clothes fit for sailing. Even the wide-legged breeches and loose shirts, such as those she wore daily, were made of fine materials of butter-soft silks and linens fit for nobility, not a sailor. She had always been grateful to be spared the discomfort her crew endured in their heavy wool.

The nude form of the Moranthese queen was seared into Alessandra's mind, and she looked to it as she cast about the clothing piles for something that might work with the woman's generous curves. The queen was shorter than she was, with wide hips and plump breasts, so anything Alessandra had would fit Lucia awkwardly, being so tall and narrow-hipped as she was, but her clothes were at least flea free—mostly. Finding a pair of black breeches and a white linen shirt similar to the one she was wearing, Alessandra took one last look around her girlhood room, a bit sad that nothing would ever be the same.

ROYCE

Lucia was gone, taken in the night. Royce's heart thundered in his ears—his queen was gone. He had been awoken by guards pounding at his door, by shouts and bells. A tall woman in hunting leathers was hurrying down the hall in his direction. He gave a sigh of relief at the sight of Ylva, his shadow. They were in the palace proper, guards rushing about, servants panicking in the corridors as the damned city's bells rang from every tower. He grabbed the woman by her muscled arm as she approached. "Is Sebastian safe?"

She nodded, catching her breath, her hand on the pommel of her sword. "We've only just arrived. Had the lad ride all night. Valeri's message said to make haste. Didn't think this was what we'd be returning to."

"Where is he?" He'd be damned if the kidnappers made off with Lucia's heir as well.

Ylva dropped her voice. "With our friend in Olde Towne. Thought it was the safest place for him when the bells started up. I left him there and made my way here as quick as I could. Is it true? Pirates made off with the queen?"

His heartbeat slowed. *Finally, a bit of good news.* He nodded as they walked, their pace a brisk one. "It's true," he seethed. "Well done, though. No one will think to look for him there."

"Where are we going?" Ylva asked.

"To pay the Vetreonish ambassador a visit."

When they came to the man's chambers, Royce was pleased to see the head of the palace guard already there with two others.

"My Lord Aldana," the man said, inclining his head. "I've got every man I can spare searching the city. The palace is sealed off, and I've been told the city's gates are closed. Thought our Vetreonish friend here might know a thing or two. Didn't want him disappearing as well. Figured you or Valeri would show up eventually."

"Smart. Thank you." Royce looked around. "Have someone find Valeri and get him to meet me here, and please," he said, gritting his teeth against the near-constant ringing, "have someone stop the bells. All it's doing is causing panic and annoying me."

"Of course, my lord." The guard bobbed his head.

Royce put his hand to the ambassador's door handle, willing himself not to throttle the man first thing.

"Shall I send my men in with you, my lord?" the guard asked.

Royce jerked his head toward Ylva. She cut an impressive figure. Royce was tall and well-built. Ylva was of an equal height, slender, but far more lethal. Only a fool could miss the dangerous aura she presented. Her jade green eyes glinted beneath the brim of her hat, and the set of her sharp jaw brooked no arguments.

"We'll be fine." Royce smiled as he and Ylva slipped into the ambassador's chambers.

4

LUCIA

Lucia paced alone and unbound beneath the ship's deck, shaking out her knotted limbs. She couldn't let herself be delivered to Ramir. There was no other choice but to escape by any means necessary. The captain was her only hope, and seduction seemed her best bet. *It may not be too terrible.* Perhaps she would be pleasantly surprised to find that beneath the salt-stained clothing and grime, the captain would turn out to be a beauty, but perhaps not. *Does it really matter?* She was getting off the ship before they reached Vetreon, one way or another.

A pile of clothes hit her in the face.

"Put those on, then come on deck," Alessandra called from the stairs before leaving her alone once more.

Lucia's lips curled. *The captain is going to be a challenge.* She pulled at the clothes, looking them over. They were a pair of finely made breeches, a linen shirt, and a thick leather belt to hold the lot together. She was pleased. It was the sort of outfit she wore to hunt, ride, or be at ease with herself. She loved her fanciful figure-hugging gowns, but to be forced into them daily to conform to a society she ruled suddenly seemed ridiculous. *When I get out of here, the first thing I'm going to do is bring breeches into ladies' fashion.* Lucia laughed, imagining the shocked faces of the elder court ladies.

"You coming, or shall I leave you down there?" Alessandra's voice echoed through the hold.

Lucia tossed her hair over her shoulder and rolled her eyes as she tugged at the belt. The breeches fit snugly over her thighs and were almost unbearably tight in the rear, but a bit loose around the waist. She was sure, even with the belt, that they were going to fall down.

"Are you alive?"

"Yes," she yelled up at the captain, stomping her way, barefoot, up the stairs. Entering the blistering heat of the day, she threw her arms up against the harsh light.

"Don't have an extra hat, I'm afraid. Best keep out of the sun," Alessandra spoke rather more congenially than before. "I'll find you some boots." She called out to a deckhand nearby. "Kier? Find Her Majesty boots." The man bobbed his head before walking away. "You ever been on a ship before?"

Lucia gazed out onto the vast blueness of the sea as she leaned heavily against the ship's railing. There was nothing else, only water. Alessandra was right. She wasn't going to jump, yet. *I'm fucked.*

"You're not going to throw up, are you?" Alessandra's face suddenly filled her vision.

Lucia shooed her away. "No. I'm not. And no, I haven't. Been on a ship, that is."

The ship lurched on the waves, and Alessandra's attention went to the wheel. "Right the helm, Smith," she called up to the stern deck. There was a shaggy young man there. Though he was three decks up, Lucia's jaw clenched as she recognized one of her kidnappers staring back at her, mouth agape. *Bastard.*

"Aye, Captain!"

The ship righted itself, and Alessandra turned back to her. "Just try to stay out of the way. The crew won't give you any trouble. Oh, and for the love of God, don't fall overboard. I don't want to have to go in after you."

Lucia watched the captain turn on her heel and leave. Lost and completely out of her element, she found a barrel somewhat out of the sun and settled down. Not a soul said a word to her as they scurried about the deck, performing their normal duties. She didn't like being still, didn't ever allow herself the time as there was too much to dwell on. *How am I going to keep myself from going mad? By planning my escape and revenge. By staring at one intriguing captain.*

Lucia spent the remainder of the day watching the crew work as Alessandra barked orders. The captain was strict with her men, but not cruel—more competent. The wind and the rolling ocean beneath them, seemed to be a part of the woman. Time and time again, Lucia's eyes returned to the tall figure striding across the deck. Her mind began to wander, imagining just what lay beneath the captain's clothes, conjuring an image of Alessandra bound and naked before her.

"You been staring at the captain all morning," came a gruff voice beside her. The man, who she understood to be the first mate, held a flagon out to her. "Ale," he said. "You need to drink. Can't have you dying before we get paid."

Lucia grimaced at the thought of sharing anything with the unkempt fellow, but she was parched. She took it, drinking deeply before wiping her mouth on the sleeve of the borrowed shirt. "Not much else to look at."

The man smirked. "Mmm."

Lucia studied him. "You really expect to come out of this with your head attached to your shoulders?"

He took the ale back. "I've got faith in her," he said, pointing to the captain, then walked away.

Lucia was shocked. The D'Allyon name was infamous in Moranth. A noble family ruined by misfortune, though Lucia knew the blame lay mostly with her dead father. She was barely half-grown herself when her father, King Teodor, started calling in the debts of any who opposed his regime. When those were not repaid, and on most occasions they weren't, land was seized and people disappeared, culminating in one dark night of slaughter and flight. It came to be known as The Purge of Moranth or simply The Purge.

Lucia had not mourned the loss of her father.

Closing her eyes, she breathed deeply, letting the cries of an albatross overhead and the rocking of the ship lull her into a doze. She was awoken sometime later by a bowl being shoved at her chest.

"You need to eat." Alessandra was standing over her, the wide brim of her hat obscuring the sun, her hand stretched out.

Lucia's stomach gurgled with hunger, and her head spun as she tried to stand. The captain was by her side, taking her weight as she gently laid her back on the deck. Lucia was embarrassed. It was unlike her to show weakness, certainly never in front of an enemy.

"You don't have your sea legs yet," Alessandra explained. "Might take a few days, if at all. Some never learn the knack."

Lucia winced before muttering, "Thank you."

She took the proffered bowl and wrinkled her nose at its contents. She hadn't meant to, she was genuinely thankful for the food, but Lucia caught Alessandra's eye roll before she was able to tuck into the beans and sea biscuits as excitedly as any of the crew.

"Well," Alessandra said, obviously taken aback, "I'll leave you to it. Just remember to take everything slow. Your body isn't used to the sea."

Lucia nodded, her mouth full. It all tasted like sawdust on her tongue, but at least she wouldn't starve.

ALESSANDRA

Alessandra paced the deck, hands behind her back in frustration. Never before had she been so uneasy aboard The Medusa. Lucia was enough of a distraction, but it was also the feeling of betrayal from her men that she was wrestling with. She returned to the helm where Rafe manned the wheel, hoping for some quiet. Rafe at least knew when to leave off.

However, Cyril couldn't seem to help himself. She felt his eyes on her as soon as she reached the upper deck. "Nice chat with Her Majesty?" he asked.

Alessandra had been uncharacteristically quiet as she went about her business, and it seemed her first mate took notice.

"Mmm," was her only acknowledgement.

Cyril tried again. "Fine-looking woman."

She cocked her head, the sun sparkling off her hair. Her gold eyes glared at him beneath the brim of her hat. "There a question in there, Cyril?"

Alessandra was well aware of what her first mate was not so subtly hinting at. The queen was certainly a comely lass—a blind man could see that—but she was never one to let pleasure interfere with business, and to Cyril's way of thinking, that's all the pretty blonde was, a means to an end.

Alessandra didn't blame Cyril for worrying she may balk. He had been a pirate for nigh on twenty years, almost longer than she had been alive, and was older than any pirate had a right to be. He had sailed and fought side by side with her father for decades, but like her father, he was an old man. He had a little home with a plump little wife in Silver Cove. The take from the queen's ransom would not only set himself and his wife up, but their three children, too. They could become merchants or traders. Live honest lives, not looking over their shoulders as the crew of The Medusa did. Alessandra knew this was the man's last chance at such a fortune.

"I mean," he began to sputter. "Well—just—with your father's passing and all, it's no wonder you might be in some need of—well, in need."

Rafe laughed, finally interjecting himself into the conversation. Alessandra tried to contain the look of embarrassed horror on her face as she and Cyril turned to scowl at the shipmate.

"What?" the sailor shrugged, not taking his eyes from the horizon. "You think Alex—sorry, the captain—can't keep her breeches on, Cyril? For God's sake, man, you trust the rest of us scoundrels with the queen's virtue, but not her?"

Alessandra's pride was pricked by Cyril's caution and by Rafe feeling the need to stand up for her, though, as always, she was grateful for the man's loyalty. She wasn't ready to admit it to herself, but her first mate's words struck some chord of truth within her. The queen was lovely and spirited, and Alessandra couldn't keep the image of her nude form from her mind.

"That will be all, Cyril. I know you have work to do," she dismissed.

"Aye, Captain." Cyril tucked his chin and swallowed before making his way to the lower deck.

Alessandra caught Rafe's bemused face. "No." She raised a finger, stopping him as he opened his mouth for what she assumed was a teasing comment.

As the sun dipped below the horizon, Alessandra found herself, once more, drawn to the queen's side. Lucia was sleeping, shivering as the temperature dropped along with the sun, her dark lashes fanning against flushed cheeks. Alessandra bent low, shaking the queen to wake her, feeling a flutter in her chest as her hand met the heat of Lucia's skin.

Lucia's grey eyes opened slowly, as if she'd forgotten where she was or the danger she was in. A lazy smile graced her dusky lips. "Come to take me to bed?"

Alessandra stood, pulling Lucia up as a bloom of desire unfurled within her. "Come on," she said, ignoring the queen's comment. That was exactly where she was taking Lucia. "You'll sleep in my cabin tonight."

"Not one for seduction, are you, Captain?" Lucia quipped.

Alessandra strode across the deck, tugging at Lucia as the queen struggled to keep up.

Arriving at the captain's quarters, Alessandra raked her fingers self-consciously through the snarls of her hair as they walked inside. She knew she was beautiful. On the occasions The Medusa ever docked long enough for her to actually get clean and wear the costly clothes her father bought her, she recognized the looks and attention she received. Knew the power such beauty afforded her. Looking in the mirror, she couldn't remember the last time she had a proper bath or took the time to brush out the long length of her dark red waves. Though why she cared about how she looked was annoying the hell out of her. What she felt for the queen, the dampness between her thighs every time the woman spoke, was infuriating. Lucia's family was responsible for the destruction of her own, destroying all she held dear. Her father must have been cursing her from beyond. To even be thinking of bedding his enemy's daughter was a betrayal.

"Now, this is exactly what I was expecting." Lucia wandered through the cabin, her eyes darting, fingers stroking the bric-à-brac that made a room a home.

"What do you mean?" Alessandra assumed the fair queen was doing more than acclimating herself to the place—more like searching for any loose weapons. She gave the ruler credit. Lucia was a fighter, if perhaps not in body, then certainly in spirit.

"I admit to being disappointed by the lack of a dragon's hoard of treasure in your hold," Lucia said. Alessandra couldn't help but snicker. "But this is perfect."

"Wasn't expecting royalty." Alessandra shrugged, her movements shadowing the queens as they roamed the cabin.

The room was truly spectacular. Piled rugs swallowed the sounds of their bootsteps, thick burgundy velvet drapes aiding to muffle the noise of a ship at sea. Ornately carved furniture, dark with age, lined the wood-paneled walls. Countless books were on their shelves, along with her father's favorite treasures from his voyages. On his desk, sat near the windows for the best light, was a jeweled dagger stolen from a prince and an intricately painted map unrolled beneath it.

Heavy leaded glass windows jutted out above the sea, letting the last of the evening's light through. It struck the dagger's hilt, reflections of emeralds and rubies skittering across the room. She hadn't supposed the room would be impressive to a queen, but Alessandra was pleased, for some reason, that it was.

There was no real intention in her mind to take Lucia to bed, much as she desired her, but she could do with a higher level of conversation than was usually had onboard. "Why don't you have a seat?" She gestured toward the small table and chairs in the center of the room.

Lucia obliged, settling back into the worn leather. "This is exactly how I always imagined a pirate's ship would look."

Alessandra could admit it was impressive, but with a handful of exceptions, the opulence came from the time before, as had The Medusa herself.

"The candlesticks," Alessandra pointed to the twisting silver holders on the table, "were given to my mother at her wedding. They've been in the family for two hundred years, so I was told. Same goes for the plates. The rugs came from my grandmother, my father's mother. She didn't want her son cold while on the high seas. I'm not overly fond of them, too itchy. The chandelier from my mother's girlhood estate, so she would always have a piece of her home here."

They glanced up to the wide circle of iron above them —the Fontaine crest of one of Moranth's oldest families, a sun in front of two crossed swords, was wrought upon it.

"Those swords were used at my coronation," Lucia said, speaking of the ancient twin blades.

"Hmm," was all the answer Alessandra gave. She wanted to remind Lucia that her blood was as noble as hers, that it was Lucia's father that had stolen the life she was meant to have. She leaned against one of the four posters of the massive bed, running the pads of her fingertips over the carved trellis of roses. "My father built this himself."

"I'm guessing he made it for your mother?" Lucia asked in a quiet, gentle voice, full of understanding.

"He did. He always wanted her to join him on the seas when she got a chance."

"Did she?"

"No. Your father had her killed."

"He killed my mother, too."

Alessandra blinked as Lucia's voice became thick with unshed tears. A rumor had circulated at the time of the queen's passing that her death was at the hands of the king. Their daughter had just confirmed it.

Lucia's stomach growled loudly with hunger, saving both women from exploring their private pain further. Alessandra, for one, was glad of the distraction.

"I'll tell the lads you'll be joining me for dinner."

Lucia perked up, sitting straighter in her chair. "Have anything better than those beans?"

"I could let you go hungry if you don't like them."

Lucia's lips turned up at the corners. "Not a complaint, more a curiosity. I've always heard how much more democratic a pirate ship is than a navy one."

"That's true, I'm certain," Alessandra answered. "Unfortunately, there's no longer a separate cook for the captain. He died some years ago. We've made do, and Cook does his best when there's call for it. I'll make certain he scrounges up something better than beans," she said, unable to keep herself from returning the queen's grin. "What I do have is my father's wine cellar, and that makes up for the food."

Alessandra moved to the cabin's door, opening it a crack. Ben was outside the door, standing guard. He snapped to attention when he saw her.

"Captain?" His big brown eyes were wide. Alessandra was suddenly struck by how young the sailor was. Though she was only a handful of years older, she felt her new position had added a decade to her years.

"The queen will be dining with me. Please let Cook know. Her Majesty has requested anything besides beans."

The young man chuckled and pulled at his cap before beating a retreat.

She shut the door and crossed the room, ignoring Lucia as she made her way to the cases of wine jumbled in a dark corner. Her fingers traced the crumbling labels before holding one bottle and then another up to the amber glow of the chandelier.

"Find something?" came Lucia's voice.

Alessandra had found what she thought was an excellent red—dark, peppery, and dry. "I think so," she answered, her eyes casting about the room for the spare musket gum worm to open the bottle.

"Ah." She caught sight of the twisted metal device already lying on the table.

She sat down carefully uncorking the wine, making sure to keep the length of the dark wood between herself and Lucia. She fully understood the queen's intentions, and while she would more than enjoy a romp with the devastatingly beautiful woman, she was aware that no good would come of it.

"Tell me what you think," she said, pouring the wine slowly into a glass.

"Thank you." Lucia took the glass by the stem, raising it to her nose. "Lovely." Alessandra watched Lucia's white throat bob as she emptied the small pour. Her eyes sparkled as they met Alessandra's. "Lovely indeed."

LUCIA

The collar of Alessandra's shirt was undone, exposing the long curve of her throat and a hint of cleavage. Lucia found the pirate captain more and more distracting with each interaction. She watched as Alessandra moved around the cabin, pointing out the remaining riches of the D'Allyon family. Heat rose in her cheeks each time the deceased members of the noble family were mentioned. What happened to them was not her fault. She, like Alessandra, was a child then. It had been her father that destroyed them, as he ruined so many others.

For the eight years of her reign, Lucia sought to right her father's wrongs. It would seem there would always be more amends to make. She almost said she was sorry for the pain, for the loss, but stopped herself. *What good will my apology do?* Lucia had to swallow back her tears when Alessandra briefly mentioned her mother's death, bringing back the nightmarish visions of a dead queen. She had been grateful for the loud interruption of her ravenous stomach.

She was warming toward her captor, but not enough to trust her.

Head and body already buzzing with drink when dinner arrived, Lucia was pleased that Cook had made an effort. Her eyes closed as the first bite of the dark, earthy venison stew hit her tongue. She thought she heard a hitch in the pirate's breathing.

"Better than beans?" Alessandra asked.

Lucia opened her eyes, licking her lips suggestively. "Mmm, so much better, and my compliments on the wine." She drank deeply from the delicate blown glass goblet, noting how Alessandra's eyes fixed momentarily on her lips. *Everything is going to plan.*

As they ate, she kept up a light, companionable conversation, finding the captain to be well-educated on a variety of topics. They mostly discussed trade. Lucia even sought the pirate's advice on her proposed embargo. Alessandra thought it a good idea for the short term as a means of destabilizing Vetreon's economy, but she didn't think it would do much to stop a man like Ramir, who cared nothing for his people.

"Aren't you worried that it will be the people of Vetreon, the commoners, that will suffer most under such action?" Alessandra finally asked.

Lucia nodded, amused by Alessandra's clear shock as she answered. "I am. That's why this whole mess needs to be ended as swiftly as possible. My current predicament," she opened her arms wide to indicate her kidnapping, "will no doubt slow the process."

"That implies you think you'll get out of this without marrying your cousin."

"Our marriage won't be happening," Lucia said matter-of-factly. "However, the embargo," she raised her glass before taking a long sip, "Royce, my Lord Treasurer, will use it to squeeze Ramir. This was a step too far. All my cousin has done is seal his fate."

A brief smile flickered over Alessandra's lips.

"You don't believe me?" Lucia asked. *Of course she doesn't believe me. She's a seafarer. She knows the odds are against Moranth. At least for the moment.*

"I believe should I fail in bringing you to Vetreon, you'll make a fine accounting of yourself in the war."

Lucia raised her glass in salute once more. "That I will."

Her plan to seduce the captain was almost entirely forgotten as the night wore on and the wine flowed. There was no longer a need for it because Lucia was already smitten. So much so that when Alessandra pulled out a pair of manacles, a moan filled with want escaped her lips before she could think to stop it.

"Ha! Don't get excited, Your Majesty. You're sleeping on the floor." Alessandra locked one cold iron cuff around Lucia's slender wrist before gently pulling the half-drunk queen from her chair. Depositing her on the wool rug as she protested, the captain affixed the other manacle around the foot of the bed.

Lucia's eyes widened with surprise as she fumbled with the iron lock before giving up. "How am I supposed to sleep like this?"

Alessandra kicked off her boots before snuggling under the heavy bed covers. "You'll figure it out, or you won't. Either way, it's better than being out on deck or in the hold with the rats."

Lucia shut her gaping mouth at the mention of rats and lay down as best she could with one arm twisted up uncomfortably. The wine helped, and even awkwardly positioned, it wasn't long before she fell into a fitful sleep.

Lucia woke to the sight of a pair of black boots beside her. Forgetting for a moment that she was fettered, Lucia attempted to jerk back, but the manacle at her wrist quickly reminded her, and she yelped at the sharp pain. *Not the most pleasant way to wake up.* Her focus shifted from her aching wrist to the boots, traveling up the length of them to a silk-clad knee, a shapely thigh, then a pistol. *How long has she been watching me?* The thought excited Lucia as the pirate's full lips and golden eyes elicited an unwanted flood of desire.

Alessandra's eyes narrowed. "You snore."

5

ALESSANDRA

The day was much the same as the one before, which was what Alessandra and the crew had hoped for. They had no need for surprises, especially with their mission and cargo aboard. She hadn't slept, and when Lucia began to wake, her frustration, fear, and general irritability fell upon the queen. Of course, it was with very good reason. Lucia couldn't know it, but last night Alessandra was near turning the ship around and sailing straight for Moranth. To her dismay, she found common ground between the two of them, which didn't make delivering the queen to that monster any easier.

Alessandra found herself torn. It wasn't right to give her to a man who would undoubtedly destroy her, but taking Lucia back home meant certain death. So, she made sure to keep her distance, unwilling to expose herself to the queen's impressive wiles. Although, it wasn't her charms that had so captivated Alessandra the night before. It was the sharpness of the her mind. They deliberated on tactics, politics, and Lucia's plans for Moranth and her people. Her eyes would light with enthusiasm as Alessandra regaled her with stories of her adventures on the high seas, and something about that sheer joy intrigued the captain.

"It was always such a romantic place, I thought," Alessandra was telling Lucia of her travels, *"the queen's city, with that palace of hers up on the bluffs. I was determined to see it up close."* She was pleased to see she had Lucia enthralled as the woman perched at the edge of her seat. *"Rafe heard rumors of old sea caves and an ancient path cut into the chalk cliffs. So, of course, I put on my finery and had Rafe and Smith row me to the beach, and sure enough, there they were, barely visible, but there was a path."* Alessandra laughed, knocking back another glass of wine. *"I'm sure I looked frightful by the time I made it into the Governor's palace, but there was a party going on, and it was dark. I spent all night there, wandering the halls of ancient Ravensbluff, heart pounding, sure I was going to be found out."*

Lucia shook her head. "I hear it's haunted."

"Now that's a ghost I wouldn't mind running into."

Alessandra could see Lucia's mind at work. "Do you think she was really as beautiful as the stories say?"

"Or as brave, fearless?" Alessandra wondered. "Maybe this will be a story one day. One that people tell."

"The pirate and the queen?" Lucia suggested, then sighed heavily. "I envy you being able to go where you want, doing as you please."

Alessandra chuckled, perplexed. "You're a queen. Can't you do whatever you want?"

Lucia's brows drew together, her face taking on a sullen cast. "No, I can't." She looked hurt.

Alessandra wondered why a queen should care what her kidnapper thought of her or her dreams of adventure. From there, Lucia turned the conversation to war, and Alessandra had done her best to rebuff the queen's advances.

———

In the light of day, she tried to set both Lucia and her own troubling feelings to the side as she pressed on with the work of captain, but as the evening drew in again, she felt a thread of excitement unspool at the thought of another night with the beguiling creature.

"You're thinking about her, aren't you?" came Rafe's teasing voice.

Alessandra lowered her spyglass, her cheeks burning despite the refreshing breeze. "No, I'm not."

Rafe laughed, not moving his hands from the ship's wheel. "You've had a grin on your face all day. Come on, Alex, it's just us up here. Pretend you aren't the captain, just my friend, and tell me all about it."

Alessandra almost laughed. Before she was captain, she and Rafe would have exchanged every detail of their latest escapades, but she was captain, so there wasn't anything she could tell, nor did she want to because it could only end in disaster. "We had dinner. We talked," she responded flatly.

Heavy steps pounded up the stairs. "Your queen's been awfully quiet today." Cyril was puffing as he reached the quarterdeck.

"To hell with the whole lot of you." Alessandra groaned. "She's not *my* queen." She didn't miss the look exchanged between her crew.

Alessandra huffed, jerked her hat from her head, then retreated to her cabin, needing a moment of quiet. Her head still pounded with the previous night's drink, and the sweltering heat was doing little to help.

She'd only just sat down on the bed, ready to yank off her boots, when a knock sounded at her cabin door. Alessandra rolled her eyes. "I'm in no mood for another lecture," she yelled, stomping across the room. She threw the door open, expecting Cyril, but was shocked when her eyes met those of the queen.

LUCIA

It was an interesting situation she found herself in. The day had gone on with no communication from her alluring pirate captain. Things seemed to be going so well the night before—too well. For a moment after dinner, she thought she had her, that Alessandra was amenable to her seduction, contrived or genuine as it was, and then came the cuffs. Lucia softly snickered under her breath. It wasn't the way such nights usually ended for her. *Alessandra has to be enamored with me; there is nothing else for it.*

She refused to let Alessandra ignore her any longer.

Feeling confident, Lucia watched from her tiny bit of shade as the captain stormed from the deck. *This is my chance.* She swept the thick braid of her hair over one shoulder, where it hung invitingly, accentuating the curve of her breast. The crew stopped and stared longingly, though silently, as she sashayed toward the captain's cabin, hips swaying in her tight breeches.

"I'm in no mood for another lecture." Alessandra flung the door open.

At seeing her surprised expression, Lucia's lips parted in a seductive smile. "I make no promises." Grinning, she brushed past Alessandra into the room. "Though talking isn't what I have in mind."

The captain stood frozen for a moment before closing the door behind them. "If you're just going to try to tempt me again, you should leave now. I'm not in the mood, and we both know it isn't going to get you anywhere."

Lucia's lips curved as her eyes, beneath lowered lashes, met the captain's. "How am I to know it won't work? I've not really tried yet." Lucia winked. Trailing a hand over the pirate's exposed collarbone, she made herself comfortable in Alessandra's space.

A low, frustrated sigh from the pirate followed her. "Sit down. You give me an excuse to break out the good food and wine, but understand," Alessandra pointed a finger at her, "conversation and food are all this is."

Lucia smirked as she sat. "I understand, Captain."

ALESSANDRA

Alessandra's lips pursed as she shook her head. *Damn the woman! Oh, let them talk! I don't care anymore.* Of course, she knew Lucia was only there in hopes of seducing her into either making a mistake or setting her free, but at that moment, Alessandra wasn't sure she cared. She wanted Lucia in the most infuriating way possible.

As the night wore on, her resolve to fend off the queen's advances softened. Lucia was so lovely, her grey eyes so inviting, and the swell of her breasts was just visible at the open collar of her shirt. Alessandra wondered what sounds she made in the midst of passion.

She hadn't meant to drink so much—she wanted her wits about her with her captive. Still, the woman's company was disarming, and whether it was the wine or the honesty, she found once again that she rather enjoyed the queen's presence. Lucia was quick-witted, only slightly haughty, and an astute observer. Her imitation of Cyril's deep barking voice had Alessandra doubled over with laughter. She could just imagine the men huddled around the cabin door, shocked by the snorts of amusement coming from the captain's quarters. Alessandra's defenses were down just enough for her not to budge when Lucia stood to bring her chair next to her own. She cursed inwardly. It had been a very long time since she'd conversed so easily with another soul, but to be so open was to put herself in danger. Lucia's eyes, dulled with alcohol, lips stained red with wine as her own must be, held Alessandra's gaze as the queen's hand ran up the silk of her breeches.

Alessandra roused herself from her pleasant stupor. "We won't be doing this. I already made that clear." She bristled, wrestling with her desire as she took hold of Lucia's wrist. It felt so slender Alessandra knew it would be nothing for her to break it.

Lucia's lips parted in a playful grin, her teeth white against the darkness of the candle lit cabin. "Oh, come on," she teased, drawing herself closer. "Let's get to know each other better. If you please me, maybe I'll let you take me back to Moranth. Give you a command."

Alessandra leveled her eyes at the queen. "No," she said, her tone serious. "There is nothing you have that I could possibly want."

Lucia raised a skeptical brow, her fingers unlacing the fastenings of her shirt.

"You're the queen," Alessandra mused. "You were the heir to the throne before that. Have you ever been told no before?"

Lucia scoffed, shaking her head.

"What I thought," Alessandra said, disgusted. "Nobles, royals, you're all the same."

"I'm not my father, you know," Lucia snapped. "Those nobles you hate, does that include you, *Lady* D'Allyon? Or do you deny who you are?"

Fury rose in Alessandra at the mention of her near-forgotten title. "The last Lady D'Allyon died twenty years ago. Killed on your father's order. That's not who *I* am."

Lucia sneered. "No, you're just a pirate, right? You don't care about anything except yourself. Then why am *I* in here with you now? Why not keep me tied up in the hold where I won't be a bother?"

Alessandra ground her teeth, her nipples peaking as Lucia baited her. "I already told you why. I won't waste a man watching you."

LUCIA

The pirate's accusations hit a nerve. She and Alessandra had been having such a pleasant time before there was mention of her dead father. There was no one Lucia despised more. For a moment, Lucia had nearly forgotten where she was, the danger she was in, so much so that she'd even offered the pirate a place in her navy. Lucia shocked even herself with those words. Alessandra was an exile. Though, as queen, the pirate's position was easy enough to fix. With a signature, the captain could once more be a lady. Of course, she would've offered anything to be free, even herself, not that it would be a struggle to do so. Alessandra was unlike any woman she'd ever known, and Lucia found herself longing to know her in every sense. Then the comparison to the king. Lucia thought she could weather any insult but that—to be branded her father's daughter. The barb sobered her up. Ending up like her father was her worst fear.

Her body began to vibrate with rage.

Alessandra had struck the first blow. Lucia thought of landing the next, provoking the pirate captain. *Don't do this, Lucia.* If she continued, she'd launch them into an unwinnable fight for either side. Instead, she slowed her thoughts, gritted her teeth, calmed her breathing, and reversed course. Her quick temper could push the captain in the wrong direction.

Lucia's tongue rubbed circles on the roof of her mouth, searching for a sweeter tone. "You're right," she began, her voice low and sensual. "Better to watch me yourself." She smiled again, her hand resting on Alessandra's thigh. "Why not enjoy me while I'm here?" She watched the pirate's pulse leap in her throat. "I know you want to."

Alessandra pushed at Lucia's hand, stood, and backed away. "Wanting and doing are two very separate things. I've no interest in being with an unwilling woman."

Lucia stood, their breasts a handbreadth apart. She didn't want to acknowledge how her stomach flipped when Alessandra said she wanted her. Getting the captain into bed was part of her plan, nothing more, but the captain's words stirred her. *Am I unwilling?* She couldn't stop staring at the pirate's inviting lips.

A moment of silence hung between them as the ship creaked, the ocean lapped, and their breathing became more shallow. Lucia's body was taut with anticipation. She wanted Alessandra. She didn't know what she'd feel in the morning, if anything, but at that moment, the imposing captain was the only thing that existed.

Lucia's brows furrowed, her fists clenched as she stayed herself, wishing Alessandra would reach for her, give her an excuse to catch her up in her arms, and take her to bed, but the pirate was still as a statue. She wondered where the captain's previous bravado had gone—where her own had gone. *Where are the teasing words, smirking lips, and inviting touch?*

Lucia felt a tug at her core as Alessandra's nipples pressed against the linen of her shirt, and her eyes darkened. Her breasts ached for the pirate's touch, her belly tightening at the thought. She couldn't move, but she so wanted to. There was something different about the pirate, different from the serving girls and noblemen's wives she was used to. Something unnamed that she longed for.

Suddenly, Alessandra's arm was around her waist, and she was being pulled into a heated kiss. Her lips parted, allowing it to deepen as Alessandra's tongue thrust against her own. The inkling of her unspoken desire washed over Lucia, but the thread was lost as Alessandra broke from their embrace.

"Why are you stopping?" Lucia rasped.

Alessandra's chest rose with a sharp intake of breath. "I need to know you want this."

Lucia had never begged for anything in her life, but she would if that was what Alessandra needed. "I—"

Alessandra froze, cocking her head to the side before her eyes widened. "Get down!" she screamed, pushing Lucia to the floor.

There was a high whistle before the sound of a tremendous booming splash outside the window.

Someone pounded on the cabin door.

"Captain!" Cyril thundered.

Lucia's eyes widened in fear as Alessandra grabbed her hand. There was another whistle, and the captain pulled her in tight, shielding her as a second crash rocked the ship. Alessandra didn't immediately let her go. "Get under the bed and stay there." The pirate's voice was firm as she took Lucia by the arm and pushed her toward relative safety. "We're under attack. I'll be back, or I won't."

"You can't leave me unarmed."

Alessandra shoved a pair of pistols into her belt before looking back at her. "There's a gun in that trunk." She indicated one next to Lucia. "It's loaded. Just don't shoot me when I come back for you. We both know that won't do you any good."

Lucia wasn't about to argue as she yanked open the chest and rifled through clothes until her hand fastened on the smooth wood of a pistol stock.

"You know how to use that?" Alessandra asked as she made for the door.

"I do." Lucia nodded before crawling under the bed, not caring about dust or the splinters jamming into her hands.

Alessandra lingered for one last moment, then she threw open the door and stormed on deck.

6

ALESSANDRA

"Where in the hell is that coming from, Cyril?" Alessandra shouted, bounding up the slippery steps to the helm. Every man topside was armed to the teeth, ready to fight. Alessandra squinted into the darkness. They were in a dangerous area of the West Sea, with lonely islands and treacherous jagged mountains jutting from the churning waves. She could just see a bit of mast and sail in the moonlight past her first mate's pointing finger as he handed her the spyglass. As she put it to her eye, a bolt of lightning lit the night.

She knew that flag—black with a nude woman in white atop two crossed bones—*The Deceit*.

"It's Defoe," she seethed, lowering the glass.

"Course it is," Cyril spat. "Only one crazy enough to try to attack with a squall like this coming on," he shouted into the gusting wind.

"Damn it," Alessandra muttered. The weather hadn't looked nearly this bad when she sat down for dinner only a brief while ago. The storm had given them no warning. They were facing not only the weather but also an adversary known for his relentlessness. She'd have rather seen the whole of the Moranthese navy before her than the lone sail of that pirate ship.

Captain Defoe of The Deceit had been a thorn in her father's side for years. Though they'd never met face-to-face, the two ships had gone head-to-head on several occasions, with no one ever gaining enough of an upper hand to declare victory.

"We can't outrun her in this," Alessandra said, ducking as another cannonball pounded into the sea. They were getting closer. "Bring her around," she told Cyril.

"Alright, you lot," the old pirate shouted. "Bring her round!"

Their only hope was combat if the sea didn't take them first. It would be up to The Medusa's gunners in the meantime. The frigate held twenty cannons, eight per side, with two at the aft and two forward. The stinging rain made it almost impossible to see. Alessandra swiped at her eyes before bringing the spyglass up once more as her ship came into better firing range. The wind buffeted her from every side.

"Fire!"

The cannons boomed around her; the sound was deafening. Alessandra watched, waiting for the seconds it took the lead balls to slam into their enemy. She grinned as they struck their target, then the world suddenly dropped out from under her.

Lying prone on the deck, Alessandra sucked in air, her ears ringing. She was soaked. Her men were all about her in a similar fashion—*rogue wave*. She pushed to her feet, only to be swept off them again.

Someone had hold of her arm as she shook her head, trying to unrattle her mind. It was Cyril. "Captain," he bellowed. "We've got to change course." His hand pointed heavenward.

Alessandra's stomach lurched at the black clouds above them. The wind was changing, and worse still, a waterspout had risen into the dark heavens before them. What had been the desirable position only a moment ago had put them in the gravest of danger. The gales of wind were pushing them ever closer to the rocky embankment on their starboard side.

"Heave to," Alessandra directed. The rain and wind nearly swallowed her voice, but she heard the order relayed and watched her men scurry off to haul at the thick ropes and adjust the sails. The ship began to swing around.

Alessandra's eyes were moving over the men, the cannons, and the lower deck when she saw Lucia stumble from her cabin, clutching her head. On her feet, she took the steps two at a time toward the queen when a jagged bolt of lightning struck the mast. Her world turned bright white for a second as the top of the mast splintered, her men screamed, and the smell of burning wood filled the air.

Her ship was on fire, her men injured, some gravely, and Lucia was about to go over the railing. Alessandra ran and grabbed the queen, seeing for the first time the gush of blood coming from her head. Lucia's eyes were wide and disbelieving as Alessandra clutched her to her chest.

"Captain!" Cyril's voice tore through her dazed consciousness. She followed the sound of an ear-splitting crack and saw the crow's nest break away and hurtle toward them.

There was no choice. Alessandra pulled at Lucia, and the two women went over the ship's rail.

For a moment, there was nothing but darkness and cold as water rushed up her nose and her ears popped as she and Lucia sank into the sea. Spluttering to the surface, Alessandra hauled Lucia with her as they gasped for air. Her gaze traveled back to the ship where Cyril stood stock still, then jumped into action.

"Smith!" Alessandra heard him scream. "Get those barrels into the water. Something for the Captain to hold on to."

The men chucked barrels and planks of busted decking. Anything that would float as the ship started to drift away. Alessandra saw The Deceit was back in range and had a good firing position as the detritus rained over the ship's side.

Lucia started pushing at her, struggling to free herself from Alessandra's grasp. "I can swim!" Lucia shouted. *Well, thank God for that!*

Alessandra caught sight of Cyril's red face above the ship's railing. He called to her, but his voice carried off on the wind, and she knew from the look of utter despair on his face that she and Lucia were on their own. It couldn't be helped. The Medusa would be dashed on the rocks if they tried to come any closer, and if he held position, The Deceit would be on her.

They'd have to swim for it. A threatening outcrop of jagged black rocks led to a beach on a desolate-looking island, half-hidden in the downpour. It was their only chance. Alessandra briefly wondered if drowning was a better fate than being marooned, but decided to risk it. *Cyril is a fine sailor. If the ship survives, he'll know where to find us. If it doesn't, we'll most likely be dead anyway, so it won't matter.*

Lucia bobbed beside her, having grabbed a rope-wrapped barrel thrown from the ship. Blood continued to trickle down her forehead, but at least she was conscious. There would have been no hope otherwise.

"We have to swim for it," she called, waving her hand toward the distant beach.

Lucia shook her head; she still looked dazed. "We won't make it! The ship?"

Lightning lit the grey sky above them, splitting it open, nearly obscuring The Medusa.

Alessandra grasped at a floating piece of the deck; she would need all her strength to survive the swim. "It's as likely to crush us as the rocks are. We have to go now while the tide is with us."

"We're going to die," Lucia yelled into the howling wind.

Alessandra nodded. "Probably," she said.

Without looking back, she began to make slow, steady strokes toward the island. The sea threatened to swallow them at every moment. It was arduous going. Lightning continued to crack overhead, the metallic taste of it on Alessandra's tongue as she swam. She looked over her shoulder every few minutes. There was nothing but Lucia, her features arranged in a determined scowl as she raised her arms and kicked her long legs.

―――

The Medusa was gone, obscured in the mist, blown far from them. The island was all that mattered. The veil of rain slackened, and the coast of the island became clear. *We are actually going to make it.* She winced as her knee scraped across shells, rending the fabric of her breeches. Her hands clawed for purchase in the cold sand. *I'm alive.* Her arms buckled beneath her as she crawled from the sea. Alessandra lay motionless on the rocky beach for what seemed an eternity and took those first few moments to thank whatever god could hear her. Had they been in colder waters, nothing would have saved them.

Lucia reached the shore shortly after, dropping beside her.

"You alive?" Alessandra said with a weary voice.

"I'm alive." She didn't sound overly confident, grimacing as her fingers probed the knot on her head. At least there was no more blood that Alessandra could see, and Lucia seemed alright.

Alessandra groaned, struggling into a sitting position; there wasn't one bit of her that didn't hurt. She glanced at the sky. The rain had stopped, but the clouds above were still low and grey. "We won't be able to get a fire going. Any kindling will be as soaked as we are."

"At least we've got a full moon. We should see about shelter."

"Know a great deal about being marooned, do you, Your Majesty?"

The queen's eyes darkened. "I know about hiding. Most of my childhood was spent doing just that." She stood, wiping her hands on her soaked clothes. "I've also been known to build a fort or two in my time. Let's go." She held a hand out to Alessandra, who took it, surprised at Lucia's strength as she pulled her to her feet.

"You sure you're the queen?" she asked in all seriousness. As much as Alessandra loved her crew, she wouldn't put it past them to accidentally make off with a well-heeled servant.

Lucia folded her arms, and the wet fabric of her shirt clung to every hard line, every soft curve. Her lush breasts and rose-tipped nipples were clear through the sheer material. Alessandra couldn't be sure if the queen caught her looking or not, but her assets were hard to ignore, even in their predicament.

Lucia glared at her. "Are you going to help me or not?" Her tone was pompous once more, the tone of a royal.

"Right." Alessandra nodded. "Shelter."

Lucia and Alessandra spent several minutes surveying their tiny sliver of beach. A few of the items the crew tossed over were scattered along the shoreline, some rope, pieces of wood, and a hat, which would come in handy for Lucia's fair skin. They gathered them up and headed inland, their wet boots squeaking as they walked.

The island looked to be a harsh, windswept, and scrubby place, with a few palm trees clinging precariously to the earth. Alessandra nodded at the swaying trees. "You know, I used to be able to climb them. If things become too dire, I can always try to get up there and retrieve those coconuts."

"I'd be impressed. I certainly can't scale a tree like I once did."

"We should go inland a-ways," Alessandra suggested. "Get out of this wind."

Lucia said nothing, just nodded and followed.

Alessandra could hear Lucia's steps as she pushed her way through the underbrush. She was determined to get through this, as she got through everything thrown at her, but she couldn't fully tamp down the fear roiling her stomach. She shivered as the wind blew through her soaked shirt and breeches.

The sky began to brighten as they picked their way through the scrub. The island consisted of mostly flat terrain, the rocky coast giving way to sand and low bushes. Alessandra turned at a moan behind her. Lucia stumbled as her eyes rolled back in her head, and her eyelids fluttered. She was fainting. Alessandra was there in an instant, catching Lucia just before she crumpled to the ground. She took hold of Lucia's arm and began to shake her.

"Hey!" Alessandra called.

Lucia mumbled something, still limp in her arms.

"Hey!" Alessandra tried again, to no avail. "Shit," she murmured before delivering a stinging slap across Lucia's face.

Her eyes flew open, focusing on Alessandra. "You're so beautiful," she breathed, still obviously dazed.

"Lucia!" Alessandra shouted in her face.

She shook her head, seeming to come around fully. "I'm fine." She stood, waving off Alessandra.

"There's fresh water," Alessandra said. "Come on. You can't pass out on me. You're too heavy to carry."

Alessandra watched as the teasing comment had the desired effect. Lucia squared her shoulders and trudged toward the waiting promise of water.

The pond, for it was that small, was fed by a burbling spring. Lucia looked at it warily, but Alessandra laughed. Dropping exhaustedly to her knees, she drank without hesitation, feeling Lucia's gaze on her. *Let her look.*

It was only a moment before her own eyes wandered too. Her gaze lingered longer than she'd meant on Lucia's pink tongue, her thirsty mouth, and the long snarls of silvery hair blanched in the fading moonlight. Lucia caught her staring, their eyes meeting as the queen wiped at her mouth.

"I'm feeling much better," she said. "Let's get to work on the shelter. Who knows what's prowling around out here."

Straightening, Alessandra blinked, nodding as a matter of course, her mind still turning the last moment over. She wanted Lucia, wanted to know what the queen's voice sounded like moaning beneath her. *What had Lucia been about to say back on the ship? Would we be entwined in my bed aboard The Medusa if The Deceit hadn't attacked?*

Alessandra finally responded, "We should set up close by. I don't want to be too far from freshwater."

Lucia's hands were on her flared hips as she surveyed the area, squinting from the dawn's light—blatantly ignoring Alessandra. "There," she pointed at a group of boulders.

Alessandra turned. *The queen is no fool.* It was as fine a spot as she'd seen and one she missed, much to her embarrassment. Three boulders, each twice as tall as a man, stood close together. The volcanic rocks converged in such a way to have created a space beneath them, not protected enough to be called a cave, but it would have to do. "That will work."

They were lucky the storm managed to be as destructive on the island as it was, or the small dagger at her hip would have been of little use securing palm fronds or other vegetation to aid their shelter. The women worked in silent determination, gathering the fronds and stacking them to be carried to their campsite. Alessandra was exhausted and scared beyond what she could admit to herself, wondering if the swifter death of drowning would have been preferable to starving on an island, wondering if Lucia was thinking the same.

Lucia was proving an adept worker, with nary a complaint. "We can weave the leaves together tomorrow to give us better cover," Lucia offered as they worked. "We've got twine from the ropes. If you let me use that dagger of yours, I can try to make a bow to get a fire started if there's no more rain, and I can find dry kindling."

"How do you know how to do all this? You're a queen. Isn't someone constantly at your beck and call to do whatever you want?"

"I wasn't always a queen." Alessandra could hear the smirk in Lucia's voice.

"Princesses have it rough, eh?"

"My mother knew her way in the wilds. Then once she was gone, I was on my own a lot. I didn't want to be in the palace. It was best to stay out of my father's way." Alessandra was shocked to hear the vulnerability in Lucia's voice, the pain of a child who'd been hurt. Then again, Lucia was the child of a man who killed his wife. No wonder the girl tried to keep her distance.

It was no secret that Lucia's father, King Teodor, was a brute known for killing any dissenters, even his wife. Alessandra was sure the welfare of the princess never crossed the common folk's minds; it certainly never crossed hers growing up. She started to ponder the upbringing Lucia had from such a man, one infamous for his cruelty. She thought of her own father, thankful for the man he was, for his kindness toward her, his love. The captain was a pirate, to be sure, one whose life depended on taking from others, from killing when it came to it, but he was never a cruel man. For all the strangeness of her life and childhood, she was loved.

Alessandra swallowed any further retort. "I'm sorry," was all she could say. Part of her wanted to know more—she was an inquisitive human, after all—but she reminded herself that her goal was handing Lucia over to her enemy to do with as he pleased. A royal wedding where neither party had any love for the other. It sounded awful, but Alessandra tried to rationalize it. *Isn't it the cost of all that privilege? Highborn women are married off at a whim every day. Why should Lucia be any different? Why should the queen's fate matter to me?*

The two finished the little structure, if it could be called that, under the wan light of a dark morning. Once completed, they crawled inside, their damp, sand-filled clothes scratching at their exhausted bodies.

"Ow!" Lucia's voice echoed in the tiny dark space.

"What?" Alessandra jerked away, forgetting the crisis of conscience gnawing at her. She didn't want to take Lucia to Ramir. Whether or not there were actual feelings, or even just lust, between her and the queen, she was beginning to think even a royal didn't deserve a fate like that.

"You stepped on my hand," Lucia accused, sounding like a wounded child.

"I'm sorry. Are you alright?"

Lucia huffed.

Alessandra could hear her rooting about, trying to find some measure of comfort on the hard-packed earth. *No more talking, I guess.* She turned over, seeking her own spot on the ground. It was almost too hot within the shelter, but it was better than the bone-deep chill of earlier. Squeezing her eyes shut, she tried to lull herself to sleep, but even as dead tired as she was, it took its time claiming her. When it came, it was filled with fits and starts, nightmares of drowning, of being pulled to the dark depths by monstrous creatures, but she must have fallen into a deep sleep at some point.

In the morning, Alessandra came around to wakefulness with a slow ease, as if she were not stranded on a deserted island. She was warm and comfortable, and there was a pleasant weight atop her. *Have we been rescued so quickly? Am I tucked safely beneath the thick blankets of my bed?* She brought her hand up to get a measure of whatever covered her, starting as her fingers brushed at long strands of salt-stiffened hair—*Lucia*. Her eyes blinked open.

Daylight came in through the gaps of their shelter as the queen lay snoring softly, her left leg between Alessandra's, her head nestled against her chest. Alessandra's heartbeat doubled; she wondered that the pounding, so loud in her own ears, did not wake the queen. Even with her bruised forehead, the purple yellowing at the edges, her hair in snarls down her back, her face smudged with dirt, and a bit of saliva escaping her sculpted lips, Lucia was undeniably beautiful in sleep.

Instinctively, Alessandra's fingers brushed at a strand of Lucia's hair that had found its way into her mouth. The queen's brow furrowed at the movement, but quickly eased, leaving only small lines of worry. Alessandra's thumb moved over them in wonder; they were so out of place in an otherwise smooth countenance. *What does a queen have to worry about?* She quickly realized what a simplification of the facts that was. She'd been captain for the course of a week and just look at the bloody state of her.

Alessandra tried to recall how long the woman atop her had reigned. They were close in age. She recalled hearing of Lucia's ascension to the throne before she had even begun her monthly courses. Alessandra remembered thinking how magnificent it must be to be so young yet have no one tell you what to do. *The foolish thinking of a child.* Alessandra thought of a phrase her father used to use, 'No leader is not weighed down by the burden he bears'. Lucia had borne the weight of an entire kingdom when she was barely out of her teens.

What would it be like to kiss those lips again? What would it feel like to have her kiss me back? The thought came unbidden.

Alessandra gently deposited Lucia onto the ground before rolling her back to the queen, immediately missing her warmth. She shouldn't be having such thoughts. What would her father say if he could see her lusting after a royal? She curled her body in on itself and shut her eyes once more, trying to block out the woman next to her.

ROYCE

He sat across from the Vetreonish ambassador, hands linked behind his head as if he were talking to an old friend at dinner. The two men were not friends. Ambassador Slrach was a decent enough fellow. He and Royce had monthly meals to discuss trade and other matters of state, but that didn't mean he trusted him. After their last meeting, one that left the ambassador with a black eye he was still sporting almost a week later, Royce wasn't sure there was any new information to be gleaned from the man. Slrach had been stuck behind a locked door for the entirety of that time, but Royce had to try.

With Lucia missing—she had yet to show up in Ramir's hands—ruling had fallen to Sebastian, and as she had previously appointed him the boy's guardian, it was up to him to find her.

Royce had come without Ylva this time. His shadow had been dispatched to Vetreon to look for answers.

"The eye is looking better," he said, pointing at Slrach.

The man glared back. It was an odd expression on his usually placid face. Royce wagered Slrach was unused to glaring.

"Right," Royce tipped his chair back on its edge, "you've been stuck in here. I've been stuck out there, trying to piece everything together, run the kingdom, and keep my generals and captains from an all-out invasion. They're rather eager, as you can imagine."

It had become clear during their first meeting that the ambassador didn't know anything about Lucia's kidnapping, but he also hadn't defended his king. Royce thought perhaps he could use that to his benefit.

"Your men would die, and you still wouldn't have your queen."

Royce shrugged. "Maybe." Lord Blanxart was a fine general, seasoned in fighting other men's battles during his exiled youth. Moranth's army was ready. But it would take more to win a war with the sea power of Vetreon.

Slrach laughed. "Without a doubt. Why are you here, Aldana? You know I don't have any information for you."

"I'm aware, but you do have the ear of your king."

Royce was willing to try anything, even on the very off chance that bastard Ramir really didn't have anything to do with the kidnapping. Royce had spies everywhere, and not one of them knew a thing other than a pirate ship called The Medusa had sailed from the capital in the early hours of the morning Lucia was taken. It would take roughly two weeks for a fast ship to get from Moranth to Vetreon. That meant there could still be a week or more before he knew anything for certain.

The ambassador scoffed. "No one has his ear."

"Lord Riffa, the queen's heir, and I are in agreement that the queen's plan for an embargo will go forward until someone tells us what we want to hear." Sebastian wasn't altogether for blocking Vetreon's merchants from the harbors of Moranth, his worry was that the people would suffer far more than Ramir, and he was right. Royce had no intention of a long trade war.

Releasing a long sigh, Slrach sat up straighter in his chair. Royce had his attention. "No one wants to talk about trade, Aldana. It's boring."

"You're right, of course, but effective. Your nobles have quite a liking for our wines and cheeses. That many sober lords and ladies are bound to cause trouble for your young king."

7

LUCIA

"How are you still asleep?" The toe of her boot prodded at Alessandra's ribs, jolting her into consciousness. "The day is half gone," Lucia said, hands on hips, once more a queen, though she knew she looked a mess.

Alessandra blinked a few times, stretched, and then sat, pulling her legs up to her chest. Her chin tilted up as she gave Lucia a smirk. "Important court business to get to, Your Majesty?"

Lucia glared, but didn't say a word. There was so much to do if they planned on surviving on the island. Perhaps the pirate had a better idea of how quickly her crew could make their way back to rescue them, but that supposed the ship was still intact and her men still free, knowledge neither had.

Lucia had woken earlier with a start, cradled in the captain's arms, secure, the direness of their situation of little concern for the smallest of moments. She'd never slept in a lover's arms before but thought Alessandra might prove the exception. Of course, Lucia would have to give her a chance first. Hours, she wagered, ticked by while Alessandra slept, and she paced. There wasn't much to see from their scrap of beach except scrubby bushes and the empty sea, but Lucia didn't dare leave the site. Her clothes, hair, everything was caked in gritty sand, but it was the pirate causing Lucia more than a small bit of discomfort. Alessandra was becoming a distraction.

The morning sun was still little more than a pale orb through the milky haze of mist as Lucia picked through the gear they'd scavenged the night before. She didn't want to think about the softness of Alessandra's lips when she had pulled her close on the ship, the heat of their bodies, the pirate's hips tight against her own, or her want thrumming in her veins. *Damn it.* Her sodden boot kicked at a bit of sand, only making things worse as the morning breeze flung the fine grains right back at her. *Ugggh! This fucking island!* Finally, when she could no longer stand her own company or the wild imaginings of her mind, she decided to wake her sleeping pirate.

"We need to look for wood," Lucia said instead of engaging Alessandra. She was too tired for wit or flirtation. "We need to make a signal fire and gather food, if there's any to be had." She smiled a rare, genuine smile as her mood shifted, her features lighting as she did. "Honestly," she quipped, "sounds like a far finer day than any spent at court. Come on."

Once out of the shelter, Alessandra shook the sand from her clothes and hair. The sun was almost overhead. Lucia noted the way Alessandra's shirt and breeches stuck to her in the thick air.

"Have you found anything useful?" Alessandra asked.

Lucia felt the heat rising in her cheeks as she tore her gaze from the pirate. "Didn't want to go too far, just in case."

Alessandra gave her a confused look. "Just in case what?"

Lucia made an annoyed sound in her throat. "In case you left me."

The pirate spread her arms wide. "And where would I be going?"

They had climbed up not a steep slope but enough of an incline to see most of the island from their purview.

"Your ship could show up, and I thought, maybe ..." Lucia's voice trailed off as she realized how ridiculous her concern was. *I'm the treasure she's guarding. She's not going to abandon me. Yet.* She flipped from thoughts of survival to anger at herself for being open with Alessandra, at her situation, at *their* situation, at the world.

Her fists clenched into balls as the rage sparked down her spine. *Fuck!* Her body shook. Lucia squeezed her eyes shut, trying to give herself the time she needed to calm down if she were to avoid upbraiding Alessandra. She hated this feeling more than anything. Lucia felt completely helpless in these moments as she fought against herself, her own body. She wondered, not for the first time, *Is it the tainted blood of my father that causes such rage in me to boil over with barely a moment's notice?*

"Hey," Alessandra gently touched Lucia's arm, her voice laced with concern, "it's alright. We're alright."

At home, Lucia had learned to mostly conceal such moments. She could leave a room without question or simply dismiss others. Here, her fury, and her inability to contain it, were out in the open.

"I just need a moment," she said through gritted teeth.

Alessandra rubbed at her eyes, and Lucia could tell she was frustrated. Lucia fretted. *Please don't be mad at me. I'm trying.*

Alessandra sighed. "It's going to be days before the crew can make the repairs to get back to us. Even then, she'll be limping. They'll have to put in somewhere to fix the mast. If The Medusa and we are lucky, and if The Deceit hasn't blown them out of the water, it's just you and me for a week at least, maybe two. I'd venture that's how long it's going to be."

Taking deep breaths, Lucia felt her temper ebb as her body regained a sense of composure. Alessandra hadn't pushed her for an explanation; she'd simply let her be, for which Lucia was grateful. "A week?"

Something changed in the captain's posture—her eyes went hard, and her shoulders squared. "Don't worry. I'll have you to your wedding soon enough, or we'll be dead." She huffed.

Lucia's mind kept turning to The Medusa, to that last moment held tight in Alessandra's arms, their bodies pressed together—the taste of her was still on her tongue. Thinking back, Lucia wasn't sure what she would have said to the pirate. Yes would have been the smart choice. She couldn't deny that a night in the surely skilled hands of the worldly captain would have proved pleasurable, but then what? Judging by the coldness of Alessandra's tone and clear determination to hand her over to Ramir, the pirate held no real warmth for her.

Lucia's stubborn gaze fixed on Alessandra. "That may be for the best. I'll not live under another's thumb, not ever again." The rage had receded to a tired determination. "If you truly mean to deliver me to my cousin, then you're sending me to my death and worse for Moranth. Ramir is my father all over again."

Alessandra sucked at her teeth, ignoring Lucia's statement. "Let's look for something to eat. If all else fails, I can try for some coconuts."

Lucia, still stiff as a board and scowling, followed as they walked further into the undergrowth.

"I've heard of plenty of people being marooned and surviving," Alessandra said over her shoulder as they went.

"I'm sure there are plenty more of those who didn't."

"Aye, but I don't plan on our story ending like that."

Our Story. Lucia's heart swelled even as she told herself they were just words. *That sounds so right. We're going to make it through this—together.*

ALESSANDRA

Being awoken by a boot to her side was not how Alessandra had thought the morning would go. Not how she wished for it to, rather. Even in the heat, she missed the familiar heaviness of her greatcoat. She'd be sweltering in it, trekking through the brambles as they had, but still, it was a piece of home. Lucia made her feel utterly lost, at odds with herself and everything she'd been raised to be. The woman was a complete mystery to her. One moment, the haughty queen. The next, a cornered animal, scared and dangerous. *And gorgeous.*

She wanted to bring up their kiss aboard The Medusa. It mattered to her for some reason, but after her rude awakening and Lucia's behavior, she wasn't about to give her the satisfaction of mentioning it. *Best to leave it alone*. If Lucia wanted her, even though Alessandra tried to convince herself that wasn't what *she* wanted, then Lucia could be the one to make the next move. Hell, she was a pirate. She didn't care what happened to Lucia or Moranth, past getting the promised payment.

Alessandra clenched her teeth as they set off to search for more freshwater or anything else of use on their little island. In her mind, she made an inventory of items washed ashore from The Medusa. There was plenty of rope, so she could make a gill net later to fish. The barrels could be used to collect dew and rainwater, and the random planks could be added to their shelter. She and Lucia could accomplish more apart, but she didn't think that to be a fine idea, especially after the queen made it clear she didn't trust her. Much as Alessandra didn't want to admit it, she too was scared, and being alone on the island would be the only thing worse than being stuck on it with Lucia.

They spent an hour or so foraging. Fortunately, Alessandra was familiar with the berries they collected. It wasn't much, but they would stave off the gnawing hunger and keep them going until something more substantial could be had. Alessandra remained quiet during their work, not getting within arm's reach of Lucia, who likewise remained aloof.

"We should go back to the shelter," Lucia finally spoke.

Alessandra's mouth dried at the sight of Lucia's lips and fingers—stained with the purple juice of berries. She imagined spending the heat of the afternoon making those stained lips of Lucia's part with cries of ecstasy. Imagined the coarseness of the sand sliding over bared skin as their bodies came together. She didn't want to fight her longing anymore.

"Sure," she agreed with Lucia.

The sun was high overhead, the steamy air buzzing with the calls of insects. They'd wandered deeper into the heart of the island, where the vegetation was thicker. The going had been slow as the path became more and more impassable. With only a stick and her dagger, it would be almost impossible to go further into the undergrowth.

Alessandra stopped.

"Hey!" Lucia snapped her fingers with impatience.

"Ssshh," Alessandra shushed, cocking her head to listen. *Rushing water. A waterfall.*

They pushed on for a dozen or so feet, nearly falling headlong into the swirling pool below.

Alessandra couldn't suppress her smile. "Come on," she said excitedly, scrabbling down the slick rock toward the clear water.

"I'm not going in there," Lucia declared.

Alessandra turned back to see Lucia's arms crossed over her chest. She arched a red brow, already halfway down the rock wall. "Suit yourself," she called back, catching a groan from Lucia before losing sight of her.

She was already halfway done stripping by the time Lucia met her at the bottom. She was tugging her soiled shirt over her head, slowly revealing the long lines of her toned body, when she heard the queen's footsteps, the skin at the back of her neck prickling as Lucia watched, silent and unmoving. Alessandra didn't pay her any mind—she wanted to be clean and cool, if only for a few moments. Lying her shirt out on a sticker bush, she loosened her belt, then dropped her breeches, scooping them up to place beside her shirt.

LUCIA

Lucia was rooted to the spot. Alessandra's shining skin, streaked with the grime of the last few days, was spectacular. Lucia's eyes wandered to the apex of red curls between the captain's thighs, heat rising in her core.

"Oh, fuck it all to hell," she muttered as Alessandra's body sluiced through the crystalline water. *We'll most likely die on the island, so why not make the most of it?* Her borrowed clothes were quickly deposited beside the pirate's.

Stepping in, she breathed a sigh of relief as the cool waters soothed her overheated skin. Dipping her head beneath the water, Lucia ran her fingers through her hair, the salt loosening its grip on the long locks. When she resurfaced, she saw that Alessandra had done the same, the captain's hair a river of red over her shoulders. Paddling closer, Lucia was stunned as Alessandra reached for her, pulling her close as if they were long-tried lovers.

Before Lucia could spare a thought, her toes found purchase below the surface, a rock, and she pushed herself further into the pirate's embrace as their lips came together. A whine stuck in the back of her throat as Alessandra's mouth opened to her probing tongue. Lucia could feel the smile lodged in the corners of the captain's mouth. Nipping at Alessandra's lower lip, her own mouth turned up in a grin as strong hands scooped her ass up into them, and she settled her legs around the pirate's slim waist.

Lucia broke from the kiss. "I thought you didn't want an unwilling woman."

Alessandra's desire-darkened eyes blinked, and her brows drew together in what appeared to be momentary confusion and fear. Her voice was hoarse with want as she asked, "Are you? Are you unwilling?"

Lucia shook her head. "No, I'm not." Her head bent to capture Alessandra's mouth once more, shivering in her arms as their kiss deepened.

Alessandra cradled her, leaving Lucia's hands free to roam the captain's stunning body, which responded beautifully to her ministrations. She stroked her hands up the small of Alessandra's back before palming her lush breasts. Her fingers tweaked the sensitive nipples, eliciting a soft moan from her pirate. Lucia ventured further, maneuvering a hand between their submerged bodies to brush at the wet curls of Alessandra's opening.

Alessandra groaned, her voice deeper this time, more urgent, as Lucia's fingers pressed against her swollen clit. Lucia was enraptured with the creature before her, her body's expressiveness, her own matching desire. Her backside was still nestled within the pirate's grasp, but Alessandra's back was arched away from her, red hair blazing as she threw her head back, eyes squeezed tight against the pleasure Lucia's skilled fingers provided. Her whole being abandoned of her defenses.

Lucia tangled her free hand into Alessandra's wet hair, her hips thrusting as her fingers pleasured the woman before her. She cried out as Lucia's fingers rolled and pinched her clit before delving into her depths. Her cries broke with Alessandra's as the pirate climaxed, her fingers digging deep into the soft flesh of Lucia's buttocks.

They clung together after, enjoying the stillness of their coupling, the sunlight reflecting in the golden flecks within Alessandra's gaze as Lucia smiled down at her. While their bodies continued to shake with diffused want, Lucia suddenly felt a moment of panic. What just happened between them was more than even she'd meant it to be. The responding glow in that molten gaze spoke to the sting of desire already spooling back up within her. She wanted more. She wanted to give and please—something that was new to her.

Lucia gave her body a shake as Alessandra held on. "I'm getting cold," she said, anxiety tightening her voice. That was a lie. With her body pressed tight against Alessandra, her head tucked beneath her chin, the slowing pounding of the pirate's heart loud in her ear, she was very warm, but she wasn't weak. To be so open, to feel so safe in another's arms. *No. This pirate kidnapped me to sell into marriage, to destroy my kingdom. This won't happen again.*

"We best get you warm, then." Alessandra smiled, tucking a strand of hair behind Lucia's ear as her ragged breathing returned to normal. Lucia shook her off, dunked her head one last time, then swam to the shore, leaving Alessandra treading water alone.

Picking up her clothes, Lucia didn't look back, couldn't for fear all her wants, hopes, her terrible need to be seen, to be understood and cherished, would be writ clear on her face. Instead, Lucia ignored Alessandra when she reached the water's edge, and Alessandra, in turn, did the same as they both dressed in tense silence.

"I can start on a gill net," the captain finally said. "You can get to work on that fire you promised."

"I promised nothing," Lucia nearly shouted.

Flustered, her fingers having a hell of a time with the buttons of her breeches, she rolled her eyes at the huffy tone of her voice. Alessandra wasn't suggesting anything ridiculous, wasn't pushing her on her feelings or anything else she didn't wish to acknowledge.

"That's fine," Lucia tried again, ignoring the confusion pulling at the pirate's brow. "I'll gather what we need on the way back."

Alessandra's gaze left hers, flicking to the horizon. "Right. We should go then."

"After you." Lucia motioned for Alessandra to set off.

Lucia was sullen as they tromped back to their site. Her mind kept going back to the moment in the water when she withdrew from Alessandra's embrace. She couldn't shake the image of the pirate's wounded expression when she pulled away from her. Alessandra's look came as a shock; it was as if she really cared for her. Lucia was uncomfortable with how that made her feel. *I've done nothing wrong.*

For all her beauty, Alessandra was a cut-throat pirate who kidnapped her and still meant to hand her over to the enemy. Although, more than a little of Lucia's discomfort was coming from the knowledge her desire for Alessandra was no longer a falsehood, if it had ever been. Alessandra and her crew would be hanged if the Moranthese navy ever managed to take The Medusa. *It's no less than they deserve, right?* But Alessandra also saved her life. Honor demanded she spare the pirate if she ever escaped her situation. Most likely, The Medusa would come back for them, and Alessandra would sail her straight to Vetreon and her waiting Bridegroom.

ALESSANDRA

It had been a quick and unexpected tryst, lasting only a few moments, but something in her had shifted. Call it intuition or savvy, but something within told her to protect Lucia. The queen had been so soft, so warm and lively in her arms. Lucia was a skilled partner, and Alessandra enjoyed the dalliance immensely. *No, there is so much more to it than that*, but they were still marooned; she would still deliver the queen into her enemy's hands. *So why should Lucia be anything other than distant toward me?* Yet Lucia's sudden coldness hurt. Alessandra realized with aching clarity that she cared for her. *Damnit*. Alessandra grimaced as she pulled the rough salt-laden shirt and breeches back over her damp skin, refocusing her mind and energy on their dire situation.

Hours passed after they returned to their camp and continued working to survive. The sun was low on the horizon when Alessandra sat back on her heels, dropping the rough lengths of twine. She'd been working on the gill net for the better part of the afternoon. Her back ached, and her hands were bleeding from when she pulled too fast or too hard on the rope. Her mind wandered as she got back to the task at hand. Lucia was there, *right there*, and all she wanted to do was reach out to her, hold her, tell her it was alright, even if she didn't believe it. She thought she understood what Lucia must be feeling; she, too, was warring with herself.

It had been her men who had kidnapped the queen, but foolish as it was, she knew their reasons for doing it. Alessandra also knew her men looked to her to see it through. She had only known Lucia for a matter of days. The men aboard The Medusa were her family, the only family she had left. She owed them her loyalty. Not only that, choosing to try to protect the queen could end up costing her the crew, her ship, and possibly her life. Much as the men loved her, a mutiny was never far from a captain's mind. Of course, none of it would matter if they couldn't get off the island.

Alessandra stood to stretch, arching her back and spreading her arms wide toward the setting sun. "How's the fire coming?" she asked as she felt Lucia's gaze on her.

Turning, she saw Lucia make a face at the smoking pile of kindling. "It isn't," she answered, tossing her bow aside and falling back, her palms digging into the sand. "I think you may have had a point about my fire-building abilities. It's been a long time since I've tried to light one of my own." She bent low, blowing slowly over the smoldering embers.

Alessandra almost laughed at the defeated scowl on Lucia's beautiful, albeit sooty, face. The hurt and anger of her previous thoughts left her as she imagined how wonderful it would be to be curled around the queen while a fire crackled before them. "Can I give it a go?"

"Please." Lucia gestured to the twigs, clearly past the point of pride.

Alessandra dropped down beside her, holding out her hand for the bow. She was impressed by the construction; it was an instrument she'd thankfully never had to use before. Yet again, she wondered at the child the queen once was. *Who taught her such things?*

"Have you ever used one of these?" Lucia asked.

Alessandra shook her head. "No, but I thought maybe you were worn out. You've been at it for hours."

Lucia wiped the sweat from her brow, leaving a streak of ash across it. Before Alessandra could stop herself, she leaned in and used her thumb to clean the soot, but her efforts did little good. The queen's hand caught at Alessandra's, their eyes meeting before Lucia guided her hand back to the bow.

"Here," Lucia said, dragging her gaze away, "hold it like this." She rested her hand firmly atop Alessandra's as she pressed her body close, using her other hand to show her how to hold the fire-starting instrument.

Alessandra's heart leaped into her throat as the heat of Lucia's body warmed her. "Like this?" she asked, using the same sawing motion with the drill and bow she saw Lucia using.

Lucia's breath hitched at her ear. "Yes, like that."

Alessandra screwed her eyes shut, waging her own battle against the desire to push Lucia to the ground and make her writhe and scream in pleasure. Her pulse thundered in her ears as she attempted to mimic Lucia's movements. She thought she felt an answering pounding heartbeat in the queen's chest.

Their efforts were to no avail, and they went to bed that night hungry and in the dark.

8

ALESSANDRA

Alessandra lay still in the darkness of their shelter for a long time, listening to the buzzing of insects, the faint sound of the ocean waves lapping at the shore, and the soft puff of breath emanating from Lucia's sleeping form. When they lay down that night, Lucia scooted as far as she could from her, not saying a word, before dropping off to sleep.

With her hand tucked under her head, eyes staring holes into the stone roof of their hovel, Alessandra huffed, shaking her head as her thoughts swirled, her legs squirmed, and her core tightened at the memory of Lucia's fingers. She was restless. Alessandra turned her head, checking that Lucia's breathing was the slow breath of sleep. Satisfied, she shut her eyes, moving her hand over her body, skimming her aching breasts, belly, and beneath her breeches to the damp curls below.

She was well-versed in pleasing herself. It could be weeks or months alone at sea, and with a cabin of her own, there'd been many nights spent in such a way, images of her latest conquest fueling her lust. As she closed her eyes, Lucia's face and body emerged from the darkness. The flesh and blood embodiment of her desire was inches away, yet there might as well have been the whole ocean between them.

Alessandra took a beat, attempting to replace Lucia in her mind's eye with one of her favorite girls in Silver Cove. The lass was buxom, with a thick fall of nearly black hair. Alessandra smiled in the dark, imagining her hands on the woman's thick thighs. In her vision, her hands were inching their way up toward the barmaid's impressive breasts, while in the shelter, her fingers rolled over her swollen clit. She thrust her hips against her palm as a gasp of delight escaped.

Alessandra froze, not wanting to wake Lucia.

The queen muttered something about fish before rolling against her, throwing an arm over Alessandra. As if her body sensed warmth, she snuggled tighter into her.

Alessandra shook her head again, this time in resignation, wanting with every bit of her being to rouse Lucia from her slumber, spread her plump thighs, and make her moan. She didn't move. She spent the night rigid with desire, not daring to stir, taking what pleasure she could in the heaviness of Lucia's drowsing embrace.

―――

Lucia's shouts of joy woke Alessandra the following morning. Stumbling out into the light, she saw the queen by the fire pit. Her hair was braided in a loose plait over her shoulder, and her face was still smudged with ash. A wide grin lighted her features as she looked at the small tendril of smoke curling its way toward the sapphire sky. Below, orange flames licked at the bunch of kindling and larger bits of wood they'd gathered.

When Lucia saw her, her face fell before going blank. The look, or lack thereof, sparked a fit of irritation in Alessandra. "You know, for someone working very hard to try to ignore me, you sure as hell won't get off me in your sleep."

Lucia blushed as she crossed her arms and turned her head like a petulant child. "I can't help what I do in my sleep."

"Or what you do when you're awake? Or are you going to pretend nothing happened at the waterfall?"

Lucia straightened and threw up her hands as she glared. "Are *you* going to pretend you won't be happy to send me to my death if we ever get off this damned island? Or that it wasn't your crew that kidnapped *me* in the first place?"

Alessandra's nostrils flared as she stopped herself from returning fire. Lucia was right. Handing her over to Ramir was exactly her intent, or it had been. After yesterday, she knew whatever the outcome, she couldn't let him have her. If her crew miraculously saved them, Lucia was going straight home. Well, after granting them pardons, of course. That was the plan she'd devised in the hours before dawn, with Lucia sprawled atop her. The queen wouldn't have much choice. She could give them a pardon or— Alessandra sighed. She knew she couldn't kill Lucia, but the crew would have to gain something for their endeavor, else they would likely pitch the queen overboard and possibly herself right after.

Instead of hurling an insult, trying to defend her actions or that of her crew, she simply said, "You don't have to go."

Lucia dropped her hands, her brow furrowing in a most adorable manner. "What do you mean?" she asked cautiously.

A trill of excitement and fear knotted in Alessandra's stomach as her heartbeat thundered in her chest. She hesitated only a moment before pulling Lucia close. "I swear on my life," she began, thumb grazing Lucia's knuckles, "I won't take you to Ramir."

LUCIA

Lucia couldn't speak for fear her voice would betray her. The loneliness she'd felt all her life dropped away as she stared into those amber eyes, her own brimming with tears. She wrapped her arms around Alessandra's waist, her toes digging into the sand as she rose to meet the pirate captain's lips. It wasn't gentle. Lucia hungrily caught Alessandra's mouth as they fell to the earth, a jumble of entwining arms and legs. Their breath mingled in a moment of absolute stillness—grey and gold eyes locked once more as they perched on the precipice. Lucia laughed in pure delight, ripping the borrowed shirt over her head, her thighs pinning Alessandra to the sand beneath them.

"Careful," Alessandra cried as Lucia threw her shirt to the side. "I—just—" she stammered. "I don't want the fire to go out."

Lucia scoffed, flicking the heavy length of her braid back over her shoulder, her bare breasts swinging before her. "It won't go out," she said, her voice husky with need as she guided Alessandra's hands to the swell of her breasts.

The pirate's breath hitched in seeming wonder as if she were an untried virgin touching a woman for the first time. Lucia's teeth bit enticingly into her lip, watching as Alessandra regained her composure. The pirate's lips quirked, and then her hands expertly roved over Lucia's body before finally finding purchase beneath her lush backside.

Alessandra nipped at the sensitive buds of her nipples, pulling and suckling at each, in turn, leaving her mark on the pale flesh of Lucia's breasts. Lucia writhed against her, a cry of pleasure escaping as her hips rolled, the motion pushing the captain deeper into the sand. With her body shaking with need, heart pounding with joy and desire, Lucia reached a hand beneath Alessandra's breeches, finding her opening wet. Lucia pinched her pulsing bud, rolling her hips in time with Alessandra's. The pirate's head lolled back, eyes going hazy, as her mouth parted, gasps and invectives escaping.

Lucia dipped her head, claiming Alessandra's mouth in a searching kiss, but Alessandra didn't kiss her back. "Wait," she said.

Lucia's brow furrowed in confusion. "I don't understand."

Alessandra sighed. "Has anyone ever made love to you?"

Lucia blinked. "What?" Her gut twisted at the aching knowledge that no, no one ever had.

Alessandra stroked her hand over Lucia's bare, freckled shoulder, the pads of her fingers brushing over Lucia's collarbone. Giving her a reassuring smile, Alessandra said, "I want you. Let me this time."

Lucia's body relaxed into Alessandra's embrace, her legs still straddling the pirate. It was a precarious position, but Alessandra managed stability, her hand cradling Lucia as she lay her down.

"You're so beautiful," Alessandra breathed as if in reverence, pressing a kiss to Lucia's hip bone.

Lucia's breath caught as, with a gentle surety, Alessandra eased her breeches down her legs. Only one other woman had ever touched her this way, but that had not been love. Lucia couldn't catch her breath as it came in gasps. Alessandra was relentless in her pleasuring. Her legs and thighs trembled as Alessandra's steady hands parted them. Their eyes met, and Lucia wondered at the desire darkening Alessandra's gaze. No one looked at her like that—no one dared.

Tangling her hands in Alessandra's thick mane, Lucia moaned as the pirate slid down her body, her hot breath puffing over the soft flesh of Lucia's inner thighs, her tongue swirling over them as she went. She lost herself to Alessandra's hands, her own tight in the captain's hair as Alessandra gave an exploratory lick at her damp curls. The pirate's tongue penetrated her, and pinpricks of light exploded behind her eyes. Alessandra's fingers dipped into her, her own soon joining, tipping her over the edge into sublime oblivion. Lucia's hips undulated, mindless in their thrusts against Alessandra's ministrations, before her entire body finally convulsed, shattering into divine release.

They lay together silently for as long as the beating sun would allow. Their skin was pink and hot when they retreated once more to their shelter, hand in hand. The little fire Lucia started needed tending, and their bellies grumbled with hunger, but Lucia was at peace within herself for the first time since becoming a grown woman. She didn't think it would last, but for the moment, she was content. Her body melded against Alessandra's as they lounged in the shade, gathering their scant strength. Alessandra's strong hand combed an errant lock of hair off her brow while Lucia nuzzled into the hollow of her neck, lips pressed to her salty skin.

"This is almost wonderful, isn't it?" Lucia said. The sun was high in the sky as their hands raised to their eyes and squinted into the day.

"I've had worse days," Alessandra quipped. Lucia could hear the smile in her voice. "We need to get the gill net out. I should have done it earlier," she lamented.

"Sorry to have distracted you." Knowing their respite had to come to an end, Lucia dusted herself off, rose, then held a hand out. There were so many questions she wished to ask, so much she wanted to know about the woman before her, but those would have to wait. Their survival depended on it.

Alessandra grinned back. "Worth it." Her thumb pressed against Lucia's chin, holding her there. "You are worth all of it." She released her and turned back to her task, missing the surprised happiness shining in Lucia's eyes. *My God, she's actually willing to risk everything for me.*

Though Alessandra swore she wouldn't deliver her to Ramir, it was not until that moment, when she saw the warmth of not just desire but something more in the pirate's eyes, that Lucia realized the depth of the feelings that had grown so quickly between them. Alessandra was taking a great risk upon herself by making such a promise to her, and Lucia finally thought she understood why. No one had ever fought for her before, risked themselves for her, not in that way.

Lucia smiled to herself in wonder that it should be a pirate who first showed her what she thought might be love. She couldn't be sure that was what she felt in turn. She'd never seen it before, never even glimpsed it. *Even if Alessandra does love me, how do I love her back? Am I even worthy of such a thing?*

Lucia said nothing as she went to tend her fire while Alessandra turned to the more skilled work of weaving a net. Lucia was happy to set her mind and body to a task rather than to the thoughts and emotions swirling within her.

They spent the remainder of the day foraging, reinforcing the minimal structure of their shelter, and gathering more wood for the fire. With Alessandra's help, Lucia was able to bring some fallen trees to the site. They were spindly things but worked as the skeleton for a larger living space. The strain and uneasy tension between the two women eased as the day wore on, their focus shifting from each other to the business of staying alive.

After working for what seemed hours, Lucia grunted. "Shit," she cursed as another sharp edge of a palm frond sliced across the soft flesh of her hand. She squeezed her hand into a tight fist, willing the pain to cease. Her eyes darted about, hoping Alessandra hadn't heard her, but she was nowhere to be seen. Lucia assumed she was foraging or checking the gill net. Being on the island had its advantages. She enjoyed putting her resourcefulness to use. Unless there was a state crisis, it wasn't something she got to spend much time doing back in the capital.

Weaving leaves together might not seem to be a great victory, but so far, despite her mangled hand, she was faring well. If she could keep at it, though Lucia wondered how much more her burning hands could take, the new addition to their shelter would have a thatched roof by nightfall. With the dark clouds rolling across the afternoon sky, she thought that might make all the difference.

More time passed, and small whipping bands of rain started blowing through their camp, but Alessandra had still not returned. Lucia was bent low, muttering against the pelting torrent, wiping at her eyes as she worked. The roof and one side of the shelter were nearly complete. She reasoned that if she could just finish lashing the last few pieces together, she could ride out the storm and get dry in relative comfort. *What about Alessandra?* The question wouldn't let her be.

The worry over her whereabouts, her safety, churned in the pit of Lucia's stomach. *Or maybe it's hunger?* Both were unfamiliar feelings for her. She could count on one hand the number of people she deeply cared about beyond the concern of a ruler, and never had a lover sparked such interest in her.

Lucia ground her teeth as she hauled the last of her panels into place and secured it. There wasn't an inch of her that didn't ache or hurt in some way, but she was proud as she stepped back into the rain and saw the shape of her day's work. *Royce would be proud, too.* She thought of her childhood friend back in Moranth, of how the fort-building skills of their youths were being put to excellent use. *Now, just go inside and get dry, Lucia. She is fine.* Her mind continued to race as the terrible thought that something could have happened to Alessandra persisted.

"Damn it." She sighed into the rain, knowing she couldn't rest without checking on her.

"What are you all up in arms about, Your Majesty?" Alessandra's husky voice came from behind her.

"Hell!" Lucia jumped. Her hands dropped to her knees as she tried to slow her pounding heart. "You startled me."

Lucia saw that Alessandra was every bit as soaked as she was, but the pirate had a triumphant grin on her face as she produced two large brown fish and a pouch full of yet more berries. *If we get off this island, I am never eating another berry again.*

"You weren't worried about me, were you?" Alessandra asked.

Lucia felt her cheeks flush. Of course she'd been worried, but she wasn't about to admit it. "No," she responded too quickly, then rolled her eyes as Alessandra's teeth bit into her lip to keep a threatening smile at bay.

"Mmmhmm."

Having had enough embarrassment for one day, Lucia shook her head, her own grin tucked into the corners of her mouth, before ducking under the new, larger shelter. Alessandra followed suit, whistling in obvious admiration of her work. A smoky fire sat in the center, a hole in the roof allowing the rain in and the fire's exhaust out. A pile of dry wood was in one corner, along with the last of their berries and coconuts on a salvaged barrel. Lucia hung her shirt over a broken crate to dry, though how efficiently that would happen in the damp climate was beyond her.

"Not too bad, eh?"

"It'll certainly do," Alessandra answered. "You're just full of surprises."

Lucia snorted. "You're not," she said, nodding toward the fish.

As enticing as Alessandra looked at the moment, Lucia was more excited by the prospect of a full belly and being dry than the beautiful creature before her.

"You had faith in me, eh?"

Lucia raised a brow. "Maybe."

Alessandra laughed. "You know, Your Majesty, if we're stuck here indefinitely, you'll have to stop acting like you're not immensely charmed by me."

Arms crossed, lips pursed, Lucia answered, "I am not charmed by you."

"Yes, you are." Alessandra grinned before giving her cheek a quick kiss.

Lucia responded with an annoyed grunt. "You just love getting a rise out of me, don't you?"

Alessandra smirked but didn't answer. "Nothing to cook these on," she said instead, indicating the fish as she held them out toward Lucia. "Take them for me."

Lucia did as she was told while Alessandra ducked back out into the downpour. She returned a moment later with a few sticks and quickly fashioned a spit, skewering the two fish and setting them to cook. Lucia's stomach grumbled loudly as the aroma of the cooking fish filled the small space. Hanging her wet shirt to dry, Alessandra laughed as her stomach answered in kind.

"Come here," the pirate gestured, taking up a spot near the fire.

"Are you asking me to cuddle?" Lucia questioned, feigning indifference.

"I'm asking you to warm me up, but if you'd rather be cold," Alessandra responded just as coyly.

Lucia crawled over, snuggling deep into her embrace. There was no one there to gainsay her, to tell her to act like a lady, or worse, a queen. No one to see her softness and mistake it for weakness. No one but her pirate.

"Mmmm." Lucia groaned as she fit herself just so within the pirate's arms.

"Comfortable?"

"I think I am," Lucia answered.

She was shocked when Alessandra picked up her wounded hand. Turning it over, Alessandra traced across the cuts before bringing it to her lips for a soothing kiss.

"You've worked so hard on our little home."

Lucia's heart nearly burst with pride and warmth at the comment and gesture. Alessandra saw her. Saw that she had taken great care in the construction of their hovel.

They stayed content in each other's arms while Alessandra slowly turned the spit. There had been women in Lucia's life, many women, but there were never moments of such stillness. She found it odd that even in their most dire situation, she felt more at ease in Alessandra's company than she ever had before.

"Are you hungry?" Alessandra asked sometime later.

Blinking, Lucia sat up with a start as she woke from her nap. "Why?"

Alessandra chuckled, wiping at the corner of Lucia's mouth. "Because you were drooling and making adorable little sounds in your sleep," she said, nudging Lucia to let her move. "Dinner is ready."

Alessandra served the still steaming fish on thick green leaves, passing one over to Lucia, who sat opposite her, the fire between them. She tore off chunks of the fish with her fingers before delicately placing them on her tongue, sucking as she pulled her fingers from her lips. Lucia paused, noticing Alessandra's stare. "What?" She looked down at herself, her bare chest, her dirty legs crossed beneath her, but saw nothing amiss.

"You somehow even make eating seductive."

Lucia swiped at her mouth, then belched. Clapping a hand to her mouth in shock, she laughed. "Yes, I'm quite the siren."

ALESSANDRA

Despite their circumstances, it turned out to be one of the best days and nights of Alessandra's life. She was completely smitten by the woman sitting across from her, firelight dancing over the soft curves of Lucia's body and reflecting in her mischievous eyes. She couldn't remember ever having felt so at peace with another woman.

Despite her confidence in her crew, Alessandra knew well the state of her ship and the skill of the captain of The Deceit; they might never leave this place. So, through a mouthful of fish, she asked what she thought was a wistful question. "Say we do get off this island, and I manage to convince the crew to take you home instead of Vetreon. What then?"

Lucia coughed, nearly choking on her food. "With you and I?" She paused. "I suppose I haven't given it much thought." Pulling her knees close to her chest, she pursed her lips for a moment before grinning. "I certainly wouldn't mind having a rakish sea captain with me at court and in my bed."

"I meant, with you, with Moranth and Vetreon." Alessandra covered, unwilling to even hope Lucia was being serious, but the queen's words gave voice, even by accident, to a notion her mind had not previously allowed. She was taken aback. Lucia fascinated her like no other woman ever had, but she was the queen of Moranth, the country Alessandra and her father had been exiled from. Even if she secured a pardon from Lucia, she could never just pick her life back up where she'd left off. *Could I? Is that what Lucia meant?* She couldn't fathom going back to her life as a noble. *Where would that leave us? It would be a great shame to sail away from such a woman, but what future is there for us?*

Lucia didn't miss a beat. "I suppose there will be a war," she answered, swallowing her mouthful of fish. "If I win, I go back to the tedium of ruling while trying to stay out of the marriage snare. My advisors are always trying to throw some idiot at me, but I have my cousin, Sebastian. He's a good lad. He'll make a fine king one day if it comes to that, or else his children will." She shrugged.

"You aren't worried about the kingdom. What could happen to it if you don't marry?"

Lucia sighed. "Bastian has been in my care since he was small. His father died before he was born, and his mother…" she blinked back tears as the emotion came through her voice, "… my father executed her shortly after Bastian's birth. He thought it smart to keep the closest thing I had to a rival at court. The boy was practically a prisoner before I became queen. He's like a son to me. His mother, my cousin, and I were close."

Alessandra cocked a brow. "How close?" She hadn't meant to tease or make light of such a momentous thing in Lucia's life, but her jealousy came unbidden.

Lucia laughed, her shoulders dropping. "Not like that. She was just a good person. There aren't too many of those in a court, especially the one I grew up in."

"Was she the one who taught you how to do all these useful things you keep coming up with?" Alessandra asked, still curious about Lucia's upbringing. *How was a princess allowed to run so wild?*

"Some of it. She and my mother were best friends, though she was younger. Sancha was her name, Bastian's mother. I suppose you know my mother's."

"Tialda, wasn't it?" Alessandra pulled the name from the depths of her childhood.

Lucia frowned, her gaze turning inward.

"Are you alright?" Alessandra asked, touching her arm gently.

Lucia's voice cracked as she said, "I just realized I haven't heard my mother's name spoken out loud since her death."

"I'm sorry."

Lucia nodded, clearly distracted by her own thoughts for a moment.

Alessandra was unsure how to continue since the conversation had drifted into such deep waters. "Least you had options in bedfellows."

"What?" Lucia questioned before realizing Alessandra was picking up the earlier thread of their conversation. "Oh, yes," she smiled. "That is true, I admit. More choices than you have on a ship, I guess."

"You guess right. Smith and Rafe are the closest in age. Smith's been on nearly as long as I have, and Rafe, after he realized I wasn't going to shag him, has been like a brother. They're certainly the comeliest of the lot."

Lucia's interest was clearly piqued as she leaned forward. "You haven't been with any of them?"

"God, no." Alessandra snorted, noting how Lucia's whole body relaxed with her words. *Was that jealousy I just saw?* Lucia need not have feared. Pretty and ready with a smile as they were, Alessandra didn't think she'd ever look at anyone the way she was struggling not to look at Lucia.

"Well," Lucia said, finishing off her fish, "we have each other for now."

Alessandra recognized the sadness in Lucia's voice for the honesty it was. There could be no future between them, much as she'd enjoyed musing on one for a moment. "You like the fish, eh?" she asked, trying to turn the conversation.

Lucia licked at her fingers, her eyes finding Alessandra's as she did so. "Mmmhmm."

The rain pounded relentlessly against their shelter, slipping through the gaps in the palm fronds and running in rivulets over the sand floor. A peaceful silence settled over the women as they finished eating.

"Can I ask you something?" Lucia began.

Alessandra thought it funny; not much else to do at the moment. "Sure, I'm not busy presently."

"Why didn't you and your father return when I issued the pardons?"

Alessandra's heart skipped a beat. "What?"

"The pardons I sent out to the families my father exiled. You and your father, your whole crew actually, were amongst them. Half of my advisors were furious with me for pardoning a pirate, even though it was my father's fault D'Allyon went rogue—nor was your father the only royal navy man to do so. A great many of our neighboring kingdom's finest ships came from men my father exiled."

"I don't know what you're talking about," Alessandra snapped, going on the defensive.

Is this a trick? Her mind began to trip over every encounter, every moment she'd spent in the queen's presence. She knew the seduction was a ruse at first, but then it seemed as though there was a genuine attraction. *I know there is, don't I? Or has it all been a means to an end, to make me want to help her, keep her alive? Is this a ploy?*

"You're lying," Alessandra said. She was simply not able to believe her father could keep something of such importance from her. At least, not at first. Then she thought about how little she truly knew about the man and how close she already felt to the woman at her side.

"I'm not lying," she nearly whispered, hurt clear in the low tones. "I've wondered for eight years, ever since I sent those pardons out, why the D'Allyon family was the only one not to answer."

Alessandra remained silent, turning her memories over in search of one that could give truth to Lucia's words. There it was. Her father, drunk in a tavern in the out-of-the-way port of Night Harbor. An argument and a messenger.

———

King Teodor had been dead for six months, and his daughter had just been crowned. Alessandra was jealous. Her own father barely let her out of his sight. He'd trusted her to take part in battles since her twelfth birthday, but only recently had agreed to her being allowed to join the crew in their carousing on land. She thought it a sign that he'd finally given up on ever making a lady of her. Her place was firmly on

The Medusa. She and Cyril had been tasked with selling a particularly fine set of porcelain taken from a merchant ship, offering her a rare chance to have the first mate's ear in private. She didn't like the road she saw her father heading down and wanted the older man's advice.

"He's angry, Alex. We all are." Cyril put one of his big hands on her shoulder as they trudged back through the dark, narrow streets of town. It was a moonless night, and the small lantern in Cyril's other hand offered little light.

Sadness and frustration filled her. "Teodor is dead," she whispered harshly. The still air was stifling even in the dead of night, and she was sweating through her greatcoat. "Shouldn't my father feel some sense of relief?"

"The death of an enemy is an empty promise. Your mother is still dead. We're still here." He opened his arms wide. "Still doing what we can to keep ourselves fed. That monster's death won't change any of it."

The scent of salt and decay hit her as they arrived back at the docks. The Medusa was moored before her.

"Get some sleep, lass."

"But my father—"

Cyril gave her shoulder a reassuring squeeze. "He'll come through this, same as everything else."

She didn't bother arguing. She knew Cyril would follow her father to the gates of hell, but she could see the danger to them all should their captain not recover. Pascal D'Allyon had never been a gregarious fellow, always had the rigid directness of a naval officer, but he was a fair and capable man, the sort who inspired loyalty. Since the king's death, though, he'd become morose and ill-tempered at sea.

When they made port, he'd find a dark tavern away from the crew and drink himself into a stupor until Cyril hauled him back aboard. Her father hadn't made a mistake sailing yet, but Alessandra was losing her trust in him, and she knew the other sailors were as well. If he couldn't pull himself together, they could lose everything.

Instead of returning to The Medusa, she decided to trail Cyril. She needed to know her father was safe. Alessandra crept along the crooked streets in Cyril's wake, staying far enough back for him not to notice her. She was good at sneaking, having grown up on a ship where the presence of a child had been a novelty. She would never have known a thing in the first few years aboard if not for her spying.

The dilapidated establishment she found her father in was on the other side of town, a tavern not even the most junior of the crew would ever dare step foot in. She nearly gagged, her eyes watering at the sickly sweet stench from within, when Cyril threw open the creaking door. Moving closer to rub at a window, she could see her father and another man, their heads huddled close together.

Cyril stayed near the door, leaving her father and the unknown man to their business. Her father suddenly sprang from his seat, blade drawn low at the man's side. Their voices were raised loud enough for Alessandra to hear the man curse. Cyril went quickly to her father's aid, pulling at him. The other man shook his head and spat on the ground before leaving through the open door and vanishing into the night.

The bright green seal of Moranth was easy enough to pick out from where she remained out of sight. It was stamped in wax across the lip of a folded piece of parchment. Word from home? *Her father scooped up the letter and stuffed it into his coat as Cyril approached. Either Cyril hadn't seen the missive, or he was being purposefully ignorant.*

Alessandra hadn't dared stay longer. By the time The Medusa's captain and first mate were back aboard, she was tucked tight in her bunk, mind spiraling with questions.

Alessandra came back to herself.

Her father never spoke to her about it, nor did she ask, and the message was never seen again. At least, not by her. Eight years. Eight years of scrabbling, living by their wits and the luck of the sea. She'd seen a hundred battles in those years, only to find out that her father could have taken her home and kept her safe. She felt ill at the prospect of his betrayal, embarrassed that she had not asked him about it when she had the chance.

Alessandra looked across the glowing embers of their fire to Lucia. "I believe you," she said into the near-dark shelter. The reflected firelight shone in Lucia's glistening eyes. "I believe you," Alessandra repeated, throwing a handful of twigs onto the smoldering flames. Her eyes burned from the smoke as she rubbed at them.

Anger flared white hot in her gut, fury at her father, at their family's exile.

Lucia's hands were suddenly tangled in her hair, her lips peppering Alessandra's skin with kisses. "It'll be alright," Lucia whispered into the night. "You can come home now. All of you can," she muttered.

Alessandra hadn't planned on bringing it up until they were once more safely aboard The Medusa, but it seemed as good a time as any. "You're offering us pardons again? After we kidnapped you?"

"I am." Lucia bit her lip nervously. "As well as a place at court."

Alessandra thought of Cyril, his sweet wife, the ever-good-naturedly suffering Margthe, and his son and daughters. Cyril could finally see the towers of Moranth again without fear of death. He could build the pub he was always talking about, overlooking the chalk cliffs.

What about me? She wasn't like her father; she hadn't chosen the life of a pirate. It was chosen for her by King Teodor, when he exiled her family, and then by her father, when Lucia offered pardons, offered a life of no more running. Still, she was a wild thing, raised by men who'd turned their back on law-abiding society. How could she hope to return to her life before?

Her father often spoke of the pirate's code of living free of any authority but one's own. For him, all kings and queens were creatures to be hated. It was Cyril who gave her the books of the ancient Moranth, tales of her ancestors long dead, kings and queens of myth, even-tempered and just. He would even speak fondly of Lucia's grandfather when he was drunk and so long as his captain was out of earshot.

To be a lady, to be the paramour of a queen, was something that could not be. Something Alessandra knew she must not dare to hope for. Still, she nuzzled Lucia's neck, smiling in the darkness as, for one night, she would let herself dream.

9

ALMONT

Almont's fingers tapped nervously on the tavern's scarred table. The Medusa was late. Not just late, missing. The pirate ship hadn't been seen since she sailed from Marshport almost three weeks prior, with the kidnapped queen of Moranth aboard. Ramir's plot had always been a gamble. The Medusa could meet with misfortune. Lucia could be injured or killed. Ships were lost at sea every day.

The king of Vetreon's secretary pulled off his velvet cap in frustration. Running a hand over his thinning hair, he drank the whisky before him in one go, then signaled for another like some drunk sailor. The air in the tavern was wet and steamy despite the lateness of the season. Almont hated the heat though he'd been born in the capital, where the southern sun beat down on the city summer or winter. He'd often wondered how his family had come to this part of the world and made the decision to stay.

The barkeep set another glass of brown liquor before him, but this time, he sipped at it—it was hardly a fine vintage requiring such slow drinking, but he wanted to take his time. Ramir had been in a rage for days, so Almont was doing his best to keep a low profile. He couldn't help but be at the king's beck and call during the daytime, but he could keep himself far from the palace at night with the excuse of information gathering.

If anyone knew of The Medusa's whereabouts, it would be the den of cut-throats and pirates in this seaside tavern, but so far, not one word had been spoken of the lost ship. *Bad luck.* His king's mood was further rattled by the ease with which Lord Royce Aldana and his protégé, the young Sebastian, had settled into ruling. Word from his spies was that the young man was a natural leader with a good head on his shoulders and the loyalty of the court.

It seemed Lucia had done well in raising the lad. With Aldana's help, the young man had enacted the embargo that was, in fact, the talk of the tavern. Most were grumbling about it, complaining that it was making it harder and harder to earn a wage without turning to piracy, but from what Almont was hearing, most placed the blame squarely on their new king's shoulders. If destabilization was what Moranth was after, they were succeeding.

Not for the first time, Almont thought of putting himself on one of the merchant ships beyond the tavern doors to make his way into the service of the Moranthese court, but there was his family. One wrong move and they would pay the price, of that he had no doubt. Almont wasn't a cruel man but thought, just perhaps, it might be better for Lucia if The Medusa had sunk.

Another coin, another glass, but then he saw a man he recognized just as the sailor was coming through the door. Slamming the drink back, he finally gave in and purchased a whole bottle, setting off to find out what he could. He was fortunate to have a head for drink. Almont didn't indulge often, but he had a naturally high tolerance for the stuff, which he had used many times to his advantage. Subterfuge wasn't nearly so difficult when the target was drunk.

"Buy you a drink, sailor?" he asked the scruffy young man, holding the bottle of rum up for him to see.

For a moment, the sailor's red-rimmed eyes widened with delight, then narrowed just as quickly to focus on the man making the offer.

"Shit," he said, shaking his head. "Whatever it is, Almont, I'm not getting involved."

Almont tipped his head in the direction of an empty table in a dark corner of the room. "Come on, Sam, you know I'm made aware any time a ship like The Deceit makes port. I know down to the penny just how much loot you pirates offload and to where." The younger man sniffed, wiping at his nose as his eyes fixed on the bottle swinging from Almont's fingers. "I know your ship came in two days ago, but nothing has been fenced, and no tax has been paid to His Majesty's purse. You probably don't even have coin for meat, much less a bottle like this. It could keep you in good spirits until you weigh anchor and sail back into the unknown."

The young man sat down heavily at the shaded table, slouching low in his chair. "You going to pour that rum?"

Almont set the two glasses down and poured the drink in a slow, steady stream before sliding a nearly overflowing cup to the fellow across from him. "This can go one of two ways, Sam—"

The sailor cut him off. "Yeah, I know. Spin a tale for you or the noose." He closed his eyes as he let the rum slide down his throat. "What if I don't have a story for you this time?"

Grinning slyly, Almont poured him another full glass. "I don't think that's true, lad. The only things sent out to The Deceit were a few weeks' worth of provisions, pitch, and lumber. You've been in a battle, maybe one that didn't go your way. To my recollection, the only entanglements your captain hasn't come out on top of have been against The Medusa. What happened?"

The man drank. "Blast it, Almont, don't you always have it figured? Aye, Captain heard it was The Medusa that stole Moranth's queen. Honestly, it pricked his pride that we weren't offered the job first."

"Perhaps whoever hired them didn't think Defoe would undertake such a foolish endeavor."

Sam tipped his glass in Almont's direction. "*Whoever*, right. Captain finally had her dead to rights, then a squall came out of nowhere, like the judgment of the gods themselves, and it was over."

Almont's heart squeezed with anticipation of the answer to his next question. "The Medusa was lost?"

The sailor took the bottle from Almont's loose grasp, poured himself a last drink, then stood. "Don't think so, but she was wounded, same as us. If she hasn't made a port yet, could be she went down. Won't know until she shows up, or doesn't." Shrugging, he moved away from the table, taking the rum with him.

"Damn it," Almont cursed under his breath, letting the man melt back into the crowd of unwashed bodies and drunken revelers. It wasn't much to go on. Like the man said, anything could have befallen the ship carrying his quarry. "Damn it," he muttered again, pushing his way to the only slightly less sticky air of the alleyway.

ROYCE

If Ramir had Lucia, no one knew it. "Shit," Royce cursed, his boot sinking into a mud-filled puddle as he made his way through Olde Towne. Ylva had sent word from Vetreon—their contacts were useless on the matter of the missing queen, but the people, already displeased with their king, were growing more so by the day.

Your plan is working, she wrote.

He'd done some digging of his own and turned up one very helpful barmaid in Marshport, who was well acquainted with the pirate ship's crew. It seemed that The Medusa had a new captain, one that shared his taste in women. *Alessandra*, his mind tripped over the name, wondering what she was like. A woman in mourning, the girl had told him. 'So sauced she could barely stand,' the wench had said when she and Royce had spoken earlier. 'Those lads were trying to pull one over on her, looked to me. Only way they could. She's a quick lass and a good tipper.' She'd clucked her tongue as if she truly cared about the young captain's well-being. *Maybe she does?*

Royce shook his boot—his stockings were soaked. It was a miserable day out, rain pelting his every step. He'd have to beg for a hot bath once he reached Uridice's. It was a long shot, but if there was something to know of the D'Allyon woman, then perhaps Uridice could shed some light on the matter. Surely a sailor of taste would have made her way once or twice to the Calan's finest brothel. The girl in Marshport had been more than helpful, insightful creature that she was, but he trusted Uridice.

Ermes was at the door of the brothel, unusual for daylight hours. Usually, the impressively large man didn't make an appearance before dark. Royce gave the man a grin as he approached, shielding his eyes as he looked up into Ermes' face. "You're even more massive than I thought. Gods, man."

Ermes' imposing form eased the smallest amount as he saw it was Royce under the hood. "She wondered when you'd show up."

"Just had you waiting out here for me, did she?"

Ermes smirked. "You flatter yourself, Aldana."

"I believe you may be right," he said, brushing through the open door.

Hands relieved him of his sodden cloak almost immediately. He turned to see that they belonged to a fine-featured redhead, her sheer blue gown doing little to hide her assets.

"My lord," she smiled.

He didn't know her, but like all the women working for Uridice, she was lovely, and more importantly, the sharpness of her mind was clear behind her pale green eyes. *Does she know who I am?*

"I've come to see your mistress," he said, brushing at his damp curls. Though tempted—he was no eunuch—Royce had yet to touch another woman in lust since the day he set eyes on his wife. A feat he still marveled at.

The redhead's eyes tilted at the corners, her lips following suit. "A man of importance, then."

Another woman swooped an arm around his shoulder. "This way, Lord Aldana. I'll let her know you're here."

He turned back briefly to get another look at the new girl. "She'll do well."

"Already is. Uridice is sure Ylva means to whisk her away, make an honest woman of her." The woman laughed. She was old enough to be his mother. Iron-grey hair in a neat bun at the nape of her neck framed a face set in perpetual sternness that belied the good-natured surliness beneath.

"Only because you turned her down, Syl."

Syl slapped his shoulder, shooing him toward a private room. Royce sat down wearily into a plush chair and kicked off his muddy boots, to the obvious annoyance of Syl.

"Don't tell me you do that in front of your wife. You've spoken of her enough for me to know she'd not tolerate it, and nor will I. Not from you." She pointed at him. He felt his cheeks flush. Syl had known him since he was far too young to have been in such a place. She and Ermes were at the heart of Uridice's household. A family Royce counted himself a part of.

"My apologies," he said quickly, meaning it.

The older woman shook her head before overseeing the servants bringing in a tub and hot water. "You've got enough on your mind, I suppose."

"That I do."

Syl nodded, saw that the others had left, and then quietly shut the heavy wood door behind her, leaving Royce to his thoughts.

———

Uridice made her appearance just as he was slipping beneath the steaming waters of his bath.

"Royce," she said as she swept into the bedchamber, an amber velvet dressing gown covering what he knew to be an exemplary figure beneath.

"Suppose I shouldn't expect privacy in a brothel."

Uridice shot him a sardonic grin, her eyes flicking to the bathwater and his naked body beneath. "Hardly what I'm after."

Royce tipped his chin toward the low settee across from him. "Have a few questions to ask." Uridice was one of the most intelligent people he knew. She was a shrewd business owner and a vault when it came to secrets. She'd been one of his most important spies for years.

"How's Sebastian?" she asked, taking a seat while smoothing the folds of her gown.

"He's handling the situation better than I would have at his age, or any age, for that matter."

"He's not a hothead like you were."

"I'm much better than I used to be."

She laughed. "We can all be thankful for that. Ten years ago, you'd have thrown us into open war already."

His tone grew serious. "Probably. I'm close enough to it as is."

Uridice's expression turned sober, her lips pursing. Royce knew the last few years had been hard for her—what Lucia had once meant to her. "Has the crew of The Medusa ever been in here?"

"Course they have. So has the crew of every other infamous ship sailing these waters. Coin is coin." Her eyes narrowed. "It's certain, then? That they took her?"

Royce splashed his face with water before toweling his hands. "I've turned up a few sailors that saw the first mate talking to someone at a tavern the night before the kidnapping, but it could have been anyone. Although, no other ship left the Calan or

Marshport within the two days either side of Lucia being taken."

"She could have been hogtied and thrown into the back of a cart," Uridice posited.

"If that were the case, I'd put my gold on Lucia already overtaking or seducing her kidnappers. She'd be back home at the palace by now. She's more than capable."

Uridice seemed to think for a moment, her golden head in her hand. "You have a point. A ship, then. One place from which she couldn't escape. Are you asking if they've been in recently? Obviously, with all the rumors going around, I would have told you if I knew anything."

"Of course, I know that. I'm more curious about the captain."

"Pascal? I heard of him only in passing from the crew. Never set eyes on the man."

"Not him. He's dead. His daughter, though, appears to be very much alive."

"Ah, sadly, I've yet to have the pleasure. I've heard she's quite beautiful."

Royce grunted in affirmation. "I've heard the same, but nothing else."

Sighing, Uridice stood. "If she's with them, she's better off than with others, at least. They're a smart crew with several old Moranthese navy men. At the very least, I don't think the ship will go down. But they are well-known anti-royalist. You need to find her, and soon."

LUCIA

As the days rolled on, Alessandra and Lucia split their time between the necessities of survival, gathering, fishing, fire-tending, and languorous hours conserving their energy during the shimmering heat of the day. After the early mornings of scavenging, picking berries, and checking the gill net, they would drop exhaustedly into their shelter. Some days were spent wrapped in each other's embraces, sleeping when they could, dreaming of a life off their island.

On a day when rain swept in early, leaving their stomachs grumbling in the grey light, words escaped Lucia's lips before she'd weighed them. "What do you think you would have been like if your father wasn't a pirate?"

Alessandra chuckled. "I'd be married and miserable, I suppose. Not much choice. Perhaps with the right person, it wouldn't be terrible."

Lucia sat up, rubbing at her eye after a drop of rainwater seeped into their shelter and dripped onto her cheek. "You really think your father would have forced you into a marriage?" It was something Lucia often wondered about her own father. *Would I be free to have my choice of consort and lovers if he were still alive?* She reasoned it was very unlikely.

Alessandra shrugged. "Maybe I would have had brothers if my mother had lived. It could have been left to them to carry on the D'Allyon name, and I would have been more free to follow where my desires led. As much as I've thought about what could have been, I guess I've never thought hard enough. I know, even as young as I was, that I was uncomfortable with being a *lady,* but I'm honestly not sure I fully know what else is out there."

"Pirate, wife, or wench." Lucia listed off with her fingers. "Not sure there is much else."

"Queen," Alessandra teased. "I suppose I could make do with that."

"Being a queen requires patience," Lucia quipped.

"And you have so much of that, do you?" Alessandra playfully nipped at her throat and was rewarded with a groan.

Lucia wrapped her arms around Alessandra. "Certainly not when it comes to you."

The sound of rain became outmatched by pleasured moans.

The downpour continued into the next morning, then the next, not letting up for four days. Their little hovel was damp and musty with the scent of unwashed bodies and a sooty fire.

"Damn it," Alessandra cursed as she looked at their meager stores.

"What is it?"

"The fish is almost gone." Lucia watched Alessandra's jaw muscle twitch. "And I can't stand being in here much longer. If this weather doesn't let up—"

"I know," Lucia interrupted, not needing to be told the dire nature of their situation. She only needed to look to her own quickly shrinking curves to know they were starving. "I'll go out," she said, grimacing as she moved her stiff limbs to stand.

"I'll go." Alessandra put out a hand to stop her, but Lucia shook her head.

"You're better at keeping the fire going than I am. You know it's true, so don't argue. That goes out, and we're done for. Let me go do this for us."

Alessandra shook her head. "I'm too tired to argue."

Lucia gave her a wan smile, then ducked out into the rain. She was soaked to the bone immediately.

She planned to make the trek down the shore to check the gill net before circling back by the brambles of berries. Humming as she went, Lucia tried to remember the words that went with the melody. It was a song her mother used to sing to her about a selkie and the sailor she loved.

The net wasn't far, but in the storm, it seemed farther. Her feet stuck in the wet sand, her breeches catching at burrs, and her back screamed as she pulled the net in. There was nothing in it.

Something caught her eye as she stood, a black smudge against the grey sky. Lucia thought she was hallucinating at first.

"It's a ship," she whispered, not believing it.

Blinking, she focused as hard as she could with the rain beating down on her.

"It's a ship!" she finally screamed, willing her words to bring the thing closer.

She sprinted for the hut as Alessandra scrambled from it to scan the horizon, her face breaking into a wide grin. "It's The Medusa! God, I've never seen anything so beautiful."

Lucia cleared her throat.

Alessandra laughed. "Present company not included."

"Are you sure it's your ship?" Lucia's heartbeat quickened. "It could be The Deceit or anyone else."

"I'd know the line of her anywhere. That's The Medusa. We're saved."

They watched for almost an hour as the stately frigate drew closer. Their hut became the fuel of a signal fire. Lucia glanced back at their temporary home engulfed in flames. After nearly three weeks alone with

Alessandra on the island, she couldn't imagine being separated from her lover and almost thought it a shame to be leaving their makeshift home. *Almost.* Lucia wasn't sure what the future would hold, but she had her secret hopes for the two of them.

"You don't think it's a trap, do you?" she asked as a dinghy was lowered into the water.

Alessandra took her hand and gave it a squeeze. "Too late now if it is."

ALESSANDRA

"You two look like drowned rats," Cyril boomed as he splashed ashore with four others.

Alessandra laughed while giving the man a fierce hug, not caring for a moment that she was his captain. She nearly went limp in his arms as the old man embraced her, unbidden tears spilling forth.

"There, lass," he whispered when her sobs could no longer be ignored. "You're safe now, *Captain*," he said pointedly. Her breathing slowed, and her body stiffened. He was right. It wouldn't do for the crew to see her like this. She nodded once, then stepped away, straightening the coat he offered around her.

"Give the queen your coat, Cyril," she said, noting Lucia's see-through shirt as she stood apart, arms crossed over her chest. *What is she thinking?*

Alessandra wished she knew, but her lover had gone quiet as the dinghy drew near.

Cyril quickly obeyed, bobbing his head as he handed over the worn garment, which Lucia took with a "thank you."

"Come on." Alessandra held a hand out to her. The little boat bobbed on the shallow surf as two sailors held it tight. "Let's get off this damned island."

"Right."

Alessandra caught a flicker of sadness flash across Lucia's face and sighed. *I shouldn't have called it that.* The island had been their home, the first place they'd been together. If not for their island, they would both be dead, or Lucia would be married to her sworn enemy. The rocky strip of land had kept them alive, had given them the time to find each other. She shouldn't have cursed it.

Lucia took her hand, letting her help her through the choppy waves into the boat waiting for them. It wouldn't have done to have survived the island only to be swept out to sea. When they sat, Alessandra made sure to tuck the queen into her side, wanting her to know that she was still there, that they were still alright. Dropping her head in exhaustion against Lucia's shoulder, she noted Cyril's glances, though he said nothing.

"How's the old girl?" Alessandra asked as they pulled alongside the ship, her hand shielding her eyes as she sought out any visible damage.

"She's still sailing," came Rafe's enthusiastic voice. Alessandra's eyes darted up to where her friend was hanging over the railing, a broad grin on his face.

The starboard side was pockmarked by cannon fire from where the heavy lead balls had slammed into her. Alessandra paused as she grasped the rope ladder—the rough hemp rope was a welcome familiarity as it bit into her palms. She gave her ship a reverent pat, fingers probing a particularly deep gash in the hull. Above her, men were calling to her in a celebratory air as more and more heads peaked over the railing to see her. She took a breath, arms shaking, as she began to climb.

"Did you lose any men?" She heard Lucia ask from below her.

Alessandra didn't hear Cyril's response as she was hauled the last bit of the way by excited sailors. She laughed as hands clapped her on the back and shouts of 'Captain!' went up.

"That's enough. Enough." Smiling, she shooed her men away.

The rain slacked off as Alessandra swung her long legs over the ship's railing, her hands reaching back to help Lucia. The lightheartedness of the moment fell away as Lucia landed heavily on the deck. She was unsteady on her feet, and Alessandra placed a hand at her back. The men were silent. The corner of Rafe's lips pulled up ever so slightly as their eyes met over Lucia's head, but he, too, remained quiet. Alessandra shifted her feet, feeling the gentle rock of the ship beneath her. *I'm home. They came back for me.* The relief she had felt being pulled over the rail by her crew had vanished. *They don't know Lucia as I do. She's not one of them.*

"Alright, that's enough fussing over me," she called. "Get back to it." At least the men still listened to her. They turned to their tasks, some grumbling, others whispering. It left her stomach in a knot of unease.

"Sure you two need a moment," Cyril offered, nodding toward the captain's cabin.

"Thank you," Alessandra said, plucking at Lucia's sleeve.

"I'll scrounge up some food. No doubt you need that as well."

Alessandra could only nod in thanks; her voice was stuck in her throat with gratitude toward her first mate. She ushered the queen into her cabin so they could dry off and change into some of Alessandra's clothes without the eyes of the crew on them. Lucia shrugged out of Cyril's borrowed coat and handed it off as the door thudded shut behind them.

"Smells like day-old cheese," she said, scrunching her nose before smiling as she wrung rainwater from her hair, making a small puddle on the floor.

Alessandra laughed, holding the garment away from her by thumb and forefinger. She didn't notice the smell, raised as she was in such close quarters, but was sure Lucia had a point. Opening the door, she called out to her first mate, "Cyril." Then turned back to Lucia. "I'll be right back." She smiled affectionately, not even mad at the water seeping into the planks of her floor. *We've been rescued. It's alright to enjoy the moment.*

Lucia made a face, already peeling off her wet shirt and breeches. Her eyes then raked over Alessandra's equally soaked figure. "I can feel you staring," Alessandra said, catching Lucia's gaze lingering on the worn backside of her silk breeches, nearly see-through from wear.

"Hurry back," Lucia teased, "or I'll have to make use of this bed all by myself."

Alessandra's brows raised as Lucia slunk toward the bed, her damp skin glistening in the daylight. Her mouth went dry at the sight. "Is that all you think about?"

Lucia pouted her lips over her shoulder. "No." She sighed. "But it's all I'm thinking about right now. Oh, and food."

"Make use of that washbasin first." Alessandra pointed toward the stand in the far corner of the room, noting her own hair and clothes had left puddles of water as she closed the door firmly behind her.

Amusement lit Cyril's face as Alessandra handed over his coat. "I'll always know it was worn by a queen." The man looked around, then bent close to her in a conspiratorial posture. "We aren't going to Vetreon, are we?"

Alessandra turned her gaze to the sea; the air was stifling as the rain turned to a fine mist. The ship's rigging creaked above her as the silent crew pretended to work while awaiting her order.

"What makes you say that?" she asked carefully.

"The way you looked at the queen before we boarded—like she carried every hope and dream you ever had along with her. You care for her."

Alessandra shook her head. "I can't give her to Ramir. I didn't want to before."

Cyril's nostrils flared. "And now you won't."

Alessandra felt her chest tighten, her teeth grind. *Should have brought my sword.* "No."

"The crew won't like it," Cyril grumbled, but she wasn't sensing danger from the man, so her body eased.

"And you?" Cyril was as close to a father as she had left. She didn't know if she was prepared to defend Lucia with her life if he went against her.

He crossed his arms and widened his stance, blocking most of the crew from her view. "Don't like it either. Doesn't make any matter to me if some royal has to marry another blue-blooded cunt they don't care for."

Alessandra's fingers twitched at her belt, again wishing she were armed. "Tell me there's a but coming so I don't have to worry about a mutiny."

Cyril tapped his fingers on the hot wood of the doorframe while sucking at his teeth. "Won't be a mutiny from me. Too old for it. Too old for any of it. Why I agreed to the kidnapping in the first place." He jerked his chin toward her cabin. "The money we'd make off her, I'd be done with this life forever. Buuut," he drew the word out, "I'd not take the woman you love from you. I'd not do that to anyone. I know what it is to look at a woman like that. Like they're the air you breathe. She can't stay here, though. You know that. She isn't one of us, and while she's on board, we've got more trouble than I care to think of."

Alessandra sagged with relief. She wasn't sure if she could take Cyril in a brawl—old as he was, he was still strong as an ox—but she'd been willing to try. "I know.

Still, it's better than sealing her fate by taking her to Vetreon. We can't be together, but she'll be safer if we take her home."

The man's eyes widened at the mention of returning the queen to Moranth.

Alessandra smirked, nudging him with her shoulder. "You trust me, Cyril?"

"Aye." Cyril's hand landed heavily on her shoulder.

She was grateful for the man's friendship. "Good. I'll speak with her now. Best shove off while we have the tide."

"The men will know we aren't heading the right way."

"Give them the order, Cyril. I'll deal with them in a bit, then you and I will speak."

Taking a deep breath, allowing the feeling of home to settle around her shoulders, Alessandra glanced once more at her crew, her family, before heading back to Lucia.

LUCIA

She was thankful to be alive, to have been rescued, yet her tears would not come. She felt them at the ready, along with a lump in her throat, but they were more akin to sadness than joy. *Will Alessandra still want me now we are back on the ship? Can our rela-*

tionship hold strong now she is back amongst her people?

Lucia had felt ill at ease among the throng of pirates she'd encountered, even when Alessandra had nestled her safely in her arms in the dinghy. They were no longer in the world they had built for themselves—unforgiving as it had been, Lucia missed it. The men that lifted her onto The Medusa, the ones that had cheered for Alessandra, were strangers to her. They greeted her with no such warmth, just stared as she was sequestered in the captain's cabin.

When Alessandra went to speak with Cyril, Lucia was left wondering what the captain was thinking. If she, too, was turning their tryst over in her mind, unsure of what lay ahead. Sex, though, Lucia understood, and sex with Alessandra, in particular, had yet to disappoint. It was how they connected when everything else was going to hell. Lucia tried not to take her lover's quick exit as a rebuff, but Alessandra's absence so soon after the rescue, stung. She had hoped to have a bit longer with her paramour before the pirate set her aside.

The air was still in the captain's quarters as the sunlight fell in golden shards across her bed. Lucia had done her best in the few moments since Alessandra left to make herself presentable. She'd used one of the heavy silver combs that lay by the desk to get the worst of the tangles out of her hair, then scrubbed her face and body before draping herself over the heavy blankets and furs covering the large bed. Catching a glimpse of herself in Alessandra's mirror, Lucia noted with a pang the loss of some of her curves. She was no longer exactly voluptuous, but she still thought she cut a fine enough figure. A fact proven by Alessandra's jaw hitting the floor as she opened the door onto the scene Lucia had created for her.

"Fuck," Alessandra muttered under her breath. Crossing the room in three long strides, she grabbed a discarded shirt. "Put your clothes on." She scowled, tossing the garment at Lucia.

Lucia was perplexed, crushed. *We have been rescued. We are together. Why on earth does she look as though the world is ending?*

"I'm taking you back to Moranth!" Alessandra announced.

Lucia's mouth fell open. "You can't."

"What do you mean I can't? Nothing's changed." Alessandra threw her arms in the air. "This is what we talked about. You're the queen. You can pardon the men and me, as we discussed. Don't you want to go back?"

"You trust me to do that?" She couldn't hide the awe in her voice.

"To pardon us? Yes." Alessandra sighed, pinching the bridge of her nose. "Besides the pardons, I know I can't deliver you to Ramir, I already told you that, but you can't stay here."

Lucia felt as though she'd been slapped across the face by Alessandra's sharp tone. Her eyes brimmed with tears before she caught herself. Refusing to give Alessandra the satisfaction of seeing her cry, Lucia blinked the tears away and put on a mask of forced indifference.

"Don't you want to go home?" Alessandra asked again, softer this time.

Lucia's nostrils flared as she tamped down her fury. She wasn't angry at Alessandra, but with their circumstances. She sought for but found no other solution. She was a queen, and the woman she loved was a pirate. *Love? Yes, that's exactly what this is. Was.* It could never have lasted; she knew that deep down. For all their fine words and imaginings on their island, reality had set in for both of them.

"Very well." Lucia stood to pull the shirt over her head, then clasped her hands behind her back and nodded. "You and your crew will have a pardon when I'm returned safely to my kingdom." She had wanted to hold on to Lucia the woman a bit longer, but the words ringing in her ears were those of the queen of Moranth.

Alessandra looked at the floor before raising her eyes. "I have your word?" she asked, voice hoarse.

"Yes, you have it." Lucia patted the bed beside her. Alessandra was right. She was a queen—running from her duty wasn't in her. Nor would she wish to unduly put Alessandra and her crew in danger, which was exactly what they'd be in if she stayed on board. Ramir wouldn't let up until he had what he wanted. *I could abdicate, but then what, and to who? Sebastian is still a boy. And where would that leave me? With Alessandra?* Lucia paused, trying to get the word for the pirate captain right. *Spectacular? Brilliant? Every fucking thing I could have ever wanted.* Still, Lucia couldn't see a path forward for them.

Her pragmatism kicked in, and she smiled up into Alessandra's golden eyes. "Come here," she teased, stretching her arms overhead. There was no point in spoiling their remaining time together with regret.

Alessandra groaned. "You've already seduced me," she said, climbing atop Lucia. "It won't change my decision." The sadness in her eyes was only there for a moment as Lucia brushed a thumb over her lips.

"I know," Lucia crooned. "So let's not waste time."

ALMONT

Almont sat before the Moranthese ambassador, Lord Maret. A far too capable man.

"Ambassador, please, you must understand. We had nothing to do with your queen's disappearance, and for Lord Aldana to insinuate such a thing is reprehensible. Surely you know King Ramir has nothing but the highest regards for his cousin, which was why he sent a proposal of marriage not two days before her kidnapping."

Maret sucked on his cheek, clearly not believing a word he said.

Almont hated the theater of politics. Both men knew if they were lucky, they would only get half-truths from the other, and yet they had to meet, had to go through the motions.

"I would say the timing of your king's proposal and Her Majesty's kidnapping were more than coincidence. I would say Ramir did so in hopes that, for some unknown reason, we would not suspect him. I also think that things haven't gone to plan. Your ruse would have only delayed the inevitable, anyway. Had the queen been forced into marriage, the Moranthese people would not have accepted Ramir's rule." Maret's dark eyes glinted. "We will not submit again."

Almont laughed, surprised the ambassador was being so open in his criticism. He had tried to tell his king the same thing when the plan was first hatched. Moranth had a formidable army, especially with Lord Blanxart at its head, nor had it been long enough for the people to have forgotten their last king. Ramir was cunning and smart, but still young enough to believe he could do anything.

"We don't have your queen," Almont blurted, his tone frustrated.

Maret raised his wineglass and took a sip. "I know. I also know that until she is found, one way or another, Vetreon's ships will not be docking at Moranthese ports and vice versa. The whole world clamors for our exports. Yours, not so much. Wellingisle provides our wool. Gold and silver come from our trade partners in Trethia. Our alliance with Vetreon has been built on familial ties for the last four hundred years. It exists because we allow it to. You don't even have the wood to build your own ships." The ambassador set his wine down with a firm thunk against the table. "Quite frankly, Almont, without us, you're fucked."

Almont cursed as he slammed the door of his rooms behind him. Maret was right, of course. He had to find Lucia. He had to find her and hang the whole thing on anyone but Vetreon's court. More importantly, he had to find her before Ramir did.

10

ALESSANDRA

They lay tangled in each other's arms as salt spray drifted in through the open window. They were at sea. Alessandra rose on her elbow to palm one of Lucia's breasts before skimming a hand over the tautness of the queen's stomach.

"I have to go tell the crew we aren't getting paid." She stood, running a hand through her snarled hair before dressing.

Lucia raised her brow. Her mouth quirked in jest. "You don't think they'll share your goodwill toward the queen of Moranth?"

Alessandra didn't return the smile. She was scared. Her hand swiped down her face as she scanned the room for fresh clothes. "I've spoken to Cyril. He's loyal. He will be able to keep most of them in check, but I need to come up with something." She paused, standing naked in the middle of the room. "Will you look at that?" she said, smiling. "Cyril's had them bring all my things up." Every one of her chests were arranged neatly within the captain's larger cabin; her clothes, her sword belt, even her books sat stacked by the foot of the bed. She hadn't noticed before.

"He believed in you." Lucia joined her, fitting her body against Alessandra's back. "Just like I do."

Reaching behind her to find Lucia's still plump backside, Alessandra gave it a squeeze. "You'll have to get dressed eventually, you know. Come find something you like."

They opened one trunk after the other. "This will do for me." Alessandra decided while Lucia still searched. Pulling her breeches up, she thrust her head through the neck of a clean shirt before tucking the white linen in, then shrugged into her coat with a happy sigh. Lucia had found the same sort of outfit of silk breeches and a linen shirt, just as they'd worn on the island.

"Not a gown?" Alessandra asked, anxious to see her lover in something akin to her court dress.

Lucia huffed as she dressed. "Absolutely not. I mean to live the pirate's life for as long as I can. Speaking of, in regards to your plan, don't pirates just sail about until they find some unwary target?"

Alessandra buckled her sword belt around her waist, then checked her blade. Testing it against her thumb, she was pleased to see that it was still sharp enough to split a hair. "Not on purpose. That's a good way for a captain to find themselves with a mutiny on their hands. I've no wish to be marooned again, however pleasant the company." Alessandra winked.

"There'll be war with Vetreon now," Lucia said, tying a red and gold silk sash around her waist. "Provided we make it back to Moranth alive, I could use a good captain with a warship and a loyal crew."

Alessandra licked her lower lip, eager to tip the queen back into her bed. "Going to press me into service, eh?"

As if she could read Alessandra's mind, mischief lit Lucia's eyes as she plopped back down on the bed. "Don't give me any more ideas unless you're willing to stay in here all day." She smirked, leaning back invitingly on her elbows.

Alessandra shook her head before perching her ornate hat over her combed locks. She wasn't clean—that wasn't going to happen until they reached port—but it would have to do. The mirror caught Lucia's reflection. Alessandra paused, glancing back one last time at the goddess lounging on her bed. Even fully clothed, she was devastating. This was what she was risking her life for, for whom she was willing to die.

"Fuck," she murmured and pushed the door open.

Alessandra stepped onto the deck to find a crew divided. Men stood about in clusters, talking, clearly not doing their routine duties. She had been in her cabin with Lucia barely half an hour, but it had been long enough for rumors to provoke the crew.

Cyril closed in quick. "Smith's trying to whip them up," he warned her. "Rafe and most of them are with you. Now that they've sobered up, they don't want to get caught up in this anymore. But Smith won't hear of it. He thinks this is our chance to get rich. Greedy bastard," Cyril spat as if he had not been the one to plan the kidnapping in the first place.

Rafe joined them; his square jaw clenched, worry clear in his eyes. "I'm afraid you're going to have to deal out some punishment, Captain."

The deck creaked beneath her footsteps. "Won't be the first time."

Alessandra stepped toward her crew as her voice, long used to shouting commands, boomed over the deck. "We have a decision to make, lads." All came to a standstill. "I'm hoping the fresh air has brought your senses along with it enough to realize the fool's errand that kidnapping Queen Lucia was." She looked over her men before continuing, echoing Cyril's earlier words. "I understand most of you are in agreement." There were murmurs and jostling among the crew. Alessandra held her hands high for silence. "I've never met Ramir, but I do know most of us are Moranthese, born and bred."

"Aye!" Smith's voice carried above the others. "Aye, and we were routed from our land by the queen's father. We hold no loyalty to her!" he shouted, pointing a finger toward Alessandra's cabin.

Nodding, she paced the deck with a hand on the pommel of her cutlass. "That may be true, and no one knows that more than I, but I've spent the last several weeks in the queen's company." There was more jostling, along with whoops and laughter. Alessandra would have normally considered it good-natured teasing, as it usually was, but she was all too aware the scales could tip easily in the wrong direction. She didn't need her relationship with Lucia to damage her argument. "She has offered pardons." It was not the time, if ever it came, to tell them of her father's betrayal. Such news would only muddy the waters. "We deliver her home safely, and we don't have to be pirates any longer."

Alessandra watched as many of the men nodded while speaking quietly with their neighbors. She also saw the group around Smith tighten, their faces taut with anxious energy. They wanted a fight.

"Maybe some of us like being pirates!" Smith shouted up at her.

Alessandra kept her voice light and calm. "Then, by all means, find another berth once we make landfall. I'll not keep any man in service that doesn't want to be here, but I want to go home." That wasn't exactly true, but she thought the phrasing would bring some of the men to her side, certainly those with family left in Moranth.

"Easy enough for a highborn," Smith threw at her. "You think the royal navy will just accept the rest of us into her ranks? That we'll be happy to bow and scrape to some pompous prick of a captain?"

Rafe stepped into action, but Alessandra caught at his sleeve. "*I* have to do this," she said, moving forward. His lips pursed, but he stepped back to await her command.

"Who is with me?" Alessandra asked. "Who wants to return home with a pardon and a place with the Moranthese Navy? There will be a war, and with war comes booty."

"Will you still be the captain?" asked one of the younger crew members.

Alessandra smiled. "I suppose I'll have to find some way to earn my keep."

"Being the queen's whore isn't enough?" came Smith's quick reply.

Alessandra stilled but did not respond to the barb. Smith would be dealt with soon enough. Her voice was calm and strong as she asked for the vote. "All those in favor of returning to Moranth, taking our lives back, say, aye."

Rafe was the first to call out a loud, "Aye!" followed by Cyril's more measured one.

Smith shook his shaggy head, the men in his circle tightening, heads bowed together.

"Aye." More men raised their hands, giving their blessing to the course Alessandra wished to set them on. Seeing she had the overwhelming majority, her shoulders relaxed—she could breathe. No more worry of a mutiny, at least for the moment. There might be a fight, but she was unlikely to be tossed overboard.

"Cyril," she ordered, "make for Moranth."

The old man nodded. "Aye, Captain."

"Rafe," Alessandra called over her shoulder, "please secure Smith to the mast for a flogging."

"Aye, Captain," he answered, moving past her with two other men.

Alessandra saw that Smith was alone. The throng of crew who had moments before supported him were moving away as though he had the plague.

"You going to clap me in irons next? Have your bitch queen throw me into a cell?" Smith railed as Rafe grasped him, hauling him toward his punishment.

Rafe shook his head as he responded. "You know the captain isn't like that. Just take your licks and be done with it. It's over. We'll sail into Moranth and receive our pardons. Then you can go on your way if you want. I understand you were hoping for riches, but there's no cause for all this. Alessandra has always been a friend to you."

He spoke the truth. She had no desire to see Smith, or any of her crew, harmed or mistreated.

Smith stopped struggling and nodded. "You're right. I'm sorry, I was just thinking about my Mary back in Silver Cove." He glanced up at Alessandra, who was running the long strips of the lash's leather through her fingers. Individually, they were soft. Hard to imagine them bringing the thumping pain she knew they would. "We would have had enough money to start our lives together properly."

Rafe placed a hand on his shoulder. "I understand. I'm sure the captain does as well."

"Aye," Alessandra said. "This will be over soon, and then it will be forgotten, eh?"

"Let's get on with it," Smith said as Rafe released him.

Alessandra watched as Smith squared his shoulders and stretched before pulling his shirt over his head. Turning to face the mast, he clutched at the wrapped ropes for purchase. He gave Alessandra a last backward glance, the heavy leather flog in her hand, then tipped his chin up at Rafe, a wry smile on his lips. "Might even enjoy this."

LUCIA

It was driving her mad to be kept in Alessandra's cabin like a disobedient child. Lucia paced across the room, her boots barely making a sound as they traveled back and forth and back and forth over the piled rugs. With her hands clasped behind her back and head bowed in concentration, she considered her options if things went badly. Lucia had found a dagger in another of Alessandra's trunks, which she then tucked into the sash around her waist. She was ready to attack if anyone besides the captain entered the room, but no one came.

She pressed her ear to the door when she heard Alessandra's raised voice, but the wood was thick, the voices too muffled to make out. Then it was quiet. Too quiet for her comfort. Unable to wait a moment longer, Lucia opened the door a crack and peered across the lower deck, where she saw Alessandra, coat off, shirtsleeves rolled to her elbows, hat forgotten in Rafe's hands. Lucia watched, rapt, as her lover unfurled a black leather flog, the thick strips falling nearly to her toes as a shirtless man waited, lashed to the mast.

Lucia's eyes widened as she crouched low behind a railing. The flog was the sort of instrument she'd used on many a partner. The width of the individual strands told her Alessandra didn't mean to hurt the lad. Still, Lucia's breath caught as the captain raised her hand and brought it down hard across the man's back with a heavy thud. The action caused a jolt of desire to crack through Lucia's body like lightning. *Gods.* She continued to look on breathlessly as Alessandra meted out punishment time and time again.

With every thud that landed, Lucia found herself more and more enthralled. She had never been on the outside of such an encounter before. It was beautiful. Alessandra was beautiful. Her lips were pursed, and her brows were furrowed in concentration, making sure every lick of the flogger hit the lad's back with precision to incur the most impact with the least amount of damage.

Lucia realized she was shaking with need as her lover landed each thumping blow on the sailor's back. The punishment wasn't meant to do any real harm—the act itself was symbolic more than anything—but to Lucia, who had only ever dealt them, it sent a ripple of desire and understanding coursing through her.

Lucia could hear Alessandra's labored breathing as the captain nodded to Rafe before turning back toward her cabin. Lucia hadn't even realized she was no longer hiding but standing in full view until Alessandra's gaze locked onto hers. Only then, as the pirate's long strides carried her quickly across the deck, did Lucia see her mistake.

"What are you doing?" Alessandra took hold of her arm and dragged Lucia back inside, slamming the door behind them. "You shouldn't be out there right now! It's not safe," she scolded.

Lucia was flushed, her palms clammy. "I—I'm sorry."

Her eyes searched her lover's for the answer to her body's response. *Is Alessandra's blood as hot from the flogging as mine? God.* Lucia panicked. *I'm a monster! Why do I want to be the one up there, letting her flog me?*

Alessandra rubbed at her eyes as her breathing slowed. "I'm sorry. I shouldn't have yelled at you. If anything happened to you …" She sighed, then stopped.

Lucia felt her cheeks flare.

"You enjoyed that lad's flogging," Alessandra almost whispered. It wasn't an accusation, but a realization—one devoid of judgment.

Lucia's eyes darkened with desire as her lips parted. "I did."

She was wet, could feel the stickiness pooling between her thighs. Lucia was near tears with yearning, with fear. *What if Alessandra becomes afraid of me or thinks me weak for having such fierce desires?* Even as her core throbbed with the image of Alessandra strung up between the bedposts, she understood, for the first time, that she too wanted to feel the abandon of being bound and dominated. To give herself over completely to the woman she loved and trusted. Yes, she finally admitted it. She trusted the woman before her more than she'd ever trusted another soul.

"I want you to flog me like that." There, she said it, that unnamable desire she'd always possessed.

Alessandra's brows rose as she looked from Lucia to the leather instrument still in her hand. "I'll hurt you," she said almost questioningly.

Lucia swallowed the lump in her throat. "I want it. I want you. Please." It wasn't like her to ask, beg for what she wanted—she'd never needed to—but then, she'd only just found what *it* was that she needed.

"Lucia, I've never—This isn't something I've done. I know—Rafe said when they found you that there was a servant you had tied up—A woman, I mean. I wouldn't even know where to begin. I've only ever used this," she said, raising the lash, "to punish."

"And I'm not in need of punishment?" Lucia asked coyly, her boldness returning. Untying the lacing of her shirt's collar, she exposed the long lines of her neck and a sliver of cleavage.

Alessandra swallowed hard. "Gods, woman, you are a wicked thing," she rasped.

Lucia ventured closer, her pulse racing as she imagined Alessandra bringing her to heel, her bare ass twitching as her pirate brought the flog down across it.

"I don't want to do anything you don't want. I don't want to really hurt you."

Lucia laughed. "Well, I'll tell you if I want you to stop." It seemed Alessandra was neither scared nor put off.

"I think that might make me want to go harder."

Lucia smirked. "Go as hard as you like."

Alessandra still looked uncertain. "How do you stop yourself?"

Lucia took a deep breath. She understood that this conversation was important, no matter how aroused she was. Alessandra's question was a valid one. For Lucia, there was no limit to what she could do in her palace, but finding that line had taken time. She could thank one very lovely and very patient brothel owner for that.

Uridice was one of her first lovers and the one to recognize the need to inflict pain that was a core part of Lucia's soul. Uridice taught her trust; she had never known such a thing before. When Lucia had worried she wouldn't be able to stop herself, when she wondered if she was the same kind of cruel creature her father was, it had been Uridice that gave the young princess her trust and body. Lucia learned she was not a killer, and that knowledge saved her.

She needed to place the same trust in Alessandra. Crossing the floor, Lucia wrapped her arms around Alessandra's waist, rising on her toes to press a soft kiss to her lips. "You aren't me. But if I say coconut, you'll stop."

Alessandra looked perplexed. "Coconut?"

"Have I ever said that word during sex?"

"Uh, no," Alessandra answered as understanding dawned across her face. "I see. Coconut it is." She chuckled before her face turned serious. "Now, take off your clothes," she said in her stern captain's voice.

Thrumming with desire and already close to orgasm, Lucia responded, "Aye, Captain."

Winking, she untied her sash to reveal herself inch by glorious inch, dropping her clothes dramatically to the ground. Once Lucia was completely naked, the pair locked eyes for a long moment. Suddenly, Alessandra had Lucia by the hair, pushing her down on the bed. She wiggled her bare ass, begging for the flog in Alessandra's hand.

"Remember," Lucia said, fingers tangled in the thick bedding, "coconut."

Lucia saw Alessandra unfurl the lash, letting the long strands of hide dangle. "I remember," she said as she gave Lucia's inviting backside an exploratory swat.

Lucia moaned, arching her back like a purring cat. Her body shook with anticipation for the next blow as

Alessandra's breath came in ragged starts from behind her.

"Was that alright?" Alessandra asked, her words stilted with what Lucia hoped was lust.

"Harder, please," she answered, her teeth set on edge against the pleasure, her head twisted back to watch as Alessandra reared back, slapping the flogger's thick tendrils harder across her backside. Lucia's body writhed from the impact. "Oh, God." She groaned in exaltation as Alessandra landed blow after blow across the cheeks of her butt and the tops of her thighs. Each stroke that landed caused a jolt of ecstasy to roll through her until, at long last, she climaxed in a great, shuddering crescendo of release such as she never knew existed.

Lucia lay amongst the tangled, soaked sheets, unable to move except to draw deep, gasping breaths of sated exhaustion. She watched as Alessandra sank to the bed beside her, breaths shallow and fast as she dropped the lash, her hands gently caressing the reddened flesh of Lucia's backside.

"You're amazing," Alessandra whispered against Lucia's ear as she gasped, still struggling to regain herself.

Lucia tried to speak but couldn't find the words to describe the pure joy she felt.

"Let me help you." Alessandra smoothed the damp hair from her brow, then helped her turn over before wrapping her in the thick quilt. "Are you alright?"

Lucia swallowed hard, her pulse still thundering in her ears. "I'm perfect," she breathed. "That was—" Her eyes searched Alessandra's, seeing the concern and care there. "That was perfect. I didn't know. How could I?" She didn't know how to explain that the ceaseless thrumming of her body had stopped for the first time in her life, that she was truly sated.

"You're alright. Get some rest. I'll have dinner brought later, and then we can talk."

Lucia nodded. "Thank you."

Alessandra smiled, gingerly dropping a kiss against her sweat-sheened brow before leaving her.

———

After discovering true vulnerability for the first time in her life, knowing she was safe with the woman she loved, Lucia slept. She was unsure how long she had dozed—the excitement of their rescue warring with bone-deep exhaustion. The brightness of the sun glinting off the island's beach remained in her mind's eye, keeping her from the deep rest she so needed. When she woke, it was to Alessandra's warmth. The pirate's thigh was pressed to her back as fingertips stroked across her shoulders. Lucia rolled toward the heat, grinning, stretching.

"Hello," she purred.

Alessandra smiled back. She looked tired, with dark circles under her eyes and her shoulders slumped. "Hello."

Lucia lifted the blankets. "You look like you need to get in here with me."

"It's tempting, but they're about to bring dinner in. You should put something on. I found this when you were sleeping." Alessandra nodded toward the foot of the bed where Lucia's green robe lay. The same ornate dressing gown she'd been wearing when she was kidnapped.

Lucia laughed at the sight. "To think how angry I was that first day." She slipped from the bed, slinking into the butter-soft silk. Her eyes closed for a moment to enjoy the pleasure of the garment against her skin. "How things have turned out."

"I'm glad you're here," Alessandra said, her voice nearly a whisper.

Taking the pirate's hand in hers, Lucia placed a kiss on the back of Alessandra's hand. "As am I."

"Captain?" came a voice from behind the door, followed by a knock.

Lucia sighed. "I guess that will be the food." She watched Alessandra get up to retrieve their meal. "You'll be needing a whole new wardrobe for court, you know." Lucia smiled as she settled back in her dining chair and imagined Alessandra in a fine court gown, her clean hair falling in rippling waves of red over her shoulder. She'd have them eating from the palm of her hand, men and women.

Lucia wondered suddenly and with a hint of trepidation if a more available suitor could turn Alessandra's head. She would have a sizable dowry and access to her stolen fortune. Lady Alessandra D'Allyon would be a very desirable match. *Does she want to marry? Have children?* Lucia was thankful Royce was taken, thinking what a well-matched pair he and her pirate would be.

"You're supposing I'm going to be at court," Alessandra murmured as she poured herself a glass of wine.

"Why wouldn't you be at court?"

Alessandra grinned quizzically as she cocked her head. "What would I do at court?"

Crestfallen, Lucia said, "Well, I'd be there." Her voice sounded more hopeful than she'd meant it to be.

ALESSANDRA

Sighing, Alessandra kicked a boot up on the table and leaned back in her chair. She didn't want to have the conversation they were about to. She wanted to enjoy her time with Lucia before things got complicated, which was exactly what they would be once they arrived back in the capital.

"I'm a pirate."

"You'll be Lady D'Allyon when you're pardoned."

"I'll always be a pirate to them and maybe to myself."

Things were already complicated ever since Lucia brought up the pardon. She'd have her family lands and title back, be a proper lady again with plenty of money and prestige. *Is that even what I want?* Alessandra kept asking herself that question, but she still didn't have an answer. She was enjoying her liaison with the queen, but neither of them should think it would carry on once they reached land.

Lucia's face turned red, a warning sign Alessandra was all too accustomed to. "I heard you, Alex. You said you wanted to go home."

The last thing Alessandra wanted to do was cause Lucia any pain. Being the first to give her the kind of release Lucia had experienced just an hour before meant a great deal to her. She wanted the queen always to have that, someone to support her, to be an anchor in the storm, but she wouldn't sacrifice who she was for anyone.

"I do want to go home. That doesn't mean I want to stay there. At least, not in the city. I never liked it there. There's room to breathe at our estate like there is at sea. I've been out here too long to be trapped behind walls," Alessandra said, arms stretched wide to indicate the openness of her world. She was trying to ease the blow. She wanted to be with Lucia more than anything, but being the queen's consort would mean a life of servitude she didn't have the stomach for.

Lucia leaned her elbow on the table, her wine sloshing from her glass. "But you wouldn't be stuck in the capital. You'll be head of the navy. With a war about to start, you'll be out at sea more often than not." She sounded desperate.

Lucia's anger looked to have turned to hurt, and Alessandra hated she was the cause of it. Fighting with herself, she thought, *What difference is there between sailing under the Moranthese flag or a pirate one? Why are you the one woman on earth that's made me care?*

"There's no use in arguing about something that may or may not come to pass. We have to reach Moranth in one piece first," Alessandra said, breathing a sigh of relief as that somehow seemed to calm her lover.

There was an uncomfortable silence as Alessandra cast about for a safe subject to discuss. Coming up empty, she was grateful when Lucia piped up.

"You think there could be trouble?" she asked, slumping back down in her seat.

Alessandra pushed her plate away in frustration. "There can always be trouble. Cyril has no idea where that bastard, Defoe, and The Deceit are. The man is like a damned ghost. Why he should be so dead set on The Medusa is beyond me."

Lucia ran a finger beneath her lip, clearly intrigued. "Something to do with your father, maybe?"

Alessandra shook her head. "I don't think so. He never said anything to that effect. My father respected the man as a fine sailor, a worthy adversary. My father was like that. Liked a fair fight." Her voice hardened. "I'm not. I prefer to put my enemies down for good."

"That sort of thinking would come in handy for an Admiral," Lucia offered.

Nodding absentmindedly, Alessandra stroked her thumb over her lips, letting her eyes drift, unfocused, as she thought. She wasn't close to being ready to make such an agreement, nor did she think the nobles of Moranth would ever sanction such a thing, so she avoided the subject.

"Can we talk about before?"

"Before?" Lucia asked. "Before what?"

"You. Me. The flogging."

Lucia sighed, leaning back in her chair. "Ah, that."

"When Rafe and the others kidnapped you, they said they found you with a tied-up maid." She'd yet to get all the details, but there was no escaping gossip on a ship.

Blood rushed to Lucia's cheeks. "Yes, but this was the first time I let someone do the same to me. I had no idea that's what I've been wanting for so long. Was it not alright for you?"

"Oh," Alessandra said, "it was beyond alright. I wasn't sure of myself either, you know."

Lucia grinned. "I was sure of you. I knew you couldn't, I should say, *wouldn't* hurt me. Not more than I wanted."

"It's not something you have to answer, but I am curious. Where did you learn, well, about that sort of thing?"

Lucia picked her wine back up, lips pursed in thought for a moment, before a wry smile lit her features. "A misspent youth. We'll leave it at that for now."

Alessandra was too tired to question further; the wine, food, and previous exertion all made for a delicious lethargy of body and mind. There was so much she wanted to know, but for the time being, her only desire consisted of crawling into bed and letting the warmth of Lucia's body and the lapping of the ocean waves lull her to sleep.

―――――

She knew it was a dream.

Rafe was at her side as they strode through the tavern doors. She was excited, eager.

Rafe's hand slapped hard on her back. "There's the missus."

Alessandra blinked, watching the grin on his face in confusion before turning toward the bar. Lucia was there, the hem of her simple linen dress tucked up into her belt. She was laughing with a customer while pouring an ale. Her hair was plaited, the length of it accentuating her impressive, corseted cleavage. Their eyes met, and Alessandra watched the flush creep up Lucia's cheeks as she swiped a hand across her brow.

"Well, lads," Lucia said. "Will you look what the sea has spat back out today." Her royal accent clashed with her decidedly lower-class wardrobe.

Then, in the way of dreams, time slipped, and Lucia was by her side, lacing her fingers with Alessandra's. Lucia's hand was so warm and real as she pulled Alessandra along after her. The stairs creaked as they climbed, and Alessandra knew what awaited her at the top as if she'd seen it a hundred times. It was Lucia's home, her room above the bar. The part of Alessandra that was aware she was dreaming chuckled at how perfectly the tiny space suited her lover. There was a bed in the corner, covered in heavy quilts and a costly fur throw that no barmaid could afford, and at the foot of the bed was a single chest. Books, precious, leather-bound copies, were carefully stacked and placed along walls, on makeshift shelves, and on the little desk beside a quill and inkpot.

Alessandra's core pulled tight with desire as her hand cradled Lucia's. "You know if this place ever catches fire—"

"I know. I know." Lucia smirked up at her. It seemed to Alessandra that this must be an old argument of theirs. This relationship wasn't new in her dream as it was in real life.

Time jumped again. Alessandra knew they had made love as their clothes were off, the sheets were rumpled, and Lucia's hair stuck out of her previously tidy braid. Lucia's lips were swollen, her breathing still ragged as Alessandra's fingers stroked small circles over her ribcage.

"I missed you, love," Alessandra whispered against Lucia's throat.

"Lucky for you, I'm easy to find, unlike some people," Lucia responded flatly, and the mood suddenly shifted.

Alessandra groaned as she threw the covers off and searched the floor for her clothes. "Don't ask me again." She heard herself say, anger rising within her. Lucia turned her head as her body began to shake with silent tears that broke Alessandra's heart. "You know you can't come with me." Her voice had calmed, gone soft with regret and love. "Anything could happen to you out there."

"Anything could happen to me here," Lucia shouted back.

"Nothing is going to happen. This is our home. You're safe here."

"This is *my* home. *My* tavern. You've been gone over a year."

Alessandra's heart squeezed. "What are you saying?"

"I'm saying it's me or the sea."

11

LUCIA

They sailed for nearly a week toward Moranth. The more direct route was far more dangerous and would have put them in open waters, where any other pirate or a ship from Vetreon could spot them and attack. Since the storm damage, The Medusa was only halfway operational. She could defend them and get them where they needed to go, but her maneuverability was less than optimal. As such, The Medusa found herself limping along the coastline of Vetreon and Moranth once more.

According to Alessandra, the damaged mast had been repaired at sea as best it could. They were lucky to have a spare on board in case of such a need. The replacement piece had been hoisted atop what remained of the old one, then bound together by tarred rope. It wasn't a first-rate repair, she'd said, but The Medusa didn't have a blacksmith on board to provide the preferred metal bands to hold the two pieces of wood together.

So far, the repair was holding, but Lucia noticed the worried look many of the sailors gave the structure each time they passed beneath it. For the repairs to be done properly, they'd have to put in at a harbor.

"Will she make it to Moranth?" Lucia asked, making sure they were out of the crew's hearing.

Alessandra sucked at her teeth, giving the ship a once over. "She's not good. She's never been pushed like this before. Not to my knowing, at least. The smart thing to do would be to make for Silver Cove and get the ship into a more respectable state."

Lucia's heart beat faster. "Silver Cove? Really?"

Lucia was in no hurry, finding the sea every bit as enchanting as The Medusa's captain. She loved the fresh air and watching Alessandra in command. Her respect for both the woman she loved and her crew grew daily as she learned of the inherent dangers of the sea and the rigors of ship life. Strange to remember only weeks beforehand, when she'd been dragged aboard by the same men who were perhaps not friends but no longer enemies.

Alessandra crossed her arms. "That's the smart thing, I said." Her lips twitched as she looked at Lucia. "I want to get you to safety as soon as I can. Smart has nothing to do with any of this."

It took nearly a week for the crew to stop gaping at her every time she came on deck.

"What can I do to help?" Lucia asked, yet again, unable to stand another day of tedious boredom. Though she was eager, there was little aboard a ship she knew how to do—she missed being able to bring her abilities to bear as she had on the island. Alessandra gave her an amused look, and Lucia's brows drew together. "What?"

Alessandra took off her hat and ran a hand through her hair. "This isn't the island—" Lucia tried to interrupt but was stopped by an outstretched palm. This was Alessandra's ship. "I know how capable you are, but ship life is a different animal than scavenging and shelter building. You've seen how swiftly the mood on board can change."

"Please, I can't sit around and do nothing. It's not in my nature," Lucia countered.

"Fine. The deck could always use a good swabbing, and I'm sure young Kier would enjoy the company."

Lucia followed Alessandra's gaze over her shoulder to the young man sweating as he pushed a mop across the deck. He looked up, clearly concerned at hearing his name, his blonde curls blowing around his beardless face.

Lucia pursed her lips, cocking a brow. "Swab the deck, eh?" She shrugged. "Alright."

Kier immediately straightened as she sauntered toward him.

"You got another mop?"

The young man's mouth gaped, but he managed a nod before recovering. "I'll go get it, Your Majesty." He bobbed respectfully.

Lucia stopped him with a hand on his shoulder. "I'm just Lucia here, all right?"

Kier's throat quivered as blood rushed from his cheeks to the tips of his ears. His eyes darted to his captain—after all, her word was law aboard the ship—and Lucia saw Alessandra tuck her chin in approval.

Smiling at her, he stammered, "Lucia, I'll be right back." The mop handle clattered to the deck as Kier hurried off and disappeared below.

Alessandra snickered as she joined Lucia beside the fallen mop and sloshing bucket of saltwater. "I was teasing, you know? We can find you something else to do," she whispered in Lucia's ear, giving her side a playful pinch.

"Well, I'm calling you on your bluff. Plus, I'm bored. Much as I may want to, I can't just sit around all day staring at you. Gives me too many ideas and not enough hours of the night to pursue them."

Kier returned, holding a spare mop, huffing as if he'd run the whole way.

"Thank you," Lucia said, giving Alessandra a wink.

Alessandra shook her head, grinning. "I'll let the two of you get to it. Oh, and Kier, make sure she does a good job. There's no slacking on this ship."

"Aye, Captain," the sailor acknowledged.

"And you," she said, fixing Lucia with a commanding stare. "You want to act like crew. Then the job better be done right."

"Aye, Captain." Lucia smirked, biting her lip and raising her brows suggestively.

Alessandra turned to make her way back to the upper deck, shaking her head as she went.

Lucia watched her go, then turned to Kier. "All right, lad, you going to show me how this is done and tell me why in the hell we're doing it?"

The young man laughed; his nervousness vanished. Tipping his head back, he looked up at the sky. "All the rain we've been having for one. Rainwater can get into the ship, causing rot. The old girl isn't exactly in top shape as is."

"Ah," Lucia acknowledged, bending to her task. There was so much she had no idea about on board.

By the time they'd finished, blisters pulsed across her palms, and her back ached from her shoulders to her tailbone.

Rafe walked past as Kier was taking the mop from her. "You taking care of our fair queen, lad?"

Kier straightened, mops in hand, soaked in sweat and saltwater. "I suspect Lucia can take care of herself," he answered.

Lucia's gut tightened. Despite Alessandra's reassurances that the handsome pirate was nothing more than a dear friend, she had yet to come to her own decision on the matter.

"Lucia, is it now?" Rafe's eyes narrowed as he gave her an appraising look.

"Something I can help you with?" she spat back.

Rafe's face broke into a wide, laughing grin. "Aye, lass, Captain told me to keep you busy. You're with me the rest of the watch. Come on. I've a feeling you're a natural at the rigging."

"The rigging?" She shielded her eyes against the sun as she looked up into the sky. The ropes appeared haphazardly strung across the ship at a dizzying height.

"What you've been through, don't tell me you're scared," Rafe teased.

Lucia glared at him for a moment. "Lead the way." She gestured toward the rigging.

Rafe was up the ropes lightning quick. "Let's go, sailor," he called back down at Lucia, who stood rooted to the spot.

"Damn it," she muttered, gritting her teeth, doing her best to follow.

It was the first of a handful of such days. She became Rafe's shadow when Alessandra was too preoccupied to have her underfoot. Lucia realized quickly enough that her new acquaintance was unable to resist a beautiful woman, a weakness she took advantage of. Soon, Rafe taught her the fastest ways to climb the rigging, tie new knots—which he showed her with a mischievous gleam in his eye—and how to steer the ship.

On one such day, he and Lucia were alone in the crow's nest when he said, "You're good for her, you know?" His eyes were steady; he wasn't teasing her.

Lucia's gaze shifted to find Alessandra at the helm. "She's good for me, you mean. I've been nothing but trouble for her."

His lips pressed into a tight line as he worked at the knot in his hands. "Some of us prefer a little trouble. For the captain, I think that's true."

Lucia flinched, wondering at the mate's words as she turned her attention once more to the sea. She'd never thought herself worthy of such kindness before, but her treatment onboard, not only from Alessandra but also her crew, made Lucia think that perhaps she wasn't so terrible.

She grinned, nudging the man with her hip. "You're entirely too pretty. You know that, don't you?"

Rafe laughed. "So are you."

"I have a friend back home that you remind me of." Her voice took on a twinge of sadness as her eyes searched Rafe's. "He was in love with me, or thought he was. I know you and Alex—I know there was, or could have been, something between you."

"Alex?" Rafe's eyes crinkled with a genuine smile as his hands ran over the smooth wood of their little perch. "I'm not going to lie and say I wouldn't let one or both of you do as you wish with me. You're made of different stuff than the pretty lasses we sailors are used to, but love?" He chuckled. "Nah, don't know that I'll ever have that sort of fine thing you and the captain have." Lucia's heart beat faster. *Is how I feel about Alessandra so obvious?* Rafe didn't seem to notice her discomfort and continued, "Not in me. Not in that way. Too big a world, too many warm beds."

Lucia felt relief wash over her at Rafe's words. She liked him immensely and thought him an important and loyal friend to Alessandra, but she wanted to be sure of where the pirate stood. *Friend or rival?* She felt she had her answer and was glad of it.

Rafe's acknowledgment of her and Alessandra's relationship made it seem real, for some reason, that the time the lovers spent on the island was not just a passing thing. What they shared was right and true, even if the two of them had not yet spoken such words aloud.

"Can I ask you something?" Lucia ventured nervously.

Rafe's eyes searched the horizon for signs of danger. The endless sea was unfurled before them, not a cloud to be seen nor another ship. "Not much else to do up here but talk and stare. I don't suspect I'll be spending much more time in my life with royalty."

Lucia took the prompt. "Do you think she could be happy with me? Happy with giving all this up?" Her hand swept across the calm seas and clear sky. She was barely sure she could give up her new existence, and it was becoming harder and harder for her to imagine Alessandra confining herself to any one spot, much less the stifling life at court. Even her Admiral, old Lord Girona, spent much of his time in the capital, not at sea.

Rafe rubbed the back of his neck, tugging at the dark curls of his hair. "Strange to even think about her not being on this ship." He breathed deeply. "She loves the sea. You've seen that. She belongs out here, even if she wasn't born to it. It's where she belongs now."

Lucia's gut clenched. She had seen the way Alessandra was when her mind was bent to sailing, how intent she was when pouring over her charts in the evenings. When they neared a landmark, she would tell Lucia how it got its name or explain why they needed to sail in the way they did to avoid unseen danger. Alessandra knew the ocean and her mysteries like the back of her hand.

"What you two have, it won't last. It can't unless one of you bends. One of you gives up a piece of yourself." Tears pricked at the corner of Lucia's eyes as Rafe spoke. "I'm not saying any of this to hurt you or because I'm jealous, or anything of the kind. I think you're practical enough, even for a royal, to know the world won't always let you have what you want."

Lucia swallowed hard. Her chest ached with the truth of Rafe's words. "And what I want is her," she whispered.

ALESSANDRA

Lucia was no longer the queen aboard The Medusa but part of the crew. After days of sailing, after surviving their marooning, the men began to look upon her in a more favorable light. Even Smith, whose mutiny had been put down, begrudgingly grew fond of her. Besides Alessandra, the sailor was the most proficient man aboard with a blade, and he and Lucia bonded over their love of swordplay. While Lucia knew how to hold her own with the slender rapier, or so she'd said, a cutlass, with its wider, curved blade, was a new thing to her.

She'd asked Alessandra to show her how to use the traditional seaman's sword, so she could be 'a real pirate', but was waved off. "I'm a terrible teacher," she'd claimed, which was true in most things. Alessandra had been fighting with a cutlass since she was a child, but she couldn't fathom how to break it down for her paramour. While Smith, hot-headed as he could be, had been in charge of training new sailors in combat for the last several years. It was the one place where he was typically calm.

Smith was not pleased at first with the prospect of working with the queen, hanging his head while muttering a curse when Alessandra had asked, not ordered, him to show Lucia a few tricks with the blade. Lucia had told her she knew how to fight, but it remained to be seen.

Rafe had been walking by and heard the conversation. He gave Smith a playful shove. "If you don't want to show her, I will," he'd said.

Alessandra smiled. It would have been awkward for her if Rafe hadn't liked Lucia, but he genuinely seemed to. In fact, Lucia was in Rafe's company almost more than her own. She thought of Lucia naked, spread before her. *Almost, and certainly not where it counts most.*

Smith laughed. "You're a terrible teacher, Rafe. Ugh." He held his hands up in resignation. "Fine, I'll do it. Can't have *Her Majesty* learning from a third-rate swordsman."

Rafe cuffed him over the ear. "Second rate, at least."

Alessandra rolled her eyes but was pleased she had Smith's cooperation.

Lucia found her in her cabin after their first lesson, eyes sparkling, dripping sweat, with a wide grin on her face. "God," her breathing was still ragged as she collapsed on the bed, "that was fun."

It was during such a lesson that Alessandra first saw the true flare of temper Lucia had warned her of.

It hadn't taken the crew long to notice the queen and her teacher practicing their swordplay. It had been a spectacle from the start. The men performing their duties nearby often paused to watch the pair for a few moments before returning to work. For the first few afternoons, Lucia worked on rudimentary movements with her new sword. She was a quick study, though, and by the fourth day, it was clear Smith had met his match.

Alessandra was at the helm as Cyril worked with Kier to keep the ship on course when Rafe found her. "You need to come with me," he said breathlessly. He was smiling, but Alessandra heard the concern in his voice.

A good thirty or so men were on deck, spread out in a circle, shouting and cheering as Lucia and Smith sparred. It was late afternoon, the sun low and unforgiving as it beat down on the fighters. Smith was pouring sweat, working in earnest to keep Lucia's blade at bay, while Lucia cursed each time Smith's sword met hers with a clang. Neither had the advantage. Alessandra guessed that while Smith was the stronger opponent, Lucia must have had an excellent teacher at court.

Their fighting styles were different. Smith relied on his brute strength, while Lucia's sword never stilled, nor did her body. She danced about, dodging as Smith's blade swung heavily through the air.

Rafe lounged next to Alessandra, their backs and shoulders against the ship's rail. "She's very good," he said, his eyes tracking Lucia's faster blade. "Quick study."

"Aye. Too quick." Alessandra barely heard him, her breath tight in her chest as she watched Smith and Lucia whirl across the deck, swords flashing and clanging. Smith hacked wildly, but Lucia spun, no longer in any danger. Lucia's jaw was set, her lips pressed into a thin line while Smith came at her, red-faced and cursing.

"What are they doing?" Alessandra asked no one in particular.

"Everything was fine until Lucia got in a good elbow shot to his ribs. He said something about her mother, and here we are," Rafe replied. "I tried to stop it, but she won't listen to me."

"They're going to kill each other." Alessandra called out, "Stop!"

Distracted, Lucia missed a parry. Smith's blade slashed across her shoulder, and she went down.

The deckhand looked terrified, dropping his blade at once while attempting to back away. "Shit, are you alright? I'm sorry."

Lucia roared in anger and came up swinging, the point of her borrowed cutlass arching toward Smith, but Alessandra had already pounced into action, pulling at Lucia while Rafe's blade blocked her attack.

Lucia strained against Alessandra, but she held fast.

"That's enough!"

Lucia's body shook with rage.

Alessandra dug her fingers into Lucia's arms as she picked her up off her feet. "Stop! I don't want to hurt you," she implored.

Lucia growled, "Let me go." Her voice was low and hard, so unlike her usually cool, measured tones.

"I'm not letting you go until you drop your sword," Alessandra rasped in Lucia's ear, but she didn't listen. She shook the queen and tried again, her voice dropping so only Lucia could hear her. "Enough, love."

Feeling the tension go out of her paramour, Alessandra took a breath as Lucia's sword clanged to the deck. Her eyes raked over the crew, daring any man to speak.

"I'll not have fighting on my deck," Alessandra shouted. Lucia was stiff in her arms but for her chest-rattling breaths. "Smith, are you injured?"

"I'm alright, Captain," he said, shaking his head.

Alessandra nodded, thankful he had the sense this time not to cause any trouble. "Double rations for you tonight. You've earned it." She was grateful the man wasn't wounded and didn't seem overly angry. It was a common enough occurrence for roughhousing to get out of hand on board, but it needed to be resolved quickly. A ship was no place for resentment and grudges to fester.

"Aye, thank you, Captain." He dipped his chin in her direction.

Alessandra's heart was racing. Lucia was aboard her ship, but the Pirate's Code demanded punishment. She had to put the matter before her men, despite her feelings. "Smith, since you're the offended party, I'll take your recommendation for punishment."

The mate looked Lucia over. "That's as fine a fight as I've had in a long time, lass. You're a bold one." He gave a hearty laugh, turning his attention to Alessandra. "I'm not hurt, Captain. Think a good mastheading will do."

Alessandra's body nearly sagged in relief. Lucia would have to climb to the top of the damaged mast and stay put until she was allowed to come down. As punishments went, it was a light one. She'd have to remember to thank Smith later.

Even knowing Lucia was hurt—a thin line of blood was seeping through the rend in the queen's shirt—Alessandra still dropped her to the ground. "Go on," she said, her voice purposefully harsher than she wished. She ached to pull Lucia back into her arms, to look into her eyes and find the reason for her actions, but she couldn't. Not in front of the men. She was the ship's captain. She hoped Lucia, of all people, would understand.

Lucia didn't say a word as she uncrumpled herself, standing slowly as if every movement was a painful effort. Once upright, she shook her wild hair from her eyes, straightened her shoulders, and turned to Smith, their eyes meeting as she gave him a nod.

Alessandra gave her a tight smile, wanting to reassure her that all would be well, then pointed toward the rigging and mainsail. "Up you go, get climbing. You can come down at last watch."

LUCIA

Her eyes flicked from Alessandra to the crew, who were watching, waiting. Rafe caught her attention at the back of the crowd. He dipped his chin in an encouraging nod while Cyril stood by, his arms crossed. Refusing to look back at Alessandra, Lucia's hands gripped the rigging, fresh callouses unfazed by the sharpness of the rope as she climbed.

"Back to work, everyone," Alessandra shouted from below.

Lucia looked down to see the men scattering and Alessandra staring up at her. The captain turned, her long strides carrying her quickly toward the helm, leaving Lucia to continue her climb alone. The wind whipped at her hair as she reached the top. The sun was just dipping below the horizon. She shivered. Cursing, she wished for a coat as she sat, arms wrapped around her knees, feet tucked up under her. She felt like a naughty child. *Last watch cannot come soon enough.* Pain seared across her wounded shoulder as she shifted her weight against the mast.

Lucia was embarrassed. She hated it when anyone saw her in that furious state, struggling to self-govern. She was especially mortified for Alessandra to have seen her that way. It was never supposed to go so far. Smith was a wonderful teacher, and their teasing banter was a thing she'd grown used to over the several days of their practice, but she was eager to push the sailor, to bring all of her skill to bear.

"Damn it," Lucia cursed at herself as angry tears fell. She hadn't meant to hurt him; the move had been instinct, drilled into her since childhood. He gave her an opening, and she took it. It was clear he hadn't expected it, and when he'd called her mother a whore, his eyes dark with momentary rage, she'd seen nothing but her father, heard his voice, and she'd wanted to kill him.

It was a daily effort sometimes to keep that anger at bay, especially at court, but she couldn't let anyone know what lurked within her.

A memory nagged at her, one she hadn't allowed herself to think of for nearly twenty years. One that scared her perhaps even more than those of her father. She thought back to the one time she remembered seeing her mother like that, eyes dark with the ferocity of her emotions. How Lucia figured she must have looked when she attacked Smith.

She had been no more than five or six. Her mother had taken her into the woods beyond the city for a rare outing away from court. Of course, there were guards and servants in the party; the king never allowed his wife to go anywhere without a guard. Lucia wondered as she grew older if it had been for her mother's protection or to keep her a prisoner.

Lucia was always hungry for her mother's attention, to be close to her. Her mother was her safety, though the queen could be prickly.

Lucia could still see the gown her mother had been wearing as if the woman stood before her. It was one of the queen's favorites, robin's egg blue with seed pearls stitched into a whirling pattern of stars and moons.

Lucia had been climbing over her mother all day, as a child would do, completely unaware of her mother's growing frustration. The queen had asked young Lucia to stop pulling at her, at her clothes, at the waves of her long hair. The queen's maids attempted to soothe the little princess, but on that day, Lucia only wanted her mother. Pulling free from the grasp of a sweet Wellingisle girl charged with caring for her, she wrapped herself around her mother once more, only to hear the sickening rip of her mother's fine gown.

The queen's hands were suddenly like tight manacles on her skinny arms. The big grey eyes that usually held such love for her were near black with fury as the maid shouted, 'Your Majesty, no!', tearing Lucia from her mother's grasp as the queen dropped to the ground, shaking.

Lucia remembered her crying, 'I'm sorry'.

She wondered what would have happened if not for her maid. Her mother had never once raised a hand to her—she was always a warm, comforting presence in her life—but Lucia saw something else there that day, and it scared her. *What if both of my parents were monsters? What does that make me?*

―――――

Lucia struggled back down the ship's rigging in the dark, her limbs nearly frozen stiff, and her lips chapped after being exposed to the buffeting wind for hours. Alessandra was waiting at the bottom for her, and perhaps more importantly, so was Smith. He was holding out a mug of ale, which she took gratefully.

The man gave her a crooked smile, his eyes crinkling with mirth. "You're crew now." He chuckled, clapping her shoulder as she drank through chattering teeth.

"Fantastic."

Alessandra wrapped her coat around Lucia's shaking figure. "Let's get you inside and warmed up. I remember how miserable a mastheading can be."

"Misspent youth?" Lucia asked, echoing their discussion about her own adolescent years.

Alessandra's eyes lit up as she caught the thread of Lucia's thoughts. "And we'll leave it at that." She winked.

Lucia saw Alessandra mouth 'thank you' to Smith as she walked from the deck, arms tight around her, and the shame she had felt on the mast became a deeper grief.

Once they were alone in the captain's cabin, Lucia sat silently on the bed, letting Alessandra chafe warmth into her arms and hands.

"I'm sorry," she finally managed. It wasn't enough, or everything she wanted to say, but it was all she was capable of at the moment.

Alessandra knelt before her. "I know." She smiled while working on getting Lucia's boots off.

Lucia nodded slowly. During the hours she'd been up in the rigging alone, she'd thought of what to say to the woman she loved. To explain what she felt when Smith's blade had met her skin, how she had seen red as the pain blazed across her arm as every bit of frustrated wrath she'd ever held had shown itself.

Lucia's voice was almost a whisper. "I think I would have killed him if you hadn't stopped me." Her eyes were unfocused, staring through the captain.

Alessandra guided Lucia's ale back to her lips. "Finish this," she chided. "It'll help warm you up. Then I want you to take this wine out on the deck and share it." She held up a bottle in her other hand. "What you did today wasn't unforgivable. In fact, you gave the lads something to talk about, which is always welcome on a ship, but the wine will help any lingering misgivings."

"But—What I did—What I could have done. I thought I had it under control, but I don't."

"You didn't kill him," Alessandra cut in. "You wouldn't have. I trust you. You would have stopped yourself."

"How can you know that when even I don't?" Lucia wondered.

"Because I know you." Alessandra kissed her gently. Her lips were soft and warm against Lucia's cracked and cold ones. "Are you warmer?"

Lucia finished her ale. "Aye." She'd stopped shaking, finally—though she couldn't quite shift the thought that she might not know herself.

"Then, come on." Alessandra held out her hands, pulling Lucia from the bed.

The pair stepped onto the deck together. The men were warming themselves before the small fire, drinks in hand, while a sailor played a merry tune on his fiddle. All talk and song ceased as Lucia approached Smith. She offered him the bottle of wine first.

"No need for this," Smith said, taking a long swig. "But," he grinned, "it's appreciated." He took another drink before handing it off to Rafe.

As soon as Lucia began passing around the fine bottle of wine, the crew forgot any sin she might have committed, if any ever existed in the first place, and an atmosphere of celebration took hold. Smith begged her for a dance, which she accepted with a smile, letting him spin her about while the crew cheered and laughed along with them. *They have forgiven me. They don't think I am a monster to be pitched over the side. Perhaps this is where I belong, too.* Doing her best to shake the melancholy pulling at her, she surprised them all with a bawdy song, climbing the ropes halfway, the bottle of wine in hand, accompanied by Rafe's lute.

Lucia saw Alessandra watching in stunned delight and couldn't help but tease her. She reached out her hand, knowing the resonance of her voice, calling to Alessandra, then leaped back, laughing with the men, and finally, the captain. It was the most raucous night aboard any could remember.

As she and Alessandra tumbled into bed that night, Lucia rose onto her elbow to stroke slow circles along the pirate's spine. "This is a family, isn't it?"

"This sort of thing doesn't go on at the palace?"

Lucia had given hints of her life in the palace as a fearful but willful child, though they rarely spoke of her life before being kidnapped. Lucia shook her head.

"Yeah, I suppose it is a family."

12

ALESSANDRA

They slept each night curled around each other. Alessandra, who had to share her bed for the first time in her life, realized the same must've been true for Lucia. The queen of Moranth was not a still sleeper; they'd found that out on their island. Lucia would strike out, mumble, then roll herself up in the sheets, leaving Alessandra shivering in the cooler climes as they sailed closer to the capital.

One night, after desperately tugging at the bedsheet to no avail, Alessandra finally gave up. Pulling on a robe, she went to her father's desk and lit a candle. Yawning, she rubbed her eyes, then unlocked the small center drawer. It was a drawer she hadn't yet had the will to open, knowing what she would find there. The sound of her breath was loud in the night as the key clicked in the lock. Her breath stopped as the drawer slid open. She felt like a child about to be caught—as if her father would return to admonish her at any moment.

She believed Lucia when she told her about her father's refusal to return to Moranth, but there was so much else she didn't understand. Her fingers ran reverently over the black leather binding of his journal as she placed it on the desk. Alessandra knew what she hoped to find within those pages—she wanted answers to all her questions. *Why didn't he take the pardon? Why didn't he tell me? What kept him on the seas when we could've returned home?* Perhaps even his hopes for her would be on the pages there.

Lucia grumbled something in her sleep, and Alessandra's lips curled in a fond smile. She shook her head as she caught herself watching the sleeping queen. No matter what Lucia tried to tell her, she wasn't sold on staying in Calan.

She turned her gaze back and opened her father's journal. For the most part, her father's neat hand laid out the typical life at sea—a proper captain's log—but interspersed between the rows of figures, weather reports, and any encounters with enemies were other, more tender musings. He wrote about her mother and how much he missed her. About how much he missed his daughter in the days before she'd joined the crew full-time. He made mention of his pride the first time she climbed the rigging and her skill with a sword.

Alessandra flipped through the pages to where she thought there might be mention of the king's death, Lucia's coronation, the pardons, or anything of the sort. What she found was a man full of contradictions, sadness, and above all, anger. For all his words, her father remained a mystery.

LUCIA

Lucia awoke, noting the lack of warmth in the bed as her hand searched for Alessandra. She wasn't there. Her eyes opened to the sight of her pirate slumped over her desk, snoring softly. Stretching, she sat up and started to dress. Her clothes, salt-stiffened and bleached in areas, no longer felt borrowed. Her hair was streaked with almost white-blonde pieces, and her hands and face had turned a warm shade of amber despite wearing a hat almost constantly. Rubbing her hands together to warm up, she felt the calluses on her palms from working with the ship's rigging. She liked them, liked how her body responded to the work. *What will the council think of me when I return?* Lucia smiled. Her attention shifted to her sleeping lover. *What will the council think of her?*

Lucia meant every word she said to Alessandra, but the captain's hesitancy gave her pause. She was putting herself out on a limb for the pirate. Should Alessandra betray her, it could mean death for Lucia. Her hands stroked over the ruby cascade of Alessandra's hair. Watching her pirate's kissable lips, Lucia thought the risk was worth taking. Alessandra saw her for who and what she was and didn't flinch.

The ship's going had been intolerably slow for the crew and captain, but for her, the pace could be slower still if it meant she could eke out a few more precious days with Alessandra. She knew things wouldn't be the same, no matter how much she wanted them to be, once they reached home, even if Alessandra did come to stay with her at the palace, become head of her navy, and take back up the mantle of Lady D'Allyon.

"Why can't it just be the two of us?" she whispered.

Alessandra murmured, rolling her head to the side. The movement revealed beneath her cheek a bound journal with the Royal Moranthese Naval insignia embossed on its cover. Lucia squinted down at the page covered in flowing script. She was unable to read it from her angle, nor did she want to pry, but she wondered who wrote it. She'd seen Alessandra's cleaner, more concise writing enough at that point to know it wasn't hers. *Her father's, perhaps?* Alessandra didn't often speak of the man, but Lucia was curious as to what the noble-turned-pirate was like.

Alessandra muttered something unintelligible again before scrunching her face up and opening her eyes. "Ow." She groaned, stretching her body and twisting her back, her spine popping as she did.

Lucia laughed. "Sleep well?"

Alessandra stared bleary-eyed at her while awkwardly covering the journal.

"I didn't look," Lucia said. Her stomach churned at the idea that Alessandra still felt she couldn't fully trust her, not when she'd literally put her life in her hands.

Alessandra uncovered the journal, then pushed away from the desk to slump back in her chair. "It's my father's," she said, waving a hand over the book. "I couldn't sleep, and I—I don't know. I just thought maybe he'd tell me what to do."

Lucia's eyes softened, her hand stroking gently over Alessandra's mussed hair. "And did he?"

"Did who, what?" Alessandra asked, her mind clearly still foggy with sleep.

"Did your father come to you in your dreams?" She nodded at the journal. "Or did you find your answers there?"

"I dreamt about my mother." Alessandra's voice was barely above a whisper. If the pirate rarely spoke of her father, her mother was an even scarcer topic. "She was brushing out my hair, singing to me. She never did that in life. My maid always did."

A pang of memory echoed in Lucia's chest. "My mother tucked me in every night. My father was usually drunk by then or with another woman, so it was our special time."

Alessandra caught Lucia's hand and smiled up at her. "Maybe it could be our special time, too?"

Lucia gave her hand a squeeze. "Only if you let me brush out those snarls."

"The queen of Moranth brushing out this mess?" Alessandra laughed. "I'll hold my breath." The laughter left her eyes, and her tone grew serious. "My father wanted to take me home when you sent those pardons." Lucia's brows drew together as she pulled up a chair beside the desk. "He thought it was what my mother would have wanted for me, but he was still so angry." Alessandra sighed, running her hand through the tangles of her hair. "I think mostly he was scared. I don't want to live like that. It's not an answer for you, not yet, but I don't want to lose you because I'm scared."

Lucia's face lit at her lover's words. "How about we just keep sailing until you decide?"

"Ha! Another matter to discuss. I looked at the charts last night. We do need to make that stop. I can't expect my men to sail into enemy territory completely unable to defend ourselves, and at the rate we're going, we'll run out of food before we make Moranth."

"So, I get a reprieve, eh?"

"For now, I suppose. How would Your Majesty like a week or two in Silver Cove?"

Lucia's brows raised, her heart rate jumping. "Pirate's Island?" She grinned, unable to hide her excitement, calling the island by its colloquial name. "I'd love to."

Alessandra returned the smile. "We'll have to disguise you, though I don't think anyone will mistake you for a lad."

Lucia stood to find her reflection in the mirror. She was still slimmer than when they'd first met, the island taking a toll on her voluptuous curves, but as she turned to glance at her rear in the tight cloth breeches, she was pleased to see those curves returning, though not fast enough in her opinion.

"I barely leave the palace anymore," Lucia lamented. "Not many would recognize me in my own city, let alone in Silver Cove."

"Maybe," Alessandra tapped her chin, "but I'm sure everyone knows it was the crew of The Medusa that kidnapped you by now." She waved a hand. "I'll think of something."

ALESSANDRA

The following day, Alessandra found just the inspiration she was looking for when she caught Rafe whistling a tune alone at the helm as he steered the ship.

"Need you to head south," she said. She had, as of yet, not discussed the stop at Silver Cove with her crew, knowing most, if not all of them, would be pleased.

Rafe gave her a puzzled look. "We changed our mind about Her Majesty? Have you two quarreled?" he teased. "I had no ulterior motives in showing her those knots, you know."

She snatched the hat from his head in excitement. "The maid, of course!"

"Um, the maid?" Rafe snickered. "Ah, that girl. Fine bottom on her. What's that have to do with our heading?"

Alessandra rolled her eyes. "We won't make Moranth at this rate. The first ship that sees us will blow us out of the water, and we're running low on food. I should have made this decision days ago."

"Decision?"

"We're going to Silver Cove."

She didn't wait for an answer, just bounded off in search of Lucia, her plan coming together.

When Lucia heard Alessandra's idea, she laughed. "You want me to pretend to be the queen's maid?" Lucia cried in disbelief, then stopped chuckling. "It might just work."

"No one knows for certain it was us, but if we go ahead and admit it, then who's to say we didn't take her mouthy servant as well?" Alessandra explained, watching as understanding dawned on Lucia's face.

"Mouthy servant?" Lucia tucked her head beneath Alessandra's chin, her lips traveling up her long neck to press against a leaping pulse point.

Alessandra groaned at the attention. "A lovely wench I managed to seduce."

Lucia clucked her tongue. "I believe I'm the one who seduced you. Where will you tell people the nasty queen of Moranth is?"

"Pitched her over the side," Alessandra teased. "Or perhaps she's already been delivered to Ramir, who, for some reason, has yet to disclose this information publicly. If I divide up my take in the hold, it's enough to make the lads seem like they've gotten their share of a queen's ransom when they go to town. Enough money to spend themselves blind. They deserve it after everything."

Lucia looked taken aback. "What about you? What of your needs?"

"My father was a smart man. He didn't drink all his money away like most of our men, even if he did try for a time. I'll be fine. I've a house, modest but mine, and a share in a profitable tavern. I won't starve if that's your concern." She pulled Lucia onto her lap, not mentioning her father's hidden treasure. "Besides,

I'll be holed up with the prettiest creature on the island. I've no need to show off anything else. I have you."

"You do have me, you know," Lucia whispered, her forehead against Alessandra's. Lucia pressed a soft kiss to her lips as Alessandra's mind swirled with thoughts of the adventure ahead.

13

LUCIA

Cyril clapped a hand on Lucia's shoulder. "Welcome to Silver Cove, Mireia," he said, calling Lucia by her new false name. She liked the sound of it, liked the freedom it gave her. The two had become friendly enough. She knew he wasn't as enamored with her as most of The Medusa's crew were, but she suspected a grudging admiration had developed. He certainly had hers, not just for his seamanship, as he'd proven when returning the struggling ship to their island to rescue her and Alessandra. More than that, despite being the instigator of her kidnapping, which she could never again hate anyone on board for, it was clear he loved Alessandra, and for that, she could forgive him almost anything.

She stared out at the small harbor as the ship anchored offshore. Three tall-masted ships sat at the mouth of the cove, including The Medusa. Sapphire waters shifted to turquoise shallows, with a pink sand beach beyond. The town was spread out in the island's valley before flat land gave way to dense, green growth and gentle slopes. Lucia's heart raced at the sight. "Will your family be waiting for you?" she asked the first mate.

His face brightened. "Aye, they'll have seen the D'Allyon flag and know it's us. Margthe will be here, at least. My children are grown, living their own lives, but I'm sure I'll see them tonight."

"How long since The Medusa was back here?" Lucia wondered, not knowing why she hadn't thought to ask Alessandra before.

"Eight months and twelve days." Cyril gave her a sidelong look as she shifted on her feet, worrying at her lip. "The captain doesn't have anyone here for you to concern yourself with," he said, guessing at Lucia's sudden nervousness.

She turned to give him a grateful smile. It hadn't been until the words were out of the first mate's mouth that Lucia realized just why she had been so anxious to reach the island. Cyril had named her worry. *Why wouldn't I think Alessandra had someone waiting for her, as much of the other crew did?*

For the last several days, ever since Alessandra made the announcement that they would be returning to Silver Cove, all Lucia heard was talk of loved ones and sweethearts, favorite barmaids, and other sports to be had. It left her feeling a bit lost as she tried to imagine herself fitting into Alessandra's home. She had just been getting the hang of ship life, and this would be yet another new world for her to try to navigate.

Cyril leaned in. "I've never seen Alessandra care for anyone the way she does you, Your Majesty."

"We're ready," Rafe called up from the ship's lowered dinghy.

Lucia's head twisted from side to side. "Where's—"

Alessandra swung down from the mast in a dramatic fashion. "Looking for me?"

Lucia laughed, pulling her close for a kiss. "Maybe."

"Come on." Alessandra tugged Lucia toward the rope ladder. "Time for your first trip to Pirate Island."

ALESSANDRA

It took nearly half an hour for the lads to bring their dinghy ashore. Lucia was silent the whole way as the oars dipped time and again into the sea. Alessandra could only imagine how nervous she was. A new place, a new identity. She leaped from the boat as they came ashore, standing in the surf, arms outstretched for Lucia. The queen didn't move.

"Come on," Alessandra prodded.

Lucia shook her head and grumbled something under her breath, but she was in Alessandra's arms a second later, letting the pirate pull her through the white-capped waves. The beach ahead was dotted with familiar faces and people waving; one in particular made Alessandra both smile and curse.

Splashing to shore, she released Lucia's hand. "Give me a moment, will you?" She didn't look pleased but gave Alessandra a nod and moved off to the side of the beach, finding shade beneath a dock piling.

"You come here right now." Margthe squeezed Alessandra tight, enveloping her in the comforting scent of freshly baked bread. "You're too thin," Cyril's wife chided, eyeing her at arm's length.

Alessandra waved her off. "I'm fine. There was the slight misfortune of being marooned, is all."

The other woman's face blanched. "What? How in the name of the mother did that happen? I'll take a lash to that father of yours. I know he thinks your place is with him and that you love the sea, child, but I swear, if any harm comes to you." Her lips pursed in frustration. Alessandra followed Margthe's searching eyes. Cyril was easy to spot with his thick white hair blowing in the wind as he saw to The Medusa's offload. "Where's your father, Alex?" Her eyes narrowed, flicking over the scattered crew, most of whom Alessandra knew she'd fed at her table, cared for when ill, or consoled when heartsick. Margthe was, in some ways, a mother to them all.

Alessandra's chest tightened at the question. "Gone. It was quick, at least there's that."

Margthe made a sign to ward off evil, then pulled her close again, whispering, "I'm so sorry, child." The older woman's eyes misted as she pulled away. Sniffling once, she then set herself to the task at hand. "Let me tell these fools where to find me, should they need me." Her hands cupped around her mouth. "Oi! You lot!" The men all turned as the stout woman shouted at them. "Most of you know where to find me. Those of you who don't, there's always a hot meal and a place to sleep it off. Third house on the right past the town, green door."

Cheers went up, and several men gave their first mate's wife appreciative hugs before they melted into the streets of Silver Cove. Cyril turned from his conversation with the harbormaster to give his wife a wave. Margthe held a hand aloft in acknowledgment.

Alessandra hung back, her lip between her teeth as if she were a child about to endure a scolding. Up until that point, Lucia had stayed beneath the pier; her hat pulled low over her eyes, the too-large coat shrouding her womanly figure.

"Mireia," Alessandra called to Lucia.

"Mireia?" Margthe gave the newcomer a long look as Alessandra pulled Lucia into view. The woman's eyes seemed to bore into Lucia's soul before she cursed beneath her breath and shook her head. "She's every inch Queen Tialda's child," she muttered, gesturing at Lucia. "Gods, Alex! What were you thinking, bringing her here?"

Lucia's body tensed. "You knew my mother?"

Margthe didn't answer. Instead, she gazed in stony silence at the approaching figure of her husband.

As Cyril ambled toward the group of women, Alessandra thought she could see the pulse leap in his throat at his wife's stance—her lips pursed and fists on ample hips. He gave a tight smile as he joined them. "Never was any good at pulling the wool over your eyes," he ventured, an arm going around Margthe's shoulders.

She shook him off. "You've all lost your senses. I didn't believe it when I heard word it was The Medusa who'd stolen the queen. I couldn't imagine Pascal and my husband cooking up anything so foolish!"

Cyril had the good sense to look abashed, his face going beet red. "To be fair, Pascal had already passed, and Ale—the captain here, she didn't know about it until it was too late." He looked down at his shoes, clearly embarrassed. "I'm afraid we took advantage of the captain's grief."

Margthe shook her head again, her silver curls bouncing. "And somehow, here we all are. You're not sleeping in my bed tonight, Cyril Andreu!"

Lucia stepped in. "Please, Mistress Andreu, your husband has put himself in danger to save me since then, and," her gaze flicked to Alessandra, who winced as Margthe let loose another slew of ancient curses. "Well, I've grown very fond of the crew—"

"And the captain, it looks like," Margthe interjected.

Alessandra's gaze flicked back and forth as Lucia dipped her chin. "Yes, and Alessandra. Please, you have nothing to fear from me. I understand your concern with me being here, but I assure you, I'll keep a low profile and not cause any trouble."

"No point in arguing. Young fools in love," Margthe muttered. "Your mother was a good woman," she said to Lucia. "For her sake, and this one's," she nodded at Alessandra, "I'll do what I can to help, but I don't approve at all!" With that, she turned and stormed back into town, Cyril not far behind her.

Watching the formidable woman disappear, Lucia pulled her coat tight around herself as she and Alessandra followed the crew into town. The streets were loud with fishmongers shouting their wares. Gulls whirled overhead and men, fresh off their ships, caroused in the streets and spilled from taverns. "Pirate Island," she grumbled under her breath, jumping back as a mangy dog barked and snapped at her boots.

Alessandra chuckled, shooing the mutt away.

"She doesn't like me," Lucia bemoaned.

"Don't think that dog likes anyone."

Shoving her clenched fists into her pockets, Lucia exclaimed, "Margthe, not the damned dog."

Alessandra caught her lover's self-pitying tone and teased, "So, you do like dogs?"

"What?" Lucia spluttered. "Yes, of course I like dogs. But—"

"We made it. We are as safe as can be for now. Let's enjoy it," she said, giving Lucia a squeeze. "I'm buying you a drink."

"What? I thought I was lying low."

"Come on, one drink."

Lucia rolled her eyes and huffed.

Laughing, Alessandra couldn't help but be content as she wrapped her arms around her lover's shoulders. The crisp autumn air riffled her hair, the aroma of cook fires drifted on the breeze from town, and the woman she loved was in her arms. The words had yet to be spoken aloud, but Alessandra knew them to be true. She breathed in deep as the warmth of Lucia's body met hers through their clothes. Alessandra had been grappling for days on whether or not to tell Lucia her feelings, but she always stopped herself. She could only dream of a world where the two of them could stay together.

Alessandra gave Lucia a gentle nudge. "Margthe was more a mother to me than my own ever was," she explained. "And you, my dear, are trouble. It may take some time, but I know she'll come round. And it isn't you she doesn't like, just everything that comes along with you."

The two women walked from the docks past brothels and taverns, dodging weaving sailors and beckoning prostitutes. Silver Cove was a proper town full of pirates and thieves, but also fishermen and tradespeople from all over. It was small, but given the right push, Alessandra knew it could become a major port with its deep waters and close proximity to both Moranth and Vetreon. Until then, the mostly good-natured lawlessness provided The Medusa's crew with the safe haven and respite they were after.

Lucia cringed into Alessandra as an exceedingly intoxicated sailor swerved into her path, arms out. They sidestepped him easily and laughed as he went sprawling into the thick muck of the street.

"How much further?" Lucia asked, brow raised. "I'm all for enjoying the pleasures of the port, but there are limits."

"Just in here." Alessandra tugged her inside an alcove, down an alley, and into her tavern, The Bronze Sail.

LUCIA

The Bronze Sail was unlike most taverns Lucia had been in. As a youth, her exploits with Royce in the city's finer establishments became the worst kept secret of the court, and yet, her father never said a word of it. She came to believe her secret was known to everyone but the king. She doubted anyone would dare tell him the crown princess had been out drinking and reveling with a disgraced lordling all night. Royce wouldn't let anything happen to her, and there were always guards lurking about, including a bodyguard she knew Lord Valeri had sent to keep an eye on her. The man was exiled, but he did what he could to protect her. Any danger in their adventures was an illusion, but it was enough to keep Lucia from going mad in the stifling and truly dangerous court.

Lucia kept her eyes down, her hat still low as she followed Alessandra through the tavern door. It was a far cry from how she'd entered the brothels and bars of Moranth, all swagger and barely harnessed need. Her boots stuck to the floor where the sawdust was sparse, and it smelled of sweat and rum. She glanced at the men about in clusters, some at tables, some arguing in corners, on the verge of a fight.

"Well, if this isn't a sight for sore eyes," came a man's bellowing voice.

Startled, Lucia looked up and met the eyes of a red-faced, bald fellow who, aside from his lack of hair, could have been Cyril's twin.

"Come on, love, give us a hug." The man beckoned Alessandra close. "Margthe stopped by on her way to the dock and told us The Medusa was coming in. My brother with you?"

Ah, that explains it—Cyril's brother.

Alessandra shook her head while taking a seat at the bar, gesturing for Lucia to do the same. She wasn't all that eager to touch anything in the tavern, but she didn't want to offend Alessandra.

"Afraid not, Cam. Margthe was giving him what for last I saw. I'd wager you see him tonight, though. Probably need a drink and a place to sleep."

Cam set three glasses on the bar and poured generous shots. After passing them around, he wiped the bar before leaning on his meaty elbow. "That business with the queen?" His lips twitched as he gave Lucia a once over, then tipped the rum back in one go.

"Aye," Alessandra said, nudging Lucia with her elbow. "We're all glad to have seen the back of that harlot, aren't we, Mireia?"

Lucia took the shot. Coughing as the cheap rum burned down her throat, she nodded. "Aye, the strumpet."

"And just who might this be, Alex?" the barkeep asked, pouring three more glasses.

Lucia's heart pounded in her chest; her accent was a dead giveaway that she was from the capital and, more precisely, the court. *Damn it.* She cursed herself for not being more careful. Then again, if she were the queen's maid, it was reasonable for her to have assumed some of Her Majesty's mannerisms and even her accent.

"Mireia—" she began.

"The queen's maid," Alessandra cut her off. Giving her a wink, the pirate grabbed her. She yelped as she found herself deposited on Alessandra's lap. "Couldn't resist this face." Alessandra grinned.

Lucia gasped, shocked to be so handled in public, but very much enjoying their ruse. If being Mireia the maid was what it took to get this level of attention from Alessandra, she could keep up the charade indefinitely.

Cam's bushy brows rose, but he gave them a warm enough smile. "A rare beauty indeed to hold your attention, Alex. Welcome to Silver Cove, Mireia."

ALESSANDRA

An hour later, Alessandra was holding up a slightly inebriated Lucia as the queen's footsteps shuffled along the path to the D'Allyon cottage.

"All I'm saying," Lucia rambled on, "is that The Bronze Sail needs someone with a bit more polish looking after it. The space is wonderful." Her arm moved in a wide arc above her head, mimicking the tavern's surprisingly high, vaulted ceiling. Her foot turned on a pebble, and Alessandra smiled while steadying her. "There's this place Royce and I used to go, down in Olde Towne. It doesn't look like much from the outside, but—" Lucia paused, wiping a hand across her brow. "It's hot, isn't it? How far away are we?"

"Just up the path out of town, by the sea. It's right by Cyril and Margthe's place. Rafe threw up a shack there as well last year. We've got our own little village in the making."

Lucia sniffed, fanning her hand in front of her nose. "Hope it smells better than this one does."

Not five minutes later, two white-washed stone houses came into view, tucked picturesquely into the green jungle landscape. They didn't fit in with the other architecture of the island, the wattle and daub of the town's buildings, but were quaint in their own right.

"That Rafe's?" Lucia pointed toward a humbler structure further down the coast, made of wooden planks in the typical style of the island.

"It is."

"And yours? Margthe's design, I believe?" Lucia stared at the two out-of-place structures, sounding more sober than before.

Alessandra's brows furrowed. "Why would you think that?"

"They clearly aren't Moranthese in design, nor Vetreonish. Margthe hasn't lost that much of her accent, you know," Lucia said.

Alessandra was still at a loss, nor had she ever given the older woman's accent a thought. Margthe sounded like Margthe, nothing more, nothing less.

"She's from Wellingisle, isn't she?" Alessandra blinked, realizing she'd not once thought to ask her second mother where she'd come from. "My mother was born there," Lucia continued. "All her household staff when I was little were from there as well. I used to hear stories about the villages on the coast, white houses with bright shutters and thatched roofs. They always sounded like fairy stories to me. You know," she stared at Alessandra's bright hair, "you look like you've got some Wellingislander in you."

Alessandra shrugged. "Who knows? I fear the reality of our homes is less than romantic, but they'll keep you warm in winter and cool in summer. I didn't know your mother was an islander," Alessandra said, unable to disguise the shock in her voice.

Though Wellingisle was said to be the most beautiful jewel in the Moranthese crown, the far-flung island was also home to her most rebellious people. A land of mists and wild legends. The only thing Alessandra could truly remember of them, from her scant knowledge of history, was that every so often, the islanders got tired of being ruled over by a faraway king and caused a bit of trouble that was soon put down. It hadn't been a true threat to anyone since the ancient Queen Tialda's short reign over a thousand years before.

"How on earth did your mother come to be the queen of Moranth?" she asked, immediately regretting the question. She was certain Lucia didn't want to talk about her mother, and with good reason.

Lucia stopped walking and went stock still as her gaze followed the line of swaying palm trees to the sea. "The last man to rebel against my father had a very beautiful, marriageable daughter. I think my father's nobles believed he married her to ease tensions, but knowing him, it was one more way of asserting his power over them. He never loved her. I don't think he even liked her, not that the man liked anyone."

Alessandra caught Lucia around the waist, tucking her chin into the queen's shoulder. "Must be where the wildness in you comes from," she breathed against Lucia's neck. "I'm sorry, I shouldn't have asked."

"It's all right," she said. "For some reason, I like talking about her with you."

"I like hearing about her," Alessandra whispered against Lucia's temple. She'd lived amongst loss long enough to know the dead needed remembering in order that those left alive could heal. "Let's get inside. We both need a good scrub."

They continued along the path silently, hand in hand. When they reached the cottage, with its sun-bleached door, Alessandra had to stoop to get under the low entryway. "The one time being short comes in handy," Lucia teased her, walking through easily. Alessandra paused, remembering all the times before when she had returned home with her father. When it had been just the two of them, and he allowed himself to be her father, not her commander. Her breath hitched for just a moment, the weight of his absence hitting her as it had not for weeks.

Lucia's smiling face emerged back into the sunlight as her hand grasped Alessandra's. "Come on."

The air was still within, the light from the open doorway casting the room in deep shadows. The ceiling was high inside, every wall was washed in a warm white, and a soot-blackened hearth took up much of the cozy living quarters. A table made of driftwood planks was wedged tight against a wall with three fine chairs, plundered from a ship a few years back, pulled haphazardly around it. A low, battered velvet settee provided the only other seating.

"Help me with this." Alessandra stood by the closed, heavy shutters. They had been pulled and latched from the inside to protect against battering storms and animals. Lucia shoved at the yellow-painted latch, nearly tumbling through the opening as Alessandra put her shoulder to the shutters and pushed. As they creaked open, dust mites shimmered in the sudden bright rays of sunlight, and the room changed from its former haunted self into a room for the living.

Alessandra scratched at the back of her neck, suddenly embarrassed by her home. "Like I said, it's not much—"

Lucia's arms were around Alessandra's waist. "It's perfect. A place all our own." She stood on her tiptoes, pressing a kiss to Alessandra's cheek. "I was promised a bath, though I'm guessing there isn't a hidden hot spring or the like."

Alessandra chuckled in answer. "You're perhaps imagined a steaming bath, perfumed oils, and soft towels. The tub is there." She pointed to a large metal washbasin. "I'll pump your water."

Twenty minutes later, Alessandra was sweating from carrying water as Lucia glared at her from the tub, where she stood shivering. "The first thing we're doing when we get to the palace is having a proper bath. I can't remember the last time I was warm," Lucia complained.

Alessandra grinned, standing nude herself after rinsing outside at the water pump. "That sounds lovely," she admitted, sidestepping a splash of water from the tub as Lucia turned. "But I can think of more than one way to warm you up," she said, scooping Lucia into her arms.

"More than one way, eh?" Lucia questioned as she dropped the rag into the bath, letting Alessandra carry her away.

The cottage was small, but Alessandra had her own room, which she stumbled toward, arms and lips entangled in Lucia.

"You best not forget being warm this time." Alessandra smirked as she laid Lucia on the bed, spreading her lover before her.

She could tell Margthe was not pleased by Lucia's presence at the dock, but the woman had enough sense to know it was useless arguing against them. Alessandra was past caring about hiding her love. Whether or not Lucia realized it for what it was, remained to be seen. But Alessandra knew. She was sure. She loved Lucia.

Hours after their lovemaking, when the sun was dipping low and the cool evening breeze picked up, Alessandra and Lucia made their way across the rocky dunes to Margthe and Cyril's home.

Margthe was crouched at her hearth, where she had a pot of stew going, her eyes on briefly meeting

Alessandra's before cutting to watch her husband as he sauntered over, giving her backside a pinch. She responded with a glare as Lucia and Alessandra sat at the table, hand in hand.

"Leave off, love," Cyril whispered against her cheek. "For all that she's a royal, she's a good lass." He hadn't spoken loudly, or for her benefit, but Alessandra had strained her ears to listen, catching the words. It was as she feared, Margthe didn't approve.

"You trust her?" Margthe asked, her concern clear. She'd been the one to care for Alessandra as a child during the long months The Medusa was in port, the one to mend her clothes and her spirits, the one the fiery-haired little girl would had run to when she needed a mother's warmth. Margthe knew the dangers of the sea— had married a sailor, after all. She knew each time she sent her loved ones off that it might be the last she saw of them, but those were accepted risks. Alessandra imagined what she must be thinking. Being the lover of a queen, a *hunted* queen, was bad enough, but for it to be the queen of Moranth, that was something else.

Cyril shrugged at her question. "I trust the captain." Alessandra felt her cheeks go red as she pretended she couldn't hear them, but her grip on Lucia's hand tightened.

Lucia caught her gaze, furrowing her brow. "What is it?" she whispered.

She brushed a kiss over Lucia's knuckles. "Nothing."

Margthe rolled her eyes. Her voice was loud enough in answer that Lucia turned. "And she'd be the first not to be fooled by love, eh?" She shook her head. Pulling away, Margthe checked the bubbling stew, which filled the cottage with a most enticing aroma of frothing tomato, fish, and potatoes. She reached up and pulled out a handful of dried rosemary from where it hung, along with other herbs.

Lucia pulled her hand back. "She's not happy with us, is she? I told you she didn't like me."

Alessandra grunted. "She just doesn't know you."

Lucia pulled Alessandra into her embrace, throwing her leg up onto the bench to support her as a slow smile of utter contentment spread over her lips. As she did, Alessandra watched Margthe's shoulders drop, the tension in her body ease.

Margthe sighed loudly, took a breath. "Stew's done," she said, hands on hips. "Cyril, you help me. I know you two are starving, and I'll not keep you waiting on the others," she called warmly to Alessandra and Lucia.

Lucia's eyes widened at her first bite of the spicy, brothy stew. "I've never tasted anything like this," she noted, clearly delighted by the simple fare as she dipped her bread into the stew bowl.

"Well, I should think not. This is a fisherman's stew."

Alessandra smiled at the look of appreciation on Margthe's face. There was no better way for Lucia to win her over, than complimenting her cooking. "You like it?"

"Absolute perfection." Lucia smiled, downing another bite.

Margthe watched, nodded her approval. "Now, Alex," she turned her attention from the young queen, "Cyril says The Medusa is in a rather rough shape. How long will we have you? This," she pointed at her and Lucia, "won't be kept a secret for long. Certainly not through the winter. It won't be safe, and you know it."

Breaking into a grin, Alessandra asked, "Trying to get rid of us already?"

The older woman's brow rose. Alessandra sighed, acknowledging the seriousness of the question and their situation. "I'll get the shipwright out in the morning, but aye," she said, "rough is right. It'll be a few weeks at least, I would think. And I'm not as oblivious as you might think to the danger here as well as abroad. Clearly, the faster we can deliver our cargo," she nodded at Lucia, "the better for all of us."

Margthe's eyes narrowed as her gaze flicked back to Lucia. "Not so ready to return, are you?"

Cyril coughed, looking uncomfortable as he gave Alessandra's arm a pat. "Margthe isn't saying she doesn't want you here. Either of you," he said, nodding toward Lucia.

Further discussion was saved by the sound of children's shrieks and laughter reaching them through the open windows. "That sounds like trouble," Alessandra said.

Everyone at the table looked happy for the distraction as a throng of small children, followed by their exhausted looking parents, rushed into the cottage.

Lucia tensed around Alessandra as Cyril and Margthe's her children and grandchildren piled in, their loud voices echoing in the small home.

Alessandra twisted her neck, giving Lucia a quick peck on her cheek. "Just be your adorable self."

"Alex!" one of the children called, a knee-high girl with blonde curls.

Alessandra gave the child a wide smile, extricated herself from Lucia's arms, and crouched down to scoop the girl up.

"You're so pretty," the little girl said in wonder, her eyes on Lucia. The queen, in her too too-large clothes and messy hair, snorted at the compliment.

"Why thank you, and so are you," she said graciously.

The rest of the evening was spent dodging racing, shouting children, and shoveling in mouthfuls of stew when there was a break in the chaos. Every once in a while, Alessandra chanced a glance at Margthe, who for her part, stayed quiet, observing from her seat at the table, with a rotation of grandchildren on her knee. Lucia and Alessandra were on the floor with some of the children—Lucia looked miserable and as out of place as she could. *And why shouldn't she? The way she was brought up.* Alessandra enjoyed the little ones and would always invite them onto The Medusa to play pirate for the day or traipse into the woods with a pack of them, hunting for buried treasure. But she had known them all since birth, spent every winter at the brightly glowing hearth beside them. They were her family as much or more than her crew. This was her home.

Of course Margthe is worried about Lucia being here. The fragility of the life she and Cyril had rebuilt at Silver Cove suddenly became clear to Alessandra as she sat watching Lucia struggle with Laia, their toddling granddaughter. The girl had hold of Lucia's hair. *I should probably help*, she thought, watching as Lucia's lips set in a thin line. One wrong word and this world could cease to exist. She knew there were agents of both crowns on the small island, always hoping to find some interesting bit of news or gossip to report. They had no authority, but that didn't mean people didn't turn up dead or missing from time to time. *If anyone knew Lucia was in their home.* Alessandra shivered. Even amongst family, the unease wouldn't leave her.

Thankfully, not one of Margthe's and Cyril's children or their spouses seemed to doubt Alessandra's story that Lucia was, in fact, a maid. She had been introduced as such, and then the matter dropped, with only one moment of awkwardness arising when one of Margthe's sons-in-law made an inappropriate quip about the queen's rumored proclivities. Lucia's cheeks turned red, and Alessandra went still before Cyril's booming laughter broke the tension, and he moved the conversation along. No one seemed to notice the false tone or, or that Margthe stayed silent.

LUCIA

Lucia was deep in thought as they walked back toward the cottage several hours later, the moon lighting their way.

"Are you alright?" Alessandra asked.

Lucia didn't answer because she was trying to anchor herself in the moment. Alessandra's hand rested at the small of her back, the roundness of her hip pressing against the pirate's as their fingers brushed together. It was comforting. Lucia hadn't said a word since they left Margthe and Cyril's.

"You don't have to explain, but I want you to know I'm here for whatever you need," Alessandra offered as they continued along the path.

"I'm fine," she grumbled, tugging free of Alessandra.

"Hey." Alessandra stopped her. "You're not fine." She grasped Lucia's hand and brought her close again, tipping her chin up.

Lucia felt her eyes brimming with unshed tears as she tried to look anywhere but at her lover. "That was just—It was overwhelming for me. I'm sorry," Lucia answered, dropping her chin in embarrassment. She always meant to have fun in such circumstances, always wanted to enjoy them in the same way those around her seemed to, but she just couldn't. It was in those moments when she felt ashamed that there was something so different about herself that kept her at a distance from everyone else. In the past, she had tried to put it down to being a princess, then a queen, as it wasn't safe for her to be close to people. Most, if not all, were incapable of being trusted. But even as Mireia, even pretending to be someone else, she still couldn't relax, couldn't quite connect in the way she thought she should.

"There's nothing for you to be sorry about. I'm sure you aren't used to that kind of ruckus. Honestly, I've lost count of the number of grandchildren Cyril and Margthe have at this point, but it's a lot. It's alright. Shit. I should have paid you more attention. I'm sorry."

"It's my fault. I'm so awkward."

Alessandra scoffed. "You think that was awkward? Wait until you see me at court."

Instead of turning uphill toward her cottage, Alessandra steered Lucia toward the beach. Lost in thought as she was, she didn't protest. Grateful once again that Alessandra intuitively knew when not to press her. "Where are we going?"

Alessandra gave Lucia's backside a playful swat. "You think I don't know how to help you unwind at this point?" Lucia couldn't help but chuckle, her body responding instantly to Alessandra's insinuation. "I'm taking you to the beach. We can pretend we're back on our island."

They crested a little rise, Alessandra sliding a few feet down the rocky hillside, her hand outstretched for Lucia's. "I'm going to have my way with you," Alessandra said.

Palm trees rustled overhead in the darkness as stars spiraled out into eternity like blazing diamonds above them. Lucia followed Alessandra, scrambling down the steep incline after the nimble pirate. She yelped as the ground gave way beneath her, but Alessandra's sure hands were there, her thumbs brushing over the softness of her stomach as Lucia found herself lifted onto the powdery beach.

"I'm going to have my way with you," Alessandra repeated breathlessly. "And I'm going to make you come until you can barely remember your own name."

That is certainly a distraction I can appreciate. Her feet tangled with each other in her haste. She would have fallen if not for Alessandra's hand in hers. "Finally got my sea legs. Now I can't walk on land," Lucia said, laughing.

"You might be getting ahead of yourself on that one, darling." Alessandra sank to the ground, kicking off her boots. Lucia did the same, nestling into the shelter of Alessandra's body, the sand cool through the silk of her breeches. The pirate was warm, the long planes of her snug against Lucia's softer body.

"I've never seen anything more beautiful," Alessandra whispered, brushing Lucia's locks over her bare shoulder.

"Nor I," Lucia echoed, her eyes flicking over Alessandra's lean curves as she tugged at her own breeches. She struggled, her fingers finding the fastenings difficult in the cold night air. "I know this isn't exactly romantic, but could you help me?" she asked bashfully.

Alessandra snickered, pressing her forehead to Lucia's as her deft fingers worked at Lucia's buttons. "There you are." She said as her steady hands slid the breeches over Lucia's hips, down her thighs, and finally off. Alessandra found purchase under Lucia's backside and hefted her on top. "Perfect," Alessandra said.

She settled onto Alessandra. *This is home.* A low whine began in Lucia's throat as Alessandra's hands stroked up her legs, her thighs, the pirate's fingers working themselves between their clits. Lucia's body was rigid with pent-up need. "Oh," she groaned, thighs sticky and shaking as Alessandra deepened the pressure on her clit. Lucia's breathing grew shallow as her hands glided along Alessandra's waist. Pushing at her shirt, she palmed the captain's perfectly formed breasts before dipping her head to pull one of the pirate's dusky nipples between her lips.

"Ugh, God. Lucia," Alessandra moaned. She pushed them up to a sitting position. "Turn around," she ordered.

A dead tree, dry and sun-bleached, lay white on the beach beside them. Alessandra somehow managed to scoot back against it with Lucia still in her arms.

Doing as she was told, Lucia dropped her head back against Alessandra's shoulder, her core tightening as kisses trailed along her neck. Her back arched against the pleasure Alessandra's fingers were giving her as they toyed with the hem of her shirt, roved across her belly, and squeezed the fullness of her breasts. It was nearly too much. Her body rocked against Alessandra's as incoherent pleas left her throat. She wanted more, needed it. A hand snaked between her thighs, just brushing teasingly at her opening.

"Alex," Lucia mumbled, turning to kiss her, tongues slipping against each other as the pirate's other hand continued to caress her breast, pluck at her nipple. Lucia's thighs began to shake, her breaths becoming gasps. Alessandra sunk two fingers deep inside her, thrusting in quick succession, thumb rubbing at her swollen clit. "Please, please," she begged.

"I'm not done with you yet. Get back on top of me." Alessandra groaned before moving once more, settling herself between Lucia's splayed thighs. Her tongue lapped slow, torturous strokes against Lucia's sex, sucking, licking, hands digging into Lucia's plump ass.

"I can't—" Lucia exclaimed. Hot wetness flooded down her thighs as she came.

After a few moments of stillness, their breathing returned to normal as the waves crashed around them. Lucia rolled into Alessandra's arms and sat up, hands on thighs, head tipped back, basking in the moonlight.

"That was exactly what I needed," she said.

Alessandra rose up on an elbow, the briefest of smiles darting across her lips. "I know."

Lucia couldn't fathom her good fortune at ending up where she had, nor could she believe she'd soon be back in Moranth, a queen once more.

14

LUCIA

With the door open, a salty morning breeze floating through the house, Lucia and Alessandra sat at a small driftwood table in the cottage's kitchen with Margthe's loaf cake between them.

"Good morning, my ladies." Rafe's figure filled the open door as sunlight spilled through behind him.

Alessandra scoffed. "We are not *your* ladies."

The corner of Lucia's lips pulled up. The chain of command and the strictness on board The Medusa was relaxed on the island, and she saw firsthand the camaraderie it allowed. It reminded her of how she and Royce had been before her coronation—*how I hope things will be once more, should I ever make it back.*

Rafe beamed. "You two know I'm close by, right? Just in case you ever have need of more company."

Lucia wished she had something to throw in the man's general direction. She settled for a gentle shove and a playful smile of her own. "Leave off, you scoundrel."

"Really, Rafe," Alessandra chided. "We could hear the noise you and whoever she was, were making all night. I don't think you'll ever lack adequate companionship."

Flashing his teeth again, he shook his head, his dark curls shining in the morning sun as he sat at the small wooden table. "I'm here to offer my services," he held out his hands as their brows rose, "as the lovely Mireia's guide in Silver Cove while you, Captain, are busy with the shipwright."

"Oh, yes. Please!" Lucia said, hearing the obvious excitement in her voice. She knew she needed to keep to herself and not be seen, but her curiosity was hard to contain.

Alessandra leaned against the table, arms wrapping around Lucia protectively. "It's too dangerous. We were already foolish going to the tavern."

"Ah, come on now, Captain. She'll be under my protection, and there's something here I thought she might like to see," Rafe protested.

Alessandra gave the two of them a half-hearted glare.

"Please, Alex, there's nothing to do here besides cooking—which I have no idea how to do—or sleeping. I'm bored."

"You could hunt. I keep hearing about your skills with a bow," Alessandra suggested. "Rafe knows all the game trails."

"Later," she whined. "Let me see something, just a little bit of the town."

Alessandra groaned and turned to Rafe. "And just what does Lu—Mireia have to see in Silver Cove? I dare say she's seen the insides of at least one filthy tavern."

"It's a surprise," Rafe answered. "No taverns, I promise."

"Oh, Alex, please, love," Lucia wheedled. "You know I'll go mad here, and isn't it safer if I'm with Rafe than alone, just in case someone does find out who I am?"

"Fine, fine, but Rafe," Lucia saw Alessandra fix her friend with a stare, "if anything happens to her, you'll bear the blame."

He gave a sloppy salute. "Understood, Captain!"

―――

Half an hour later, Lucia had a scarf and hat covering her ashen locks as the coat Alessandra had given her on board hung from her narrow shoulders, the cuffs constantly in need of pushing up as they flopped down over her hands.

"I feel ridiculous," she said frustratedly as she and Rafe made their way into town.

"It's not my favorite look of yours." He laughed. "This way."

They sidestepped a suspicious dark puddle with a man sleeping beside it, a bottle in hand, then ducked down a narrow alley. A knot pulled tight in Lucia's stomach as the daylight shrank and the walls grew closer the deeper into the alley they went. Her mouth was dry as her heart thundered in her ears. *Can I really trust Rafe?*

"It's just up here," Rafe said, pushing Lucia behind him as a man pressed by. "Here we are." He was clearly pleased with himself as he watched Lucia's reaction.

They were in front of an old building, older than most of what she'd seen in town. The timbers were white oak, pale against the shadows of the street. Lucia's eyes widened as she saw the symbols above the doorway; a crescent moon framed by two stars. "Rafe, this is—"

"Aye," he whispered. "I thought you would want to see it."

Her fingers reached out to trace the name carved into the doorpost. *Tialda*. The ancient queen and saint that her mother was named after. "I thought all of her shrines were destroyed."

A smile ghosted over his lips as he shrugged. "Not all of them."

Lucia wondered at his quick friendship, at all the kindness shown to her by people she had feared all her life. "Thank you for bringing me here."

Rafe nodded. "You go in. I'll keep watch."

Lucia ducked under the low entry, her skin prickling as her feet crossed the threshold of the holy place. It was dark inside, a cavern of a room lit only by smoking votive candles. Above the dancing candlelight was an image of St. Tialda, her blonde hair shimmering with gold pigment, her sword raised as she rode her war chariot into battle. A queen who had died defending her people.

Lucia knelt before the fresco, head bowed. Her father had ordered every shrine to the legendary queen destroyed after he murdered his wife, an effort to remove even the name itself from the memory of Moranth's people. Lucia's heart squeezed tight as she thought of both young queens killed too early. She couldn't help but think of her own plight and the unknowable fate that was laid before her.

Her lips moved silently as she asked for guidance in keeping her people safe, then she slipped into a one-sided conversation with her mother. "I miss you," she whispered, her voice loud in the quiet room. Her throat bobbed with the effort to choke back sobs. "I should have helped you!" Her balled fist slammed against her thigh. "I should have found a way to kill him for you."

"Thought you were keeping a low profile, Mireia," came a familiar voice from behind.

Startled, Lucia turned to find Margthe standing at the entrance to the shrine. *How much did she hear?*

"I wanted to light a candle for my mother," Lucia said, swiping at the tears slowly rolling down her cheeks.

Lucia saw something change in the other woman's stance as Margthe nodded to the altar below Tialda's painting, pale beeswax candles flickering in the shadows there. "I light one every week for my boy," she said, gently taking Lucia by the elbow and drawing her close. "Why don't we light ours together?"

Lucia couldn't speak but allowed herself to be maneuvered to the altar. Margthe gave her an encouraging smile and handed her a lit taper before lighting her own. Lucia had never held much esteem for religion as her mother had brought her up in the ancient ways of her homeland, where the saints were merely thinly veiled aspects of the primal gods and goddesses of the land. Still, she would ask for their help, whether or not they could hear her.

With Margthe beside her, a quiet prayer on her lips, Lucia wondered what her mother would have been like if she were still alive. *What would she think of me and the choices I have made?* Her gaze sought out Margthe's, their eyes meeting over the flickering candles.

"Come here, child," Margthe said, crossed arms unfolding as she beckoned Lucia forward.

As if propelled by an unseen force, Lucia nearly collapsed, sobbing into the large woman's embrace. Racking cries filled with the anguish of a helpless child echoed off the chamber's walls as she shook within Margthe's strong arms.

"There, lass. Let it all out." She stroked Lucia's back in slow circles. "Your mother would be proud of the woman you are," she said kindly as Lucia's arms wound tighter around her.

"You don't know me," Lucia sobbed, her cheek pressed against Margthe's cloak, soaking the fabric.

"I don't know you, but my husband has come to care for you, it seems, as does Alex. That girl is like my own child. I'd do anything in my power to keep her from harm. Are you going to hurt her?"

Lucia stilled in the woman's arms. Pulling away, she wiped her sleeve across her nose and tear-streaked cheeks like a child. "I don't know. I worry I'm like my father. I'm so angry so much of the time."

Margthe regarded her with shrewd eyes. "You angry with her around?"

"No, not as much," Lucia whispered, acknowledging it for the first time, even to herself. Alessandra's presence helped tether her in the best way. "She trusts me. She doesn't ask me to be anything but myself. For all I know who that is."

Margthe took Lucia's hand in hers. Sitting on one of the wooden pews, she pulled Lucia down gently beside her. "I didn't really know your mother. She was just a child running about with wild hair and scraped elbows, giving the boys hell when I left the island, but she had a temper, a quick, furious one. It came on like a summer storm and was gone just as quick. Now, your grandmother, I did know."

Lucia was enraptured. She had never before heard anyone speak so freely of her mother, and she knew hardly a thing of her mother's family—*forbidden knowledge*.

"She was just the same. It was always best to stay clear when they were in a mood, but they were good to their core." She gave Lucia's hand a motherly pat. "I'm sure your mother did what she could to protect you, but I don't doubt the world you grew up in was an unhappy one. That can change a person, make them believe they aren't worth the ground they step on."

Lucia was crying again, slow, silent tears. It had taken being kidnapped to find herself among people who saw her not for the queen or the monster's daughter but for the Lucia she was always fighting for, the child her mother couldn't fully protect from the evils of her father's court.

"Look at me," Margthe crooned as if to an injured child. "You can't live your life scared of becoming something you aren't. There wasn't ever an ounce of kindness in your father, not a bit of warmth or compassion. From what I hear, the same could be said of the new king of Vetreon." Lucia flinched at the mention of Ramir. "But," Margthe continued, "I've never heard one word of the like in regard to you. A monster wouldn't be here in a shrine with tears and snot running down her face." Her gaze skittered away as a wry smile turned up her lips. "Now, I have heard tell of other, shall we say, interests you have. So long as you and Alessandra find pleasure together, well, I can't find fault with you there."

Lucia blushed, thinking this was becoming like the uncomfortable conversation she knew mothers had with their daughters on their wedding nights. Conversations she had never had. She gave Margthe a smile, and when Cyril's wife opened her arms again, Lucia sank silently back into them, finding a mother's comfort she had almost forgotten.

ALESSANDRA

Alessandra groaned. She didn't have the coin. Not enough, at least. Nor did she have the time.

"I don't want to put my men in more danger than is expected," she said to the shipwright. The gangly man had spent the last two hours going over The Medusa, and his assessment wasn't promising. The ship needed a new mast, and there were patches to be made in the hull and other repairs. "What's the best you can do for the money and the time? We just need to make it to Moranth in one piece." It wasn't a fact she was advertising, but she'd known Will Sullivan nearly her whole life, and in his business, it was discretion that kept a head on his shoulders.

The fellow scratched at his stubble, shaking his head. "Heard you got yourself into quite a bit of trouble."

Alessandra's hand grazed the hilt of her cutlass. It wasn't really a threat, more a gentle reminder, one Will seemed to take.

The shipwright ran his hand over a rail. "She won't be limping anymore," he said, his hand indicating The Medusa, "but she needs a major overhaul. I'll do what I can. She'll get you to Moranth, but if there's trouble, I don't guarantee she'll get you out of it."

Alessandra sighed, resigned that it was the best she could hope for. "How long?"

He rubbed at the back of his neck. "Fast and cheap?"

"I know, Will, but it's what I've got."

"I'm only doing this because it's you," he responded. "I can have her ready to sail in a week."

Alessandra thumped the man on his back. "I won't forget this," she said.

Her thoughts turned to Lucia as she made her way back to the cottage. It had been a long morning and the idea of falling into bed with her for the remainder of the afternoon seemed a perfect one. Their last week together before the world became real again.

"Alex." Rafe startled her as she came up her path.

Nearly jumping out of her skin, Alessandra had her cutlass half-drawn. "You scared me." She smiled, hands on her knees as she worked to slow her racing heart. Noting the worried look on his handsome face, she grabbed at him. "Is Lucia alright?" She forgot to use her false name in her haste to get to her cottage door.

Rafe's arm went around her waist, his body blocking her way. "She's fine. She's safe."

"Then why do you look like that?"

His hands dropped to his sides as he hung his head. "I took her to see the St. Tialda shrine." Rafe winced as Alessandra took a sharp breath. "I'm sorry, I didn't know. I just thought it would be nice for her since her mother was named after the saint."

Alessandra raked her fingers through her unkempt hair and shoved past him. Margthe was at the hearth, a pot of stew bubbling, while Lucia sat alone at the table. Her face was tear-stained, her eyes full of anguish, as her hands lay limp in her lap.

Margthe turned from tending the fire and motioned Alessandra over. "Help an old woman up." She huffed as Alessandra assisted her. "That should be ready in another hour or so; just keep it simmering." She gave Alessandra's arm a squeeze, then inclined her head in Lucia's direction. "She's had a day. Rafe and I will leave you to it. Then you and I are going to have a talk."

"Thank you." Alessandra sighed, settling herself in a chair beside Lucia as Margthe and Rafe retreated.

"My father killed my mother." Lucia's voice was hollow when she spoke; she sounded exhausted.

Alessandra slipped her hand into Lucia's. "I know. I'm so sorry."

"I was there." Lucia's voice caught on the words.

Alessandra's eyes snapped shut, her heart aching, as so much of Lucia's hurts suddenly made sense. She sank to her knees before Lucia, arms enfolding the queen in safety. "You were a child. You were just a child." Alessandra comforted her, lips whispering against Lucia's thighs.

"No one would help her." Lucia gasped through sobs; her voice was hoarse from the strain. "The guards just watched as he strangled her." The tears kept coming. "Eighteen years, and I've never told another soul. I thought he was going to kill me, too. He could have, you know, and no one would have stopped him."

Alessandra gently pulled Lucia from her seat, cradling her as her own tears fell. "I'm so sorry, my love. I'm so sorry."

"You're going to leave me." Lucia whimpered against her chest.

"I won't, love. I won't," she whispered. "I won't leave you."

She rocked Lucia until she felt her go still in her arms, the sobs turning to quiet breathing. Alessandra's breath left her body in a racking sigh. Her word was sacred to her, and she had just made a promise to Lucia that she wasn't sure she could keep, but she would try. Quiet as she could be, Alessandra eased Lucia's head to the floor, then grabbed a plush blanket. Knees creaking as she stood, she settled the thick wool over Lucia's sleeping form, then silently left the room.

She found Margthe and Cyril alone in their cottage. Cyril was leaning back in a chair, patting a full belly, a pipe between his teeth, while Margthe was winding a skein of yarn, her fingers wrapping the thread into a ball for knitting.

Margthe tipped her chin in question. "How's the poor lass?"

Cyril grunted, maneuvering himself to his feet. "Think I'll take a walk," he said by way of exiting the conversation. Margthe's eyes followed him to the door before motioning her forward.

Alessandra sank heavily onto the floor before the fire as Margthe stroked her hair like she had when she was a little girl. "I shouldn't have let her go with Rafe." Her words were slow with the weight of the afternoon.

The stroking stopped. "No," came Margthe's soothing voice. "That was dangerous for us all. You're the captain now. Not a thing you do doesn't come back on us all."

"I know." Alessandra stretched out her legs, letting her head fall back against the other woman's knee. "Why couldn't she have just been a pretty wench with a taste for the sea?"

"Had that dream, did you?"

Alessandra groaned. "How did you know?"

"I used to have them about Cyril. He was a farmer in mine. It was a happy enough fantasy, but he'd never truly been himself if he gave up the sailor's life."

"In my dream, she asked me to choose, her or the sea. I wouldn't even let her come with me—I was too terrified something would happen to her." *I wouldn't let her in real life either, but damned if I know how to refuse her.* Alessandra turned to catch Margthe's laugh.

"Queen or barmaid, she would never have been easy."

"No. Nor am I, I know." Alessandra sighed.

There was a tug on her hair. "The two of you belong to each other now. You need each other."

She can't be right, can she? I've neer needed anyone. "Margthe," Alessandra pleaded, "don't put that on me along with everything else."

"Ha!" she barked. "I'm thinking you'll not get away from that woman in this life or the next."

15

ALMONT

Almont struggled to keep pace with Ramir's long and sure stride as he surveyed the palace guards. The soldiers were standing at attention in the orange and gold of his house, their breastplates and helmets gleaming under the unseasonably hot sun. Having been warned in no uncertain terms by Moranth's ambassador that should any link to Ramir or his court be found in their queen's kidnapping, there would be war, Vetreon was readying itself.

"That bitch is still alive, I know it," Ramir spat as he paced, arms behind his back. "Where have you been? I've been out here for nearly an hour."

Almont wiped the sweat from his brow as it ran, stinging his eyes. His voice was hushed as he spoke, "Your Majesty, forgive me, but I've just had word. You're right. She is alive."

Ramir's pacing stopped mid-stride—dark eyes bright as he turned his head slowly away from his men to bring all his focus on Almont. With a flicker of a smile, he said, "Tell me everything."

"Your Majesty." Almont dipped his head in the direction of the guard.

"Right." Ramir rolled his eyes. "You men are the finest lot of soldiers in all of Vetreon." His voice was clear and strong, the voice of a leader. "I've no doubt that you are more than capable of putting down any threat to our land that may arise. You have my thanks. Dismissed." The soldiers relaxed, falling out of formation and going back to their tasks.

Ramir pulled at the sleeve of Almont's silk jacket. "Walk with me," he commanded. Almont followed.

The royal seat of Vetreon was more a fortified castle than a luxurious palace, speaking to centuries of warfare. Ramir's father, being Moranthese, had brought as a wedding gift to his Vetreon-born bride, a renowned gardener. The man had done what he could to create a bit of lush grandeur to the ancient hilltop home of Vetreon's royal family. It was to those stepped gardens Ramir took Almont.

"Very well, Almont." Ramir finally stopped to let the man speak.

"Majesty, I've had word from our man in Silver Cove."

"Pirate's Island?" Ramir rubbed at his chin. "Makes sense. Go on."

"He swears all holy that Lucia is there with the crew of The Medusa. He said when the ship pulled in, her captain kept a crew member close. *Very close*. One that happened to have an impressive figure, as he put it, and a long blonde braid."

Ramir sneered. "Then we have her. Send word for this man to secure my bride."

"Majesty, if I may." Almont waited for his king's approval to continue. Ramir flicked his fingers in acquiescence. "Our man in Silver Cove has no ship, no crew. He's not the sort who can handle a job like this. He's there mainly to ensure our nobles aren't skimming from us with their trade tariffs. What I suggest is sending someone else. Someone with a ship and men used to battle, should one erupt, maybe even one we could pin the whole affair on, should it fall apart."

Ramir, his arms crossed, looked out over the burbling fountains and blooming flowers. "Get to it."

"The Deceit is docked in an inlet just down the coast. She's a fast ship, and her captain is second to none."

"Defoe, yes?" Ramir sucked at his teeth. "Is there a reason you know his whereabouts, yet he remains a free man?"

"Majesty, Defoe is a *generous* man, and his generosity extends to the royal treasury."

"I see. Very well, make it fast, though. If you know where Lucia is, then so does that bastard, Aldana."

ROYCE

Royce shut his ledger as a knock came at his door. "Enter," he said, expecting the man who walked in. Ambros Tomas was tall, made taller by his plumed captain's hat, which he tucked beneath his arm as he approached Royce's desk.

"My lord." He nodded, standing straight like the navy man he was.

Royce waved his hand at his brother-in-law. "Sit down. Enough with the formality."

The younger man smiled as he sat. Ambros was the youngest captain in the royal fleet and his sister's favorite brother. Vivienne, Royce's wife, had five. Ambros landed in the middle of the brood and, more often than not, could be found at his sister and Royce's table when on land.

"You're the first to hear this news," Royce said. He thought he should be happier to know Lucia was alive, but there was still a vast sea between the queen and Moranth, and a great deal he didn't know. He hated not knowing everything.

Ambros leaned closer. "What news is that?"

"I've found Lucia."

A wide smile broke across the captain's face. "The brigands have been caught, then? She's safe?"

Royce sighed. "She's alive and sailing with The Medusa. And I do mean *with*." Ambros' brows nearly met his hairline. "Exactly. She's at Silver Cove, and from what my man says, she's bedding the fair captain as well."

"Course she is." From Ambros's laugh, Royce suspected the younger man was recalling some of the more colorful stories he'd related of the princess Lucia had been. "You have someone, then? In Silver Cove?" Royce quirked a brow, and Ambros smiled. "Foolish question."

"I need you to go intercept The Medusa, Ambros. Not engage. Not destroy. Intercept and escort."

"You can't believe a pirate ship like that is just going to let a Moranthese vessel pull alongside? It could be a trap."

"I want you to take all precautions. Don't trust anyone but Lucia. I know this puts you and your crew in a difficult position, but it could be our only chance to get her back safely. Ramir has agents in Silver Cove as well. We have to get to her first. The last thing we need is The Medusa getting overtaken. I've been made to understand Ramir has sent The Deceit after her.

"Shit," Ambros cursed. "You want me to go after two of the best pirate crews on the seas?"

"I do."

Ambros stood and replaced his hat, straightening it. "We'll be gone with the tide, my lord."

Royce nodded. "Thank you."

———

He caught up with Sebastian just as the young man was about to enter the council chamber. The guards on either side were at attention, working in unison to open the two massive doors. Royce put his hand out, slamming one, to the astonishment of the guards, and plucked at the royal heir with his other. "Walk with me," he whispered, leading Sebastian down a deserted hall.

The young lord frowned as he shook Royce off. "We have a meeting. What's going on? Do you have some news?"

He gave the lad a smirk before turning his head to make sure they were alone. "I'll give it to our fair queen. She knows what she's about." Sebastian looked puzzled. "She's on Silver Cove *with* the crew of The Medusa. My man says she's—" He stopped, unsure how much he should reveal. Lucia was like a mother to the boy, and Royce wagered he had no desire to know about her love life. From what the message said, it seemed as though Lucia was doing more than all right and enjoying the company of The Medusa's lovely young captain. "She's unharmed," he settled on.

The weight of the world looked to lift from Sebastian's shoulders. "We have to get her help," he said excitedly. "Can your man get her out, bring her home?"

"I've told him to try to make contact but not draw any attention to her. From what I understand, she's as safe as she can be for the moment."

"But the pirates?"

"Like I said, your cousin knows what she's about. Our man believes the captain of The Medusa means to bring her home and earn herself a pardon."

Sebastian paced the hall, a finger to his lips. "The Medusa was the D'Allyon ship, yes?" Royce nodded, pleased that his protégé was putting the pieces together for himself. "You said, 'herself'. The young captain is then Lady D'Allyon?"

"She will be if the queen grants her pardon, yes."

"Is there anything we can do to help? Can we not send a ship? The whole of our navy?"

Royce snickered. "Your loyalty is admirable, but if we send a ship in, we'll be starting a war we won't win. Silver Cove is a world unto itself, untouchable. Trade won't survive if we have every pirate fleet on the seas after us, and *only* us."

"Then we send a ship to intercept The Medusa and act as an escort."

"Indeed, my lord," Royce said proudly. "I've already done it. I've sent Ambros after her. If luck holds, Lucia will be back here in one piece within a fortnight."

LUCIA

It had been a shit day for finding game. A blowing rain had come in overnight, and the animals Lucia had successfully tracked earlier in the week seemed to have disappeared. Crouching down, she blew at a stray lock of hair, a small sickle blade in hand. Her bow, on loan from Cyril's grandson, was slung across her back, easy enough to get to if she needed it.

She'd woken early that morning, pressing a kiss to Alessandra's forehead as she slept, sheets tangled beneath her, before leaving for the woods. That had been hours ago. Her breeches were soaked to her knees from the morning dew, and her stomach growled, but she didn't want to return empty-handed. She spotted the same sort of mushrooms Rafe had pointed out on their hunt days earlier and stooped low to cut them from their stems.

A twig snapped behind her.

With an arrow notched as she spun on her heels, Lucia searched the mist for any sign she was not alone. She stayed still and silent for a moment or two.

The hair at the back of her neck stood on end, but she could see nothing. A low rumble of thunder rolled through the thick undergrowth, and she cursed, sliding the bow back over her chest as she began her trudge back to the cottage.

Lucia had made herself right at home in the seaside cottage she shared with Alessandra. The two had been cohabitating on the island for a little over a week. Lucia had begun to think it would be a shame to leave the simple life behind. It was quiet once they were away from the rowdy town, so she could sleep late, wrapped in her pirate's arms.

There were no council meetings to attend, no affairs of state to decide. It was with a heavy heart that she looked to her future. She deeply missed Sebastian and Royce, but had no desire to return to her old life. She felt terrible for not getting a message to them, letting them know she was all right, but that would have been foolish, and knowing Royce as she did, she thought he probably already knew she was alive.

Instead of worrying about what she couldn't control, she had settled down into the role of *wife?* She wasn't exactly sure. She didn't think she particularly needed to figure out a title for her relationship with Alessandra, though the crew, and increasingly Margthe, had begun to treat her as such. She wasn't much for cooking, despite the older woman doing her best to teach her, and cleaning was best left to Alessandra, who grew disgruntled when unable to find her favorite pair of polished black boots or a battered book that Lucia had put away.

What she could do, and enjoyed doing, was foraging and hunting. Thanks to years of practice, Lucia was deadly with a bow. After a day of following a game trail through the thick underbrush with Rafe, she had gone home with enough rabbits to provide Margthe for days.

Lucia paused, taking a breath at the cottage's threshold—*it will be ending soon, as everyone knows*. Dripping wet as she entered the house, Lucia set the bow and quiver of arrows by the door, then wrung out her hair and stripped off her soaked clothes.

Alessandra's hands wound around her naked waist as the pirate's chin tucked into the crook of her damp neck. "Mmm," she purred, "my wild huntress."

"Your huntress has returned with nothing to show for her troubles, I'm afraid."

With her lips grazing Lucia's long neck, Alessandra sighed. "Thankfully, I'm very easily pleased. Besides, you know we can always eat at Margthe's." She squeezed her tighter, and Lucia couldn't help but give herself over to the tranquility of the moment. The rain pelting against the thatched roof, dripping onto the small porch, added to her sense of calm. And of course, the mere presence of Alessandra.

Lucia didn't want her to leave, but she knew Alessandra was set to meet with the shipwright. "Don't you have somewhere to be?"

Alessandra's hands roved from her hips, cupping Lucia's breasts. "Nothing is more important than this moment with you."

Lucia's body moved in time with the thundering of Alessandra's heart beat. She ground her rear back against Alessandra's pelvis as she threw an arm up, cradling her pirate's head in its crook.

Alessandra gave a restrained purr in answer, the sound reverberating down Lucia's spine. Her fingertips caressed the curve of Alessandra's cheek, as her mouth kissed tenderly along an earlobe, the pirate's jaw, finding Alessandra's lips soft and ready.

Once the morning rains had passed, Alessandra rose from their bed as Lucia watched, already bereft at the passing of their respite.

"I won't be gone too long," Alessandra said, tucking her shirt into her breeches. "Hopefully, Will has plugged up all the holes, and she'll stay afloat long enough to get you home."

Lucia likewise, left the warmth of the tangled sheets, pulled a shirt over her head and shimmied into pants.

"Will can take as long as he likes," she grumbled low enough that Alessandra couldn't hear much.

"I didn't catch that," she said, slouching into her coat.

"Nothing." Lucia pouted, but only briefly. *I have to go back and face what's to come. It's my responsibility and no one else's.* "Will you be back for dinner?"

Alessandra chuckled. "Are you going to cook it?"

While perched on the edge of the bed, face turned up to her lover, Lucia beckoned Alessandra forward. "Come here," she said. Alessandra bent low and caught her mouth in a kiss. Lucia fisted her hands in the heavy wool of the coat, not letting go until she'd had her fill. Her tongue darted across Alessandra's as her nipples peaked. They'd spent nearly half the morning abed, but she wanted more. Alessandra's knee landed next to her thigh.

"Damn it, woman." Alessandra groaned as their cores met. Her voice was tight, her lips still a breath from Lucia's. "I have to go."

"Ugh." Lucia let her go with a slight push. "I know. I know."

Alessandra's brow rose, a smirk on her lips as she ran her tongue over them. "You'll save that thought, though?"

"If you're lucky."

Lucia took the opportunity of Alessandra's absence to settle down with a book, a weighty tome on the history of seafaring. It held very little interest for her but let her attempt to focus on something other than the feeling of unease that had been with her since the woods. She sat by a crackling fire, the promise of dinner at Cyril and Margthe's ahead, but still couldn't focus on the book in her hands. The words kept slipping from her mind, untamable on the page.

She was sure she hadn't been alone out there, hunting. She hadn't told Alessandra about her suspicions. It would only worry her. Alessandra had been uncomfortable leaving her side since she'd returned from St. Tialda's shrine and Lucia couldn't risk having her time in the woods taken from her as well.

The storm shutter banged loudly against the window, and Lucia jumped, dropping her book to the floor. "You're being ridiculous," she muttered to herself, picking it up and sitting back down.

Am I being ridiculous? What if someone recognized me at the tavern that first day or saw me in town with Rafe? Lucia had not ventured back into town after that morning in the sanctuary of St. Tialda. It had been unwise on all their parts, and Margthe had privately given them all a talking to about it.

To Lucia, her words had been kind, just as they had been the day the woman had found her crying. 'You're not alone anymore,' Margthe had told her. 'You must stop living as if you are.' Simple enough advice, but it was as if the understanding of it had not clicked until the woman said those words aloud. Lucia had always lived for her kingdom and her people, but not for herself. She wasn't sure what Margthe had told Alessandra, but the pirate had been loath to leave her side since, even more so than she previously had.

Alessandra would be returning from the shipwright any moment, and with her return would come the announcement that their time in Silver Cove would be over. Lucia tried to soothe herself from the thought, despite her grief at leaving and the rawness of her nerves, by going back to her book.

Becoming hungry, she was just sitting down at the table with a wheel of cheese in hand when a knock sounded at the cottage's door. She jumped again, then shook her head in annoyance with herself—surely it was Margthe, or one of her brood, come to call. Still, she took the loaded flintlock pistol from where it hung above the hearth before she went to the door, cursing herself for not using the rusty lock, having grown complacent in her happiness.

Her fingers just brushed the brass knob when the door flew open. A man of middling height, age, and looks stood before her, his eyes wide as she leveled the pistol at his chest.

"Who the hell are you?" she asked, heart racing.

"Your Majesty," he inclined his head slightly, "Lord Aldana sent me. My name is Ferran. I have a ship at the ready. We can be gone and on our way to Moranth before the brigands even realize you are missing."

Lucia's brows drew together. "I'm not being held captive." She bit her tongue. "And I'm not the queen," she quickly amended in a passable Wellingisle accent that would have made her mother proud.

The man's dark eyes gleamed, a knowing smile forming. "You must forgive me, but I was at your coronation, Majesty. I could never forget gazing upon the most beautiful creature in the land."

Lucia backed away, her hip bumping painfully against the dining table. "I'm not going with you."

It made sense that Royce would have his spies looking for her, but it also made sense for an asset of Ramir's to pretend to be from Moranth. There had been no news of her since her kidnapping, and possibly less of The Medusa—*Until we made port.* Her gut tightened. They were close enough to the capital for word to have reached her court, plenty of time for Royce to have dispatched a crew to rescue her. *But I don't need rescuing. I am precisely where I want to be. I am with Alessandra. Where is she?*

Lucia kept the pistol aimed at the man. He looked like a spy, completely average in every sense. "How do I know it was Lord Aldana that sent you? You could be a spy for Vetreon just as easily."

"Majesty," he took a step toward her, "forgive me, but you're coming with me whether you want to or not."

ALESSANDRA

Alessandra brought her hand to her eyes, shielding them from the setting sun. The shipwright's crew had done a far finer job than she paid for, and she had every intention of thanking Will properly if they survived the trip back to Moranth.

Will looked pleased with himself. "What d'ya think, Captain? She gonna float?"

She knew he was teasing her. The Medusa's mast was new, and some fresh sails had been placed where shrapnel rendered the old ones useless. The Deceit's cannon had made quick work of the gorgon figurehead, her once lush figure and curling snakes no longer recognizable—she still looked a fright. The important thing, though, was that The Medusa would sail, as Will had promised. In her current condition, and if the winds were favorable, they could make the capital in a matter of days. The thought filled Alessandra with dread. Lucia would once more be a queen, and she a pirate.

"Captain!"

She turned to see Smith racing toward her, a hand squashing down his red cap to keep it from flying off. The young sailor doubled over as he reached her, taking great lungfuls of air.

Heart racing, Alessandra grabbed him by his shoulder. "What is it, Smith?"

"The tavern," he stammered. "Rafe's been stabbed."

The pair ran full tilt into town and through the doors of The Bronze Sail.

An unusual stillness hung over the tavern as Alessandra followed Smith in. At the time of day, there should be at least a dozen or so half-drunk sailors telling embellished tales and having a laugh or a fight. Instead, Alessandra found tables overturned, and her boots crunched on broken glass as she moved closer to the tight knot of her crew.

Kier was in a corner; his lip bloodied, his eyes turning black. Two of The Medusa's sailors stood, arms crossed, in front of him. Rafe was still on his feet, though two more men supported him under his arms, and a red stain bloomed from a tear in his striped shirt.

Cam came lumbering to her side. "Glad to see you," he said. "Hope that shipwright fixed you up, Alex. Time for you lot to be on your way."

She grasped the man by his arm. "What the hell happened here?"

"I'm sorry, Captain, I'm sorry," Kier muttered through ragged breaths.

Her jaw clenched. Two of her best mates were wounded. Her tavern was in shambles. *For what?* She felt ill. "Rafe," she pressed her hand to his blood-stained shirt, "you alright?" *What will I do if he isn't?*

He's my best friend and a fine sailor. I need him if we're going to war.

His cheeks were ashen, but he gave her a wry grin. "I'll survive," he slurred, head nodding as he faded in and out of consciousness.

"Set him down there," she said, pointing to an upright table and chairs. He winced as he took a seat. "What happened?" she asked again, leaning in close. No one seemed to want to tell her the truth. It wouldn't have been the first time there was fighting amongst her crew, but there was a different air to this quarrel that she needed to understand.

"Captain," Rafe's eyes were glassy, but his grip on her shoulder was strong, "the lad told someone about *her*."

Her breath caught. *Lucia.*

Alessandra's eyes darted around the room. Kier was clearly drunk, as were most of the crew, probably not much help. *Cam.* She stood, knocking a chair over in her haste. The tavern keeper was back behind the bar, clearing away shattered bottles. Alessandra slammed her fist down. "I need to know everything."

"It was busy, so I don't know everything," he started. "Kier was in early, before the rest of the crew. Had words with his fiancée, from what I gathered, and came to drown his sorrows. Next thing I knew, he and Rafe were tussling. A few of the crew joined in, but mostly to separate the two fools. Then Rafe was staggering, and Kier had a bloody knife in his hand." Cam gestured at Kier, still crouched on the floor, muttering. "He must have said something to the wrong person, is all I can figure from what Rafe was shouting at him." He shook his head, sighing. "That wasn't the queen's maid you brought in here, was it?"

Bile rose at the back of Alessandra's throat. Lucia was in danger. Imminent danger.

Smith and another crew member yanked Kier from the floor, his shirt covered in vomit. "Where do you want him, Captain?" Smith asked.

Her world was coming apart at the seams.

"Get them both to my house. Rafe will need to be looked at, and Kier needs a hot bowl of stew more than anything." Alessandra turned all her focus onto Smith, knowing that if she were going to be in a fight, he was the best she had to take with her. "You drop him." She nodded at Kier. "You're with me." She didn't wait to see who picked Kier back up, only heard the thud of his body meeting the wooden floor and the hurried bootsteps following close at her heels as she made for her cottage.

With full darkness a heartbeat away, Alessandra and Smith were both panting as they closed in on the home, their swords jangling at their sides, when a scream, *Lucia's,* tore through the night, followed by the sound of a pistol discharging.

"No," Alessandra whispered.

She charged hard at the open door, her sword drawn and Smith on her heels, when something—*Lucia*—crashed into her. Both women went tumbling to the ground as Smith jumped aside. Disengaging as quickly as she could and hauling Lucia up with her, Alessandra's blade was back at the ready when a stranger appeared at the door, his sword drawn. Smith stepped in front of both women, giving them the briefest of moments to catch their breath.

"Are you hurt?" Alessandra said, eyes and hands checking her lover for injuries.

Lucia was gasping for air, her hair wild, the flintlock pistol loose in her hand. "I'm fine. I'm fine," she said, pushing at Alessandra. "Don't kill him, Smith."

The pirate shot a glance back, confusion clear on his face. "What?"

The unknown man stepped forward slowly, warily. "I'm just here for Her Majesty. Lord Royce Aldana sent me to get her home safely." He held out a hand, his sword clattering to the cottage's floor. "I swear I didn't mean her any harm. She attacked me."

"Damned pistol misfired," Lucia spat.

Alessandra saw Smith trying to hide his smirk by wiping a hand across his mouth. She took Lucia by the arms, not sure whether she wanted to laugh or cry with relief that she was safe. "Is that true?"

Lucia's throat bobbed, eyes cutting to the side. "I don't know. I assume both Royce and Ramir have men looking for me. Either way, if I'm going home, it's with you. I told the bastard I wasn't in any danger, but he *insisted*."

Alessandra's mind tried to make sense of the night's events as her stomach flipped. Lucia had a chance to leave her, and she hadn't taken it.

"Did you see who Kier was talking to?" she asked Smith.

The sailor hadn't sheathed his sword, but it was held lightly by his side. "Aye, Captain, only just. He was leaving as I was sitting down. This," he pointed the tip of his sword at the flustered stranger, "isn't him."

"Shit," she spat.

"What are you talking about?" Lucia asked.

Alessandra searched the darkened landscape. There was nothing there except two swinging lanterns making their way up the hill toward them as the sound of her drunk crew's singing carried across the way. "Let's get inside," she said, gently pushing Lucia toward the safety of her home.

Once inside, Alessandra sat down heavily, swiped her hat from her head, and shook out her loose hair. She wanted to make sure Lucia was safe before she got into what she figured would be a lengthy conversation. "Smith, find something to tie ..." She opened a hand in invitation for the agent to speak.

"Ferran," he muttered. He was backed into a corner, unarmed, but Alessandra wasn't taking any chances. Even if he was who he said, that didn't change the fact he had tried to force Lucia to go with him.

"Tie Ferran up. We'll take him with us. He can sail back to the Moranth in our hold. Aldana can affirm his identity, or not."

"What?" the man interjected.

"Do you know who else on the island is after the queen?" Alessandra asked, ignoring his protest.

"The Deceit."

16

LUCIA

Alessandra, Smith, and Lucia unleashed a collective curse at the news. Defoe and his crew were the very last thing they needed.

Lucia was fuming. She was so very close to making it home with Alessandra at her side, and she'd be damned if anything got in her way. "We have to go. Now," she said, looking around the room.

Setting the pistol down, she grabbed her few belongings, an emerald silk scarf and a battered gold bangle from Alessandra. A commotion outside caused her to stop and straighten from where she'd been digging through the books to find her favorite—she wasn't about to leave without knowing who the dragon-slaying heroine ended up with, the king or the wizard.

"What is that?" Lucia asked.

Smith was still in the midst of tying up a cooperative Ferran. The spy's wrists were bound, but his legs were free. If he wanted to attempt an escape, it wouldn't be difficult, but he seemed content with his lot for the moment. Alessandra had gone into the bedroom and returned carrying Lucia's sword belt, cutlass, and hat, tossing them to her as she made for the front door.

Lucia heard her shout into the night, "Get in here, you lot!" Alessandra poked her head back in. "Lucia, clear the table. Rafe has been stabbed. Smith."

"Captain?" the sailor asked, his knotwork complete.

"Run over and get Margthe and Cyril. Tell her to bring her kit as Rafe will need stitching, and tell Cyril we'll be sailing on the tide. Hell," she groaned.

Smith nodded, then nearly collided with his mates as he ran out the door.

Lucia's eyes widened, her mind racing, as she moved her afternoon snack of cheese and an orange from the table. She was worried. She genuinely liked Rafe, and more than that, her life was clearly in danger. She was sure Ramir was behind the attack. *Why else would Defoe be after me?*

The group of men carrying Rafe and Kier stumbled through the entry. Rafe whimpered, his face possessing an unhealthy pallor as the men lay him out on the table.

Alessandra clutched Rafe's hand while standing over him. "You going to make it?"

"I'll be alright. You've got to get her out of here. It isn't safe anymore."

Lucia paused in buckling on her sword belt, taken aback by his words. He wasn't worried for himself, but for her. She stepped to the pirate's other side, taking up his free hand. Rafe flashed one of his too charming smiles, though it looked as if it pained him to do it.

"Don't worry about me, Your Majesty. You've got this one to protect, eh?" He jerked his chin toward Alessandra.

"I will." She gave his hand a squeeze. "I promise."

"What, in the name of all that's holy, is going on?" Margthe burst into the room with Cyril puffing behind her. "Rafe! Saints preserve us." She moved quicker than Lucia thought possible, shooing her and Alessandra away. "Start boiling water," she ordered over her shoulder.

"On it," Alessandra answered, ducking out to the water pump.

The little house was crammed full of people, the din growing louder. "If you don't live here, get out," Margthe said, her tone brooking no argument. The lads shuffled out of the cottage into the night, but it was clear from the noise outside that they hadn't gone far.

Lucia edged closer to the table, fascinated as the woman looked at Rafe's wound. It was a jagged, weeping thing, skittering diagonally across his ribcage. "Will he be alright?" Lucia asked, her voice barely a whisper.

"Aye." Margthe nodded, her fingers probing the cut. "It's shallow enough, but you'll be needing stitching," she said to Rafe. "What were you thinking?"

Lucia looked up as Alessandra returned with a pot of water and set it over the fire, stoking it before giving Cyril's sleeve a tug. The man had, until that moment, been leaning against a wall, staring at the silent, restrained Ferran. She followed the pair to the back room that had once been Alessandra's father's bedroom.

Alessandra was pacing. "Cyril, gather the crew. I think almost every man is here or sleeping it off close by. The tide will be with us if we move fast. The Deceit has to be on the other side of the island for us to have missed her. It'll take time for them to know what's happened and move into position to block our escape."

Cyril stopped her frantic movements by placing a hand on her shoulder. "Lass, what is going on?"

Lucia gritted her teeth. This was her fault. All of it. If she hadn't been aboard, if she hadn't been shortsighted and enamored with the idea of playing the rogue, Rafe wouldn't have been stabbed trying to protect her. "I could turn myself over," she offered. *It is the only way.* She'd come to care for and respect The Medusa's crew. She couldn't let them risk their lives for her.

Alessandra rounded on her. "Absolutely not."

Cyril threw up his hands. "Turn yourself over to who?" he asked in obvious frustration.

Alessandra gave him the basics of their situation. "Kier was drunk and gave information to a man working for Ramir, at least, I assume as much. Rafe found out about it, and they fought, though I don't think Kier meant any real harm. I'll deal with him later."

"Is that the man tied up in your kitchen?" Cyril said.

"No, he's a Moranthese spy or one from Vetreon—wrong place, wrong time. He'll be coming with us, but he doesn't seem to be a threat. The problem is The Deceit."

"Devils take them," Cyril cursed under his breath. "Sent by Ramir?"

"I believe so," Lucia whispered.

"Captain's right," Cyril spat. "We're getting you home safe." He nodded at Lucia. "And if those Deceit bastards come looking for a fight, they'll find one."

Lucia nearly burst into tears, overcome by Cyril's protectiveness. She bobbed her head. "Thank you," she said, voice thick with gratitude.

He nodded once more, and the three returned to Margthe and Rafe. The woman was finishing off her stitches, and a bit of color had returned to the pirate's cheeks, though he was far from his usual rakish self.

"Can he sail?" Alessandra asked.

Margthe breathed heavily. "He can. It's a risk to move him, though. That wound could open back up and fester, but I suppose, as stubborn as he is, the risk is the same here as at sea." Margthe tousled Rafe's hair. "No climbing the rigging or showing off for at least a week." To which he gave a solemn nod.

"Good," Alessandra said. "We have to move quick. Let's get you on your feet." She moved to take Rafe's arm while Cyril took the other.

Margthe blocked their path to lock her arms around her husband's neck, kissing him for a long moment. "You come back. Do you understand me?"

The old pirate's face turned red as a fond smile played on his lips. "Aye, I'll come back, love."

Lucia caught Alessandra's gaze, locking eyes as the elderly couple said their goodbyes. She didn't want to ever make such a pronouncement. She didn't want to ever be parted from her own pirate. She flicked tears from her eyes as they marched toward the door.

A good many of The Medusa's men were milling about outside the cottage, some sitting slouched against the house, others already snoring.

"What are we doing, Captain?" Smith asked, emerging from the shadows.

"We're getting out of here as fast as we can. Send some of the lads to round up as much of the crew as they can. We've only got a few hours before the tide turns, and then we'll be easy pickings for The Deceit."

"Aye, Captain." Smith turned, gathered a handful of sailors, and disappeared down the hill.

Lucia was struggling with her emotions—fear, excitement, rage, love—which were fighting for dominance within her as she watched the men scatter in search of their crewmates, a core group staying behind to escort them and ready the ship.

Alessandra took her by the arm. "It will be alright. Do you have all your things?"

Lucia steeled herself. Her course was set. "I think so," she said, patting her pockets, checking that her sword was secure.

"Alright, come on then." Alessandra prodded her. "We have to make haste."

Lucia stood rooted to the ground, looking longingly back at their home. "I'll never see this place again."

"You don't know that," Alessandra whispered, her fingers lacing with Lucia's.

Smiling sadly, Lucia brought Alessandra's hand to her lips, planting a kiss to her palm. "This has been the happiest time of my life."

Alessandra sighed. "Lucia, I—"

A high whistle cut through the night.

"Someone's coming, Captain," cried one of her crew.

Dropping Alessandra's hand, Lucia squinted into the night, but all she could see were the silhouettes of palm trees and clouds limned by the moon's light.

"Don't think they're friendly," the voice called again.

"How many?" Alessandra asked.

"Maybe a dozen."

Lucia glanced around, seeing about the same number of Medusa men.

"Fuck! Get Rafe out of the way."

"I can fight," he protested.

"No, you can't. Stay in cover and shut up." Alessandra pointed back to the cottage. "Someone secure the spy to a tree or something. Don't need to be watching our backs as well," she said, unsheathing her sword. Lucia followed suit, as did the men around them. "Guess we'll get to see how good you really are in a fight." She winked at Lucia.

"Guess so."

Lucia prepared herself for battle by taking deep, slow breaths. She'd never been in a true fight where killing was the goal before. Her mind quieted to a single thought, *I must survive.*

Having lost the advantage of surprise, The Deceit's men shouted, running full tilt at their opponents.

Alessandra raised her sword. "Let's make short work of these bastards!"

The men and Lucia hoisted their swords, shouting in approval before the two bands of pirates clashed on the rocky hilltop.

Lucia stayed at Alessandra's side, trusting her skill to keep her right flank safe. She dodged a man's flailing blade, knocking the back of his head with the butt of her sword as he went, then saw Alessandra skewer him as he fell. Another came at her. She was shocked by the force of his sword as hers blocked his downward strike, the hit reverberating through her body with a bone-shaking ferocity. He was a huge fellow, and the blow nearly knocked the wind out of her, but she recovered, dancing out of his reach as he brought his sword down again.

She wouldn't survive a continued assault of the man's brutal, unforgiving force, but she could make it if she kept moving. She dodged again, avoiding a wide swinging arc meant to split her in two. Rolling, Lucia came to her knees, and with a backward lash, delivered a killing stroke across the man's middle. She heard him scream but was already moving.

A hand reached out to help her up.

Smith had arrived and was standing above her, smiling. "Fine work, Your Majesty," he said, hauling her up.

She was breathing hard, but she was alive.

Groans, shouts, and curses echoed around her as the clanging of sword meeting sword fell off, and the fighting came to a bloody end.

Alessandra grasped her coat sleeve. "Let's go."

A few of The Medusa's crew were limping or lightly scathed, fairing far better than their foes, most of whom lay dead or seriously wounded. Lucia didn't have the time to think about the man she'd killed as they still needed to make it to the ship. She'd have time later to contemplate the life she'd taken, though she didn't think the man's death would weigh too heavily on her. He had been trying to kill her, after all.

They made their way to the shore, alert for another attack, but none came. Lucia and Alessandra helped Rafe into a rowboat as Smith locked the oars in place, Ferran looking miserable in the back. The others were already being ferried to the waiting ship, having been pulled from taverns and beds. All were clamoring for details of the fight. Lucia climbed the long rope ladder without aid, happier than she could have believed to be back aboard The Medusa, with Silver Cove at her back.

Alessandra shouted, "Stand by to make sail!" The command carried across the deck, and men scurried to their places, no doubt many still drunk. However, the crew knew what they were about and moved without delay. Alessandra nodded to Cyril. "Make sail," she ordered.

"Make sail!" Cyril relayed, his voice booming in the night.

Lucia watched, still in awe, as the mainsail unfurled. The Medusa was underway, pointing to Moranth.

ALESSANDRA

Their bodies lay close together in the night as the moonlight traced its way across the floor, highlighting Alessandra's desk and her mother's silver candlesticks against the darkness. Neither woman was sleeping despite the lateness of the hour or their well-earned exhaustion after a day at sea. With the repairs Will had made at Silver Cove, it would only be a handful of days until they made port.

"We'll be back in Moranthese waters tomorrow."

Lucia sighed. "Shame, I liked being a pirate. Being a queen is so tedious in comparison." She kissed

Alessandra's hand before snuggling in closer. "I told you once that I was jealous of all this, of all the freedom you have. I had no idea what I was missing then."

"Mmhm," Alessandra acknowledged, "and now you know."

"And now I know," Lucia repeated wistfully. "Do you have an answer for me yet?"

Alessandra flipped to her back, staring at the dark ceiling. She didn't need Lucia to elaborate; she knew the question she was asking. *Will I stay with her?* For weeks, she had pushed the question aside. The answers she had hoped to somehow find in her father's journal had eluded her, nor had their time together in Silver Cove made her choice easier.

The answer she kept coming back to was *yes*. *Yes,* of course she would go with Lucia. She would do anything in her power to help the woman she loved in the coming fight against Vetreon. *But at what cost?* She feared losing herself in her effort to save Lucia. *And what of my crew? This isn't their fight.* She could possibly gain Lucia only to lose her family.

The last time Alessandra had been in Moranth without fearing for her life, she'd been five years old. By that time, her mother had ingrained into her the manners and rituals deemed necessary for a lady at court. Alessandra knew the life of a noble, remembered it, remembered her discomfort in it. She hated when her family left their vast estate by the sea to come to the capital every year, as the king demanded. She hated the stiff dresses and the hours it took to put her hair into the elaborate braids and coils fashionable at the time.

Will I have to do so again, or can I keep true to my taste? Of course, her choice of clothing was the least of her worries. She would be under constant strain if she regained her title and lands, which were run by the Crown in her absence, and her new command of the Navy. Aye, it was true that ship life as an officer, then captain, was stressful enough for any one person, but it was a life she knew, the sort she was comfortable with.

Being a lady, being an admiral were challenges that were outside her scope. She would have men and ships she didn't know under her command. She would have to keep her wits constantly about her and question every single person's motive at court. On a pirate ship, things were more straightforward; most of it boiled down to wenching, fighting, or thieving. All three activities she excelled at.

Most importantly, though, was how this would change her relationship with Lucia. They would no longer be equals as they had been on their island, nor enjoy the domestic ease of their life on Silver Cove. Lucia's word would be law once they were in Moranth. *Where will that line be drawn behind closed doors?*

Still, Lucia was giving her a path forward that hadn't existed before they met. If it had, Alessandra had been unable to see it. A pirate's life might be fairly simple, but it also tended to be fairly short, and she had seen enough of life to know she wanted to live it. There was almost no greater gift Lucia could give her than to have the ability to live that life without fear. A pardon would give her that freedom.

Her hand caught at Lucia's in the dark, cradling it against her heart. "I accept your offer, Your Majesty." Trepidation lay heavy in Alessandra's voice. The new life presented to her was terrifying, but the woman at her side was worth all of it and more—that didn't mean she wouldn't mourn the loss of her old one.

Lucia huffed. "It sounds so strange to hear that title again after all this time. Please don't call me that when it's just us. I want things always to be just as they are now."

Excited as Alessandra was to have finally made a decision, she was brooding. She didn't want to be. She wanted more than anything to fling herself fully into Lucia's world without a longing backward glance, but she couldn't. "They won't be, though, you know that. You're the queen. That carries weight. I'll be under your command, your subject."

"What if I wasn't the queen?"

Alessandra's heart skipped a beat. "If you weren't the queen, then we'd all be hanged as soon as we made port." She deadpanned, not really amused but unwilling to delve too deeply into her comment. *Can't it be enough that I've agreed to stay?*

"That's not funny."

"No, nor is the thought of you abdicating. There is no way to avoid war—you've told me that—and knowing what I do of the world, I think you're right. Are you saying you think there's anyone more capable of winning it than you? You think Sebastian would be safer without you?"

"Without you and I, you mean?"

A smile crept over Alessandra's lips. "Aye, you and I."

A heavy sigh came from Lucia's side of the bed, and Alessandra had her answer. They both had a larger role to play, and it was time to step into them, or else the consequences would be dire. "Come here," she breathed, folding Lucia's naked body into the safety of her arms. "I think the two of us should make our way into the capital alone. Not risk The Medusa or the lads."

"I'm not swimming to shore again," Lucia teased.

Alessandra gave her a squeeze. "No, we can be dropped at Marshport and ride in from there.

Lucia lay in her arms until morning while Alessandra spent most of the night fretting about her looming responsibilities.

The next day dawned to a bright, cloudless sky, and the gulls circling and calling overhead spoke of their nearness to land. As Alessandra scanned the horizon from the deck, she felt hands at her waist. *Lucia.* Shaking off the usual reserve she showed while on deck, she beamed as Lucia's lips whispered in her ear, "Good morning."

"Morning," she purred, letting her head drop back to rest on Lucia's shoulder. Her eyes closed against the golden morning as salt spray danced on her lips and the soft pads of Lucia's fingers pressed firmly at her hip bones.

Though the crew knew their captain and previous captive were romantically involved, the women had been more circumspect for the last three days on deck in deference to them than they had been at port. There was a reason women weren't usually on board a ship, at least not for long periods and not in great numbers. For Alessandra to have been brought up from girlhood on board was somewhat unheard of. Yet, here she was, with her paramour, her desire sated each night while most of her crew went without. She couldn't say exactly when they would come across a Moranthese Royal Navy vessel or make it the capital itself, but it would be soon, a day or two at most. Surely, the crew would allow them these last moments without malice.

"This is heaven." Lucia sighed contentedly.

Her words brought Alessandra back to reality. "No, this is just the calm before the storm."

Hours later, Alessandra, Rafe, and Lucia were at the helm. Rafe was giving Lucia a lesson in ship steering, not being able to bear the tension of the wheel without causing further injury to his healing wound. Alessandra stood back to admire the cut of Lucia's breeches, the look of concentration on her face as she listened intently to Rafe, and the straining muscles of the queen's forearms as she manned the wheel.

"Ship!" Smith shouted from the crow's nest, wrecking the peaceful moment.

Lucia looked to Rafe as Alessandra searched through her spyglass. "Keep her steady," he said.

"It's Moranthese!" Alessandra called back. "Run up the white flag! Kier, get up here and man the helm!" The young sailor, having taken a good number of lashes and enduring a long mastheading, was back in the good graces of both captain and crew. He rushed to take up his position.

"Aye, Captain," Smith responded, removing the D'Allyon crest of a black lion on a gold background, and then unfurling a white piece of sail, one never before used on The Medusa.

It was a strange sight indeed. Alessandra momentarily cringed at what she assumed would be her father's harsh words for her decision—*A D'Allyon never accepts defeat*. Still, she was no longer a child but a woman, a captain in her own right. The decision was hers.

"Cyril, load the guns and have the lads at the ready in case we're dealing with an idiot. Just the chain shot. We aren't going for casualties."

The man laughed. "Aye, Captain."

Even with the white flag up, it wasn't unheard of for a surrendering ship to be decimated by an overly excited captain. The chain shot would cripple a ship, usually without killing too many people.

Alessandra's eyes turned to Lucia. Their lives were about to change, and neither could say whether for better or worse. "Are you ready?" she asked as if Lucia were not simply returning to her home and her previous life.

"I don't want to leave you," Lucia whispered.

Alessandra gave her a smile. "No need to be frightened. You're not going anywhere without me."

Then came a sound every sailor dreaded, cannon fire. Alessandra grabbed Lucia, throwing her to the deck and covering her with her body. The shot thundered, missing The Medusa—from the closeness of the splash—by mere feet.

"You alright?" she asked Lucia as she crouched low, edging toward the ship's rail. Another volley whistled through the air—this time, it didn't miss. The Medusa shook violently as a cannonball slammed into her.

Alessandra was at Lucia's side as soon as her ship ceased its shuddering. Lucia was holding her side, gasping like she'd taken a hit, but she nodded. "I'm fine." Alessandra could barely hear her, but she breathed a sigh of relief.

"Stay down." She chanced a look over the rail, her eyes narrowed. "Fuck." Her ship was hit. A hole was blown in her side, and a cannon was hanging halfway out. No doubt someone had lost their life. She called up to the lookout. "What do you see, Smith?"

The fog was so thick, the silence after the shot deafening, but the lookout made no comment as his eyes scanned the waters, trying in vain to discern the direction of the fired cannon. "Not much, Captain."

"God, there's two of them!" Alessandra shouted, pointing as another cannonball howled toward them. The lead ball crashed into the ship's side, sending more splinters flying.

It wasn't the Moranthese ship that had fired. Alessandra felt ill as Defoe's flag came into view. They had hidden in the morning fog and now, there was little hope for escape. "It's The Deceit!"

"Our white flag is already up. Captain, what should we do?" Cyril's face was bloody from a weeping head wound, but it appeared superficial.

Alessandra held up a hand. The Moranthese ship was still silent as she sliced through the water, but Alessandra saw The Deceit closing. This was the second time the bastard had surprised her.

"Fuck!" she exclaimed as another volley pounded into The Medusa's side, sending her diving for cover. Lucia was there, hands over her head. When she glanced up at Alessandra, her eyes were wide with fear.

"We can't just sit here, Captain!" Cyril yelled into the din.

Lucia grabbed hold of her. "I'm all right! Get out there." She attempted a smile as she shoved Alessandra to her feet. "You can't worry about me right now."

Pursing her lips in determination, Alessandra shook her head, gave Lucia one last look, then stood. *I need to get a better view.* Alessandra ducked and ran down the steps to the lower deck, weaving through her wounded crew, colliding with the starboard rail as The Medusa fired her own cannons. Her eyes watched the Moranthese ship cut sharply. Her gaze followed the projected path, and she realized they would be in the perfect position to turn their cannons toward The Deceit.

A predatory grin spread across her face. "The Moranthese ship is turning!" she called to Cyril. "They're not firing at us. Focus everything on The Deceit. I want to be done with this bastard once and for all!" Alessandra stood, her impressive height giving her men a focal point. She raised her cutlass, signaling to the men at the cannons. "Fire!" she shouted, slashing her sword downwards through the air as she did.

"Fire!" Cyril relayed.

Alessandra's eyes swept toward the helm for signs of Lucia, but smoke obscured the upper deck. She flew up the stairs, her heart racing, stopping as she saw Lucia lying crumpled on the deck. Rafe stood above the queen, one hand and his body braced dangerously against the ship's wheel. He was pale, sweating with the strain. Blood seeped through his shirt as his wound reopened, and his eyes were wide as they met hers.

"No," Alessandra breathed, imagining the worst. Cannon fire boomed around her. She kept waiting for the impact as she rushed toward Lucia, but it never came.

"She's been hit!" Rafe called to her.

Alessandra choked back a sob of relief as she watched Lucia's body take a shuddering breath even as her eyes took in Lucia's injuries. Pulling Lucia's limp form against her, she turned back to Rafe. "You're hurt," she said, eying his bloody shirt. "Kier!"

she yelled at the young sailor as he rushed up the stairs. "Take the helm. Rafe's wounded."

She saw Kier's face blanche at Lucia's state, her white shirt torn, a dozen or more wood splinters embedded along her torso. *Gods, how deep are they?* He nodded at Alessandra, swallowed, and then took over as Rafe slid to the deck, clutching his weeping side.

"I'll live." Rafe nodded toward Lucia. "She breathing?"

Alessandra stroked the hair from Lucia's face—she was pale, a gash open on her forehead, but her heartbeat was strong; Alessandra felt it as she bent to examine her, pressing her ear to her chest. "Aye!" she called back. Resting her forehead against Lucia's, Alessandra whispered, "I'm not letting you on another bloody ship." She realized that was, of course, provided they survived the day.

"Captain," Cyril hailed as his head came into view. "The Moranthese ship is firing on The Deceit!" He pointed as cannonballs pummled the smoking hull of the other pirate ship.

Alessandra left Lucia to throw herself back into her duty. Striding to the rail, she watched The Deceit for any signs of a fight. None came. A cannonball looked to have destroyed the enemy's mast. The other ship was crippled, thanks in part to the Moranthese guns. Sailors were scrambling about the deck, tending to their wounded and putting out flames as a lone figure stood motionless, staring not at the Moranthese vessel but at her.

Alessandra heard Cyril's heavy steps draw near.

"Can we sail?" Alessandra asked without breaking her stare.

"Don't know, Captain."

Alessandra turned. The first mate gazed about the deck. Men were scattered, but it looked as though they were mostly hale, just a scrape here and there from what she could see.

"Aye," he answered, his eyes fixed on the unconscious queen at her feet. "We're shot to hell, but she'll float. Is she alive?"

Alessandra nodded, turning her gaze back to Lucia. "I want you to lower a dinghy. I'll surrender with the queen, secure our pardons, or not. Whatever happens, as soon as I'm off this ship, you take The Medusa, and you put in some place safe until you hear what's happened, one way or the other."

The man grabbed hold of her arm. "Lass, that's suicide! You know what'll happen to you if she doesn't wake. Or what they'll do to you until she does!"

"It's the only way. They'll hesitate to kill me once they know who I am, but you lot," she gestured to the crew. "You'll be dead by morning. They'll want to take their time with me. Make an example of an exiled lady. That gives you time to get clear."

"She's not worth it, Alessandra!"

She jerked away from him. "She's worth it to me!" The words came unbidden, the truth of them ringing in her ears.

Lucia is worth everything to me.

17

ALESSANDRA

Alessandra's arms were screaming as she exerted all her effort in bringing the dinghy alongside the Moran- these ship, choppy seas adding to the difficulty. Lucia lay heavy against her legs; she hadn't moved or made a sound since the accident. Alessandra feared she might never see those grey eyes she loved so dearly open again.

After the battle, everything seemed quiet as she rowed hard for the other ship, with only the dip of her oars and the whoosh of the sea against the hull. There were no more screams, no more cannonballs hurtling through the air. It was a moment of blissful calm she knew wouldn't last. She knew she could very well be taking herself to her doom.

As heads appeared over the rails to stare at her, she saw a lad call out, but she wasn't close enough to hear what he said over the ocean's churning. A man in a naval officer's garb strode from the upper deck. *Must be the captain.* She racked the oars and stood to call out, hoping her voice would carry, though she didn't think they'd shoot a woman on sight. "I have the queen aboard!" The boat was close enough to the larger vessel that she could pick out the dark hair escaping beneath the sailor's knit cap as the lad yelled something toward the figure she assumed was the captain.

The Golden Egret—the gilded letters loomed large in her vision. The Moranthese ship was a war galleon, larger but slower than The Medusa and nearly as old. It dwarfed her dinghy as Alessandra came abreast, being careful not to be crushed against the ship's hull. More faces had joined the sailor staring down at her.

"She's wounded," Alessandra yelled, hoping they could hear her this time. "I'll need help with her!" she said, turning toward Lucia's bleeding, limp figure once more. Her stomach knotted at the sight.

The captain jerked his chin toward her in answer, and two large men descended the rope ladder attached to the ship quick as they could while Alessandra secured the dinghy to the ship's side. The men gave her only a cursory glance as one gingerly hoisted Lucia over his shoulder, taking care to ensure the shards of wood were not jostled, while the other climbed up behind in case the first had a mishap.

Alessandra glanced back toward the sea, watching The Medusa sail clear of the burning Deceit, then on. There was no chance of an escape for her. She had to get aboard. Her arms were like lead weights as she climbed the swaying ladder, but she eventually made it to the top, where she found herself at the tip of a sword. The man at the other end glared at her.

"And just who might you be?" the man Alessandra took for the captain asked. He was younger than she would have expected, ordinary looking, with bright, intelligent eyes, lacking malice. For all that, his saber was a hairsbreadth from her throat.

Her eyes darted behind him to where Lucia lay, a man bent low over her. "That's the queen. That's Lucia, you have to help her!"

The Moranthese captain turned his head to take in the scene behind him. "I'm aware. The surgeon will do what he can. Now, I'll ask once more for your name."

Alessandra breathed in deep and drew herself up. She didn't think they'd kill her right off. She was the daughter of a famous pirate, if not famous yet herself, and she was also a disgraced Moranthese noble. Nonetheless, her heartbeat pounded in her ears. "I am Alessandra D'Allyon, Captain of The Medusa," she said succinctly.

Recognition lit the man's eyes. "Captain Ambros Tomas. Welcome aboard The Golden Egret." The man dipped his chin in greeting as he sheathed his sword. "You are hereby under arrest for the kidnapping of Queen Lucia. You will be held in the dungeon of Calan until those with higher authority than mine decide what to do with you."

It was as much as she could hope for—not to be killed straight away. Yet, when the sailors grasped her arms, instinct took over. She scuffled with the two men, the same who had brought Lucia aboard. Alessandra elbowed one, then kicked at a third as he approached, giving him, at the least, a bruised rib.

"Stop!" Captain Tomas' voice cut through the commotion, his sailors heeding his command at once. "There's no need for that, Captain," he said. "My men are under strict orders not to harm you."

They didn't look too happy about it. The one she'd kicked was holding his side, his fists clenched, while the grip of the other two tightened noticeably around her arms. Alessandra tried to still her thundering pulse. She hadn't meant to fight. What was important was Lucia. The queen's pale hair, loose and wild against the dark wood of the deck, gave her focus.

"Orders from who?" she asked, but it didn't matter. "I'm sorry." She shook her head. "Lucia? The queen? Will she live?" Alessandra rasped, needing to know how Lucia was.

The ship's surgeon was examining Lucia, his back to them, the maroon velvet of his coat, threadbare over his narrow shoulders. Captain Tomas cleared his throat in the surgeon's direction, and the man came forward, licking his thin lips, a bony finger pointing at Lucia. "The queen is obviously unconscious. The other wounds appear superficial. I can remove the wood and clean the wounds," the surgeon said. "With a head wound like this, though, it's impossible for me to know. She will either wake, or she won't." He looked as if he was going to be ill. No one wanted to be responsible for the queen's death. "Even if she does wake," the man continued, "there is always a chance she may have suffered permanent damage."

"Never one to mince words, are you?" Tomas frowned.

"No," was all the response the surgeon gave.

Of course, Alessandra knew the same, but upon hearing it, she, too, felt bile at the back of her throat. Catching Tomas watching her, she flared her nostrils and stood straighter. *Does he somehow know what Lucia is to me? Can he use that knowledge against me? Will his men? I can't show them how truly afraid I am.*

"Secure her down below," Captain Tomas ordered as rough hands bound Alessandra's wrists and feet in coarse rope, much the same as her men once secured Lucia aboard The Medusa. She didn't fight them this time, though her body was rigid with the effort. Her path lay with Lucia's, her fate bound with the queen's.

As she was hauled below, she heard the captain say, "We'll have to come around. If the captain of The Deceit is alive, he'll be a fine trophy!"

―――――

She thought she spent three days aboard The Golden Egret, kept in the hold. During that time, she was fed, given water, and, most importantly, updated on Lucia's state.

The bowels of The Golden Egret were every bit as mundane as those of The Medusa, with wood, rot, and rats. She was used to the sound of their claws clicking in the shadows as they scampered about, but aboard her own ship, where Alessandra was free, and the cats kept the rodents primarily in the hold—where she currently was. *What must Lucia have thought in those first hours on The Medusa? Was she this scared?*

A chamber pot had been left for her; her bonds loosened enough to allow her to take care of her bodily needs. A smoking oil lantern hung from a nail on the wall. There was barely anything else there in the near dark. Speed had clearly been necessary for The Egret's mission.

Hours later, Captain Tomas stood before her, solemn. "Still no change, I'm afraid," he said. "What happened out there?"

Alessandra laughed sardonically. "My crew kidnapped the queen. We were tasked with delivering her to

Vetreon. I've no idea on whose authority or what was planned for her once she reached the enemy's shore."

His eyes narrowed. "You consider Vetreon an enemy?"

Aren't you quick? Of course they're the enemy. They mean the woman I love harm. She tipped her chin and gritted her teeth. "I do now."

Tomas pulled a chair into view opposite Alessandra, adjusted his sword in its sheath, the metal clinking as he sat. "I was sent by someone who believes you no longer mean the queen any harm. Someone who thinks you may, in fact, be attempting to bring her home. Someone who thinks you love her."

Hope bloomed, but Alessandra was wary as her heart leaped to her throat. She had no reason to trust the man before her. But what trap could there be? He had told her the matter of her life or death was out of his hands.

"Your friend had a spy? A man named Ferran?" Alessandra asked. The spy had not spoken a word of his true intent back on The Medusa.

"I'm not at liberty to say."

She scoffed. "You weren't privy to that information, you mean."

Tomas smirked. "Just so. But I am someone he trusts. It would go better for you to tell me how we all came to be here." He raised an arm and swiveled his head. "Not much else to do."

"Very well," Alessandra relented. "My crew, *not me*, kidnapped the queen. I was incapacitated at the time. Doesn't reflect well on me, but it's the truth. I came to with a stolen queen aboard my ship. Aye, Vetreon was our initial destination because what else could we do? But, gods know why, the fates intervened." She continued to speak, telling him of Defoe's pursuit, of Lucia going overboard, the island, their rescue. Alessandra talked about their time together after that, leaving out the more scandalous details. Lucia's safety was her goal, and that had remained her truest desire.

Captain Tomas didn't interrupt her tale, but sat quietly as it unfolded. At the end, he leaned in close and simply asked, "And do you love her?"

Alessandra closed her eyes, willing her voice to be strong as she spoke the next words. "I do."

Tomas said nothing, just blinked and leaned back, then hit his knee and sprang to his feet as if she'd just said the sky was blue. "If there's truth in your story, then I wish you luck, Captain."

Tomas treated her with restrained indifference over the coming days. It seemed as though he might've just believed the story she told him during their one conversation aboard his ship. He did send a man to free her from her bindings, one of the large brutes from before.

"Come to get in another shot?" she spat as he dropped heavily from the last step.

The man's uniform barely fit, tight as it was across his massive shoulders and corded forearms. He laughed at her. "Captain says he wants you untied, so that's what I'm doing." She was shocked but pleased, nonetheless.

"Oh." She wasn't sure what to say as he ambled toward her.

While he worked at the knot securing her wrists, he said, "That was a fine piece of sailing you put on." His voice was gravelly as he spoke.

"Doesn't matter. The queen took a hit." The ropes fell from her hands. The tightness in her chest lessened at the small bit of freedom.

The sailor crouched, using his knife to get at the ropes around her feet. He smelled like onions. "Ah, you've been at sea longer than most, from what I've heard. You know as well as any, it's only luck that keeps a man safe in battle." Blood rushed back into her legs as the last constraint was pulled from her. "There we are." He gave her a smile as he stood.

Alessandra rubbed at the bruises encircling her wrists. "You're being quite friendly for a royal navy man."

"When the queen took the throne, I was pulled from the prison and given another chance."

"Conscription?"

"Better than the hangman's rope."

Alessandra felt her breath catch at the mention of her possible impending fate. "I suppose. Is that why the captain sent you down here?"

He shrugged. "This crew's not a bad bunch. But aye, safer for you, maybe. I don't hold such lofty ideals or contempt toward pirates as some of my compatriots. People got to eat. We do what we do, eh?"

"That we do," Alessandra said softly. If Lucia lived, maybe she wouldn't have to anymore. *Maybe it's the only thing I'm good at.* "What's your name, sailor?"

"Finch," he said, his blue eyes twinkling.

"Finch, thank you. Please let the captain know I appreciate the gesture."

He tipped his chin. "I will, Captain."

"And the queen?"

His demeanor changed, becoming sober. "Nothing."

Still alive, at the least. I have to stay the same.

Days later, Alessandra's fate remained unsettled, but her circumstances had greatly declined. She had not seen Tomas again until the day of her removal from the ship. Finch dropped back down into the hold, a look of unease on his blocky countenance.

Alessandra sniffed at the air. Even below deck, it had changed—the dead fish stink of a wharf. "We've arrived, haven't we?"

"We have."

"I heard the gulls this morning. At least, I think it was morning."

He didn't give her an answer. "Gotta put you back in chains, I'm afraid."

Another set of steps clamored down the stairs. Captain Tomas's plumed hat brushed the ceiling of her makeshift prison as Finch approached her like she was a skittish colt, arms out, manacles dangling.

"Please, Captain," Tomas said, "don't try anything foolish. It's for your own good."

Every fiber of her being told her to fight, but she knew it would be no use. As fast as she was, there was a whole crew and who knew how many soldiers between herself and freedom.

"Where is Royce Aldana?" she asked. If Lucia had been truthful about their friendship, perhaps he would believe her.

Tomas' brows flinched. "Why would you wish to speak to the Lord High Treasurer?"

"Because he's who sent you. Isn't he?" It was a gamble, but the only one she had.

Finch had stopped short as she spoke to his captain, but at a nod from Tomas, he moved closer.

"I give you my word that Lord Aldana will be notified as soon as possible."

She looked the man up and down. She'd been given bread and water during her brief captivity. No one had harmed her. She believed him. Against her nature, Alessandra held out her hands and allowed Finch to lock the cold iron around her muscled wrists.

She was seized as she reached the deck, a burlap sack thrown over her head. Her stomach twisted into a knot of fear of the unknown as her imagination took hold, conjuring hellish devices of torture awaiting her. Alessandra's last vision was one of a smirking soldier, but there was a momentary steady hand at her shoulder and Captain Tomas' voice against her ear, muffled through the fabric. "I've already sent a man for Lord Aldana. I'm sorry I can't do more." He gave her arm a squeeze, and then his presence was gone, replaced by rougher hands and unintelligible shouts, orders she tried her best to comply with.

It was a long and uncomfortable ride to her next destination. Her breath was loud beneath the covering, hot as her body was half-dragged over slick stone floors, down seemingly unending steps—old, uneven things which caused her to stumble more than once, her lip splitting as no one cared to break her fall. She was unceremoniously shackled to the wall, and her hood was finally removed. There was a scuffle outside her cell door; a body slammed hard against it.

"That's enough, you bastard!" A man's voice shouted, then the commotion moved on.

"Welcome home, bitch." The soldier sneered but was thankfully gone without further incident.

The dungeon beneath what Alessandra presumed was the Palace of Moranth was dark. Sooty air mixed with the reek of mold. The walls, slick with the stuff, were illuminated by smoking torches that wouldn't last long. She would be alone in the dark. She preferred the hull of The Golden Egret. *Shit.*

Alessandra looked up as two figures appeared at the door. An old man, leaning heavily on a staff, with a tall woman in leathers beside him. *Could this be Lord Valeri, of whom Lucia had spoken?*

"Alessandra D'Allyon," his voice was stronger than his failing body, "you are under arrest for the charge of piracy, kidnapping, and treason."

"It still counts as treason if I was exiled?"

The tall woman's mouth quirked, but she stayed silent.

"I am Lord Valeri, the queen's chief counselor. While she is incapacitated, it falls to me to protect the realm."

Alessandra's eyes narrowed. *Is he attempting to overthrow the crown? Fuck, I hate politics.* "I thought that duty fell to the queen's heir, Sebastian Riffa." She hoped the answer signaled both her loyalty and her deeper knowledge of Lucia. Sebastian was not officially her heir.

"Lord Riffa is of no concern to you. Your only concern should be keeping your head on your shoulders."

"I'm to be given a noble's death?" she asked, genuinely intrigued. With a good executioner, a beheading would be the quickest way to go—one reserved for the higher strata of criminals.

Valeri shook his head. "You're not making this easier on yourself."

"Why should I?"

"Because, according to Captain Tomas, you're in love with our queen. Yet, you sit here throwing barbs like you welcome death. Which is it?"

Her teeth ground together. "What I say doesn't matter, does it? Lucia will live, and so will I, or she will die, and so will I."

"You seem certain the queen means you no ill will."

"If you're going to torture me, get on with it. Otherwise, leave me be."

Alessandra was unsure how long she had been there—could have been two days or two weeks—until there was another voice. It wasn't a calming, reassuring voice, but a loud, obnoxious one, cursing in a foreign language.

"Will you shut up!" Alessandra screamed into the near darkness, the effort causing the split in her lip to open back up. It wasn't as if she could sleep anyway, but the man's incessant caterwauling was going to cause her to go insane before she could be hanged.

"I will not shut up!" came a man's heavily accented voice. "I am Defoe! I will do as I please!"

Alessandra nearly lost it. She couldn't stop laughing, despite the pain shooting through her ribs from another unfortunate landing. She was locked in prison, awaiting her death, next to the man who had tried, and nearly succeeded, killing her not once but twice. She wondered who this Ambros Tomas was that luck so favored him to have captured the captains of two of the most infamous ships on the seas.

The captain of The Deceit seemed shocked that anyone would have the nerve to laugh at him as he unleashed a torrent of invectives her way, this time in her tongue, before asking, "Who dares such an affront as to laugh at me?"

"Captain D'Allyon, at your service," she called through the dungeon bars. *That* made him shut up.

"But you're a woman!" he said, sounding confused.

"That's true. Well done."

"But Pascal D'Allyon?"

Alessandra shook her head. "My father is dead."

"I'm sorry for your loss."

Alessandra was shocked at the genuineness of the words. "Forgive me, Captain," she said, "but you've tried to sink me twice now, countless times while my father lived, yet you sound as if you truly are saddened by my father's death?"

"Your father was a fine opponent. Although—Was it you commanding in our last two meetings?"

"You seem surprised."

"I am. You sound young, but I should expect nothing less, I suppose, from the daughter of such an accomplished sailor. My compliments to you."

"You don't sound much older." Alessandra blushed, glad Defoe couldn't see her. The captain spoke like he sailed, full of swagger and cunning.

He laughed. "You're not the only one raised by pirates."

That caught her attention. He didn't sound Moranthese or Treathean. "My compliments to you as well," she said. *We'll most likely be hanged together, may as well be pleasant.* "Where are you from?"

"Never had a home but the sea. Thank my mother for that. She captained Vengeance."

Alessandra couldn't believe it. The noblewoman turned pirate had been her girlhood hero. "Your mother was Lizzie Grey?"

"Is. I suppose it's safe enough to tell you she lives."

"The Grey Lady." Alessandra spoke the nickname with reverence. She wondered how Defoe came by his name and just where the legendary pirate was.

"You two," a guard's voice cut in. "No more talking!"

Tomas must have purposefully kept them apart on his ship, as she'd been uncertain of the other captain's fate. She would have to get more out of Defoe for no other reason but that she was curious.

Defoe spoke again in defiance of the guard. "You know, you owe me for not a few of my best men from that little squabble on Silver Cove." He didn't sound overly bereft at the loss.

"And you for your two attacks."

Torches passed before her door, their light shining through the small, barred opening. The butt of something heavy banged at her door.

"I told you both to be quiet!"

"A draw then?" Defoe proposed, and Alessandra knew he was speaking to her, not the guard.

"Don't suppose it matters now," she answered, expecting yet more shouting from her captor.

"Have faith, my lady. I do not plan on dying so soon. Nor should you, I think."

Alessandra squeezed her eyes shut, nodding to herself in resignation. There was nowhere to go and nothing she could do if they meant to kill her. Her wrists and ankles were shackled. Her fate rested in Lucia's hands.

No one came, and Defoe stayed silent.

She wasn't sleeping exactly, more flitting in and out of an exhausted, anxious consciousness when she heard metal clinking as keys jangled into the door of her cell. She was weak and shaky, but as her chains were long enough for her to stand, she was determined to meet her fate on her feet for as long as she could.

For the most part, she'd been left to herself after that first brief altercation with the guards, if being somewhat thrown down stairs and banged against walls could be called as such. She was given water but no food. She was almost grateful for the neglect. *Captain Tomas was a fine jailor in comparison. He even had the decency to look sorry when he handed me off to the royal guard.*

Her cell door creaked open, and she prepared to give her captors what fight she had left. If she were to be killed, she would not go quietly. As her eyes adjusted to the brighter light from additional torches, she noted the man who entered her cell was clearly a noble, well dressed and clean-shaven, with a head full of becoming salt and pepper hair. He turned to his two escorts, guards by the look of them. "Leave the torches. Wait for me outside," he commanded, dismissing them with a nod.

Someone with power.

"Who are you?" Alessandra rasped, shocked by the sound of her voice echoing in the empty chamber.

"My name is Royce Aldana."

Tomas kept his word. If anyone could help her, he could. "Lord High Treasurer. *Lord* Aldana, then."

He gave her a grin full of white teeth. She was unsure whether she liked the man or thought him far too handsome to be trusted.

"Just so. And you, I believe, are Lady Alessandra D'Ayllon."

She smirked. "Haven't been that since I was knee high. I believe you mean Captain Alessandra D'Ayllon."

"If the queen pardons you, as you say she wanted to, then that's precisely who you are, my lady."

Alessandra turned the man's words over in her mind. *Wanted?* She sank back to the damp, cold floor. Her voice nearly broke as she asked, "Is she dead, then?"

Lucia's condition had been foremost on her mind. Alessandra knew that she had not recovered, else Lucia would have seen to her release already. She believed that with her whole soul. But the guards would not speak to her except to tell her to be quiet, and Defoe knew no more than she. Alessandra was wracked with guilt over the whole affair as she lay rotting in the dungeon.

She should never have crossed paths with Lucia. The queen should be nothing to her—moreover, she should be nothing to Lucia. Alessandra cursed at herself—she had brought nothing but harm to her lover. *That's not true*, a little voice within whispered. *Doesn't matter now.*

"No. Still unconscious. Most of the council are calling for your head. I'm trying to convince them that, at the least, we keep you here, tucked safely in a cell until the queen wakes or dies." Royce's voice carried the worry of one who cared for and loved Lucia.

Jealousy sparked within Alessandra at the thought of Lucia in the lord's arms, despite assurances that had never been the case. Her eyes narrowed. "What are you to her?"

Royce stepped closer. "What are *you* to her?" he asked, his voice not unkind.

What am I to her? "Someone who cares," she answered.

Royce took a beat, then nodded. "As am I. I'm sorry I can't do more for you. I believe you. I don't know what Captain Tomas told you aboard The Golden Egret, but I sent him. He was meant to be an escort. I understand your ship ran into some trouble at the exact wrong moment. That's how Lu—Her Majesty came by her injuries?"

Alessandra swallowed the lump in her throat. Lucia trusted the man before her. "It is. I tried to protect her through everything, but it wasn't enough."

Royce sank, resting on his heels, eye-level with her. "Ambros mentioned something about an island."

"We were marooned."

"And your crew came back for you. That certainly speaks well to your nature, Captain. I'll do what I can to keep you alive. And if you are who you say you are, then welcome home."

"Not the homecoming I was imagining."

"Mmm."

"If you believe me, then can't you get me out of here? The guards ..." She jerked her chin, fighting the fearful tears threatening.

"I'm sorry for that, truly. I was attending to matters outside the city. I came back as soon as I could."

"But you can't help me?"

"The guards won't bother you anymore. You have my word, for what that's worth to you. I'll see you're given decent food, but any more than that and the council will think I'm in on it with Ramir. Trust me. It took every diplomatic bone in my body to keep Lord Valeri from putting you on the rack."

A shiver ran down her spine at the mention of the torture device. "The captain told you that, too? That it was Ramir?"

Royce rubbed at his dark stubble. "He did. Of course, the Vetreon court denies any involvement. We've set up an embargo, which has rattled the young king, but until the queen is hale, there is nothing and no one to corroborate your story."

"And if she dies, then so do I." It wasn't a question. Alessandra fully expected to be hanged for piracy and the murder of the queen should anything happen to Lucia.

Dropping his head for a moment, Royce slapped his knees and stood, much as Captain Tomas had, groaning as he did so. "And there would be nothing I could do to prevent it, Captain."

He called to the guards, "Open the cell."

"Wait," she said. "How long have I been here?"

That brought a faint smile to his handsome face. "Only two days, my lady. Sorry, Captain"

Only two days. Alessandra moaned, truly feeling the effects of her captivity. She wasn't made for such confinement, and after a life on the sea, it seemed especially brutal to be locked underground without even the hint of daylight, fresh air, or the sounds of the waves.

"You know," Aldana said as the guards opened the door for him, "my family was exiled too, but I was kept at court, insurance against my father making any further trouble. I'd almost say you were the lucky one. That your father was able to get you out, I mean. Not all the children taken as hostages survived."

She grunted an acknowledgement. "I heard something about that. My mother didn't survive either."

"I know. I'm sorry."

ROYCE

He slowly took the dungeon stairs back to the surface of the palace. *Alessandra D'Allyon. Beautiful woman, well-spoken. Interesting accent, though that's to be expected given her background. Clearly in love with Lucia.*

Sebastian had begged to come with him, fascinated as he was by pirates, but Royce refused, leaving him under Ylva's watchful eye. He'd first wanted to take the measure of the rogue lady himself. Should his friend survive, then perhaps Lucia had found her match. *If she survives.* The court of Moranth boasted fine physicians—Lucia was in good hands—but as they had told Royce, there was only so much they could do in the situation. The splinters from The Medusa were removed, the wounds cleaned, no stitching required—none had pierced deeply enough. But she remained unconscious.

His body sagged with exhaustion and preemptive grief as his foot landed heavily on the top step. *What will I do if Lucia doesn't live?* In practicality, there was much for him to do, namely, seeing that Sebastian was safe and made good decisions as he sat the throne—but it would be with a heavy heart. Lucia was so much more than his queen. She was still his dearest friend for all that they had not been so close in the last few years.

Ylva was waiting for him at the top of the stairs. "How did you find the prisoner?" The assassin-turned-bodyguard had barely left Sebastian's presence since she'd brought the heir to the throne back to the capital weeks ago.

"Where's Bastian?" he asked as Ylva fell into step beside him.

"With the queen. He swears he saw her finger twitch and sent me to find you. Poor lad," the woman said, shaking her head.

Royce's eyes narrowed, head jerking back in surprise.

"What?" she asked.

He chuckled, continuing to set a brisk pace. "It's just that I don't think I've ever heard you use that tone before. Was that empathy?" he teased.

Ylva stopped, putting her imposing physique squarely in his path. "You're lucky you pay so well, my lord," her face was stony as she paused, then her eyes sparked with mirth, and her lips split into a wide grin, "and that I'm fond of you."

Royce returned the smile—his heart had faltered for half a second as he wondered if he'd finally gone too far. "And that I'm married to your favorite cousin."

"That helps," Ylva replied.

They continued down a long hallway and climbed the set of stairs that took them to the royal suites.

Sebastian jumped up from his seat at Lucia's side as soon as Royce entered her bedchamber. "Did you tell him, Ylva?" the young lord asked.

Royce gave him a tight smile. "She did. Saw the queen's finger move, eh?"

"I know I did. See," he shouted, pointing, "she's waking up."

Lucia shifted beneath the heavy blankets, her brow furrowing, as a groan emanated from her pale figure before going still once more. Her eyes remained closed.

The heir looked crestfallen. "I thought—"

Royce put an arm around Sebastian's shoulder. He, too, had been hopeful as it was the most response they'd gotten from Lucia since her arrival. "So did I. We just have to wait."

Sebastian shook him off. "I'm tired of waiting. She has to wake up."

Royce nodded. He couldn't imagine what the lad was going through. Lucia was the only mother he'd known. More than that, should she die, the whole of her realm passed to him, a boy still years from becoming a man —no matter how level-headed and quick he was.

———

Royce could barely keep his eyes open as he sat with Uridice and Ylva in the brothel owner's private chambers. He had stayed up most of the night at Lucia's bedside, with Sebastian in a chair next to him.

"What if she doesn't wake up?" Ylva's voice startled him from his stupor.

"Treason to even speak such a thing." Uridice shook her head. She, too, looked worn, Royce noted as the trio sat before a roaring fire. It was where they always met—a place where no one would question them being.

"She's right, though," he said. "Sebastian doesn't want to believe the worst, of course, but it's been nearly three days."

Uridice turned her golden head. "I won't believe it either."

"Being morose won't help the situation. Why are we here?" Ylva questioned.

"I'm not being morose," Uridice countered. "You're the one who brought up the queen's death."

"I'm being practical," Ylva said. "There's a difference. She never made Bastian's position official. Honestly, he's lucky there hasn't been more palace intrigue around the matter."

"Agreed." Royce nodded. "Valeri and the rest of the council have been nothing but supportive. Things could have gone another way entirely."

"Everyone sees what a good lad he is. They aren't hesitant of him as they are of Lucia, either," Ylva said.

Royce nodded. He knew Lucia and he thought, most of what was in her heart, but she could be so guarded with others, and for good reason. Still, her nature and the ghost of her father's memory, were enough for many to be cautious around their monarch.

Uridice seemed to flick tears from her eye as she cleared her throat and regained her composure. "I called you here because your efforts in Vetreon have come to fruition. The countess is ready to meet. Will you be able to convince Sebastian?"

Royce took a large gulp of his wine, then winced. "Ylva tells me Mercedes is every bit as lovely as her mother, and as smart. He's going to be king, perhaps sooner than any of us would wish, but it will happen, and he will need a queen."

"Lucia would never want to force him," Uridice commented, despite being a chief player in the arrangement.

Royce had to agree. "No, but she understood duty more than anyone, and she instilled that same sense in Bastian."

"*Understands*," Uridice corrected.

Royce bent his head. His queen was, indeed, still very much alive. "Understands."

18

LUCIA

Lucia was sure she was dreaming as an overwhelming stench of decaying flowers enveloped her, and a trill of music floated in the heavy air. Everything was too close, too warm; she was drowning in softness.

"Your Majesty?" came a woman's startled voice.

Lucia groaned a response. Her throat was raw with the effort. It was as if she hadn't spoken in some time. She coughed to clear it and felt hands beneath her, helping her sit up. When she opened her eyes, the brightness of her bedchamber nearly blinded her. One of her maids was beside her, holding her in a sitting position as if she were a child, while another poured a glass of water, handing it to the first.

"Send for Lords Valeri and Aldana now!" the maid sitting with her barked at the other, who quickly scurried off.

Lucia wanted to drink deeply, but could only choke down a few sips of the cool liquid before coughing again.

The maid's eyes were round with worry as she stared down at her. "Can you speak, Your Majesty?"

Lucia coughed again, almost scared to try by the look the other woman was giving her. *Why shouldn't I be able to?* "Alessandra?"

"No, it's Charlotte, Your Majesty."

Lucia shook her head in consternation. *Where is Alessandra?*

Her chamber doors opened, and a concerned-looking Royce entered, followed by the ambling Lord Valeri.

"Thank God, Your Majesty," Royce said, bowing deeply before her, as did Valeri.

"Royce," Lucia rasped, "the pirate, the captain—"

Royce shot Valeri a look, which Lucia caught. "Alessandra?" Royce clarified. She nodded. "She's in the dungeon, Your Majesty."

"What?" Her eyes widened in panic as she tried to hurry from the bed, her weakened limbs tangling in the covers. Royce caught her, steadying her. Lucia's maids rushed to wrap her in a robe and give her their support as she worked to find her feet. *I have to get to Alessandra and make sure she is safe.*

"She's alright, Your Majesty," Royce said.

Calming a bit after Royce's assurance, she asked, "How long have I been unconscious?"

Royce was her friend; he knew her well. She hoped he would have, if not taken Alessandra at her word, at least protected her as much as possible until the truth could come to light.

"Nearly a week. You took quite a knock to the head, but it seems you'll survive." A slight smile flickered across his features.

Her mind went to the other important person in her life. "Sebastian?"

"Ylva had him safely here the morning of your kidnapping. You'll be proud of him. I barely had to lift a finger to keep this place running. Of course, he's been worried sick about you. He has hardly left your side. I'll wager our young lord will be annoyed he wasn't here when you woke."

She motioned to a guard. His face showed his shock at being acknowledged, but he lowered his spear and approached. "Your Majesty?"

"Please find Lord Riffa." She always found it strange to speak of Sebastian so formally. "Let him know I've woken and am fine."

"Are you?" Royce asked.

She arched her brow. "I'm alive. That will do for now."

The guard bowed and backed away before hurrying from the royal bedchamber.

"He's missed you terribly. We both have."

Valeri cut in. "All of us have, Your Majesty. You will be quite proud of how Sebastian has shouldered his duties." Lucia's heart did indeed swell with pride. "He's proven himself a very capable young man."

"I never doubted he would, though it did help to know the both of you were here with him. Now, I'm going to free Lady D'Allyon from my dungeon. I can't believe you put her in there."

Valeri seemed a tad shocked—at which part of her statement Lucia was unsure. *I don't care, either.*

Servants and courtiers scattered as she flung open the doors of her chamber. She ached and was weak, but terror and fury propelled Lucia through the palace halls and into the lower levels. Valeri gave up following, but Royce did his best to support her as she became winded. She tried to stem her panic in front of her courtiers, but as she leaned on Royce, her feet slipping on the treacherous stairs, the fear of what she might find rose like bile at the back of her throat. *Does she think I've betrayed her? Is she hurt?*

"Captains Defoe and D'Allyon are currently the only two prisoners," Royce explained.

"Fucking Defoe," she cursed. The man had nearly killed her, twice.

Flanked by guards, Lucia and Royce made their way down the little-used steps to the castle's lower levels. In her father's reign, the dungeons were always filled with whoever displeased him, but since she took the throne, they remained mostly empty.

"Where are their crews?" she asked.

"From what I understand, The Medusa got away clean. The Deceit is sunk, with only a handful of the crew remaining. They were sent to the city jail."

The Medusa is safe. My friends are safe.

Lucia pulled her inappropriate dressing gown around her. It was cold beneath the palace, in the depths of the dark earth.

"I wish you would have let me get a cloak for you," Royce scolded.

She was in no mood. She paused briefly to turn on him. "I know you didn't have a choice, but I swear, if anything has happened to her, *you* will answer for it."

"I did what I could for her."

She choked back a sob, catching it just in time. *I have to get to Alessandra. When she's in my arms, everything will be fine. I just have to get to her.*

The silence of the place sent a chill down Lucia's spine. She put her eye to the small opening in

Alessandra's door. No one was moving beyond the bars. *Is she alive? How can anyone survive down here?* She held her breath as the key to Alessandra's cell turned, the lock clinking, and the door swung open.

The torchlight illuminated Alessandra's sallow face.

"Gods!" Lucia rushed forward and dropped to Alessandra's side. "Get her out of these immediately!" she shouted at the guards.

A few days of unconsciousness wasn't much—her throat was scratchy, her limbs a bit heavy as if she were still waking—but three days in a dungeon had not been so kind to Alessandra. Her red hair hung in limp tangles over her shoulders. She was pale, the healthy sun-kissed glow she normally possessed overtaken by a bloodless pallor.

Alessandra squinted against the brightness of the fire as she was released, slumping forward into Lucia's waiting arms with a grunt. "Think I like it better when you're the one in cuffs," she quipped, her voice hoarse with exhaustion, wincing in obvious pain as Lucia wrapped her in her arms.

Lucia's mind raced. *She's alive! She's all right, she's alive, and we'll be fine. Everything will be all right now.*

Lucia snickered but didn't rise to the bait, worried as she still was. Her fingers traced the dried blood crusted over Alessandra's lip, her eyes briefly meeting

Royce's—they'd be having a serious conversation soon.

"I've got you," Lucia whispered against her, not caring that Alessandra was filthy and that her fine silk robe would have to be burned. "I've got you, my love." As weak as she was, Lucia could barely shoulder the other woman's weight. Royce must've noticed this and quickly stepped in to help.

"Good to see you again, Lord Aldana," Alessandra said as the nobleman offered his arm.

Royce had the grace to smile and bow. "And you, Lady —I mean—Captain D'Allyon. Your Majesty, myself or one of the guards are more than willing to help the captain. You are only just recovered."

Lucia glared at her old friend while Alessandra attempted to shake them both off. "Or I can make it myself. Honestly, Lu—Your Majesty."

"You're not touching her," Lucia snapped at Royce. "And neither are the guards."

"It's alright," Alessandra said.

It doesn't matter. We're alive, together, and safe. Lucia said nothing more as they climbed back up into the light, with Royce and a guard only a step behind.

ALESSANDRA

She could barely stand, and leaned heavily on Lucia as they made their way from the depths of the palace. Her pace was slow, shambling as her legs and feet began to work after days in her cramped confines. She offered Lucia an apologetic smile. "I'm sorry I'm moving so slowly. Everything hurts."

Lucia gave her arm a squeeze. "I'm sorry I can't be topside in a battle without nearly getting my head taken off."

Alessandra felt the knot in her stomach tighten at the memory of Lucia pale and limp on the deck of The Medusa. "I promised myself I wouldn't let you back on a ship."

"We'll see how long that lasts." Lucia smirked, then grunted, shifting Alessandra's weight.

They climbed the last flight of stairs in awkward silence as Royce and the guard hovered behind them. She'd have to let Lucia know Royce had done what he could for her. She wasn't angry at the man, honestly. She even understood the guards' initial treatment. After all, her crew had kidnapped their queen with the intention of handing her over to Moranth's rival. Alessandra would have probably done worse if she were in their position. As they reached the royal suite, Alessandra saw Lucia give the lord and guard a dismissive flick, which they heeded without a word.

The opulence of Lucia's chambers when they entered was a shock. Her childhood manors had been ancient but not kept in the best repair, nor were they very grand. Their ceilings had been low, darkened by centuries of soot—the fortress homes of country lords. The palace, Alessandra remembered from childhood, was mostly of newer construction, rebuilt after the ancient hilltop castle burned some hundred years ago.

It had sweeping white walls, rounded arches, and gardens full of fragrant flowers. The beauty of it was in its simplicity. Lucia's room carried that same measure of graceful roundness, soaring ceilings, and light-filled airiness, with an added lushness befitting the woman who lived there. Gold and blue glass tiles sparkled across the entirety of the ceiling in a glittering mosaic, and drapery of a muted blue, faded with the sun, framed a balcony that looked out over the city below.

The large bed in the middle of the room was nearly buried beneath velvet bedding and piled high with pillows. There was a fireplace big enough to stand in, with a desk pulled dangerously close—plumed pens and bottles of ink sat jumbled in no particular order across it.

Lucia's maids gaped at her. *Well, at least I've supplied the court with gossip for the next decade, and I haven't even opened my mouth yet.*

"Help me with her," Lucia ordered.

The two women bobbed, muttering, "Your Majesty," before reaching for Alessandra. Lucia relinquished her with a groan as she twisted her back.

Alessandra was already feeling her strength returning as the blood flowed back into her limbs, but she wasn't going to say no to some help. "You should have let Aldana take me." Lucia tsked and tossed her head, arms crossing over her chest. Alessandra noted the dark stain at the hem of the gold silk of Lucia's robe. "Your gown and your slippers are ruined. And there's no reason to be angry at him. He gave me hope."

Lucia's brow raised, but her posture softened, her shoulders dropping an inch. "I don't care about the gown." Her eyes flicked to her servants, still awkwardly shouldering Alessandra.

"Draw a bath for her." The two women didn't move. "Put Lady D'Allyon on the chair, there." Lucia pointed at what Alessandra was sure was some priceless chair of ornate Treathean design, the back carved into the shape of a stag's head.

Again, there was hesitation on the part of the maids, but Alessandra wagered they wouldn't dare question Lucia. She was sat down in the wide, throne-like seat. The women hurried off, only for one to return a moment later, wringing her hands, eyes downcast. *The poor thing looks like she's about to pass out. Is Lucia so different here?*

"Your Majesty? Might it be permissible for the lady to be washed before going into the royal bath?"

Lucia, who had been in the middle of pouring two glasses of wine, looked up. "What?" Her attention moved from the maid to Alessandra and back, catching the woman's meaning. "Ah, yes." She looked back at Alessandra. "Sorry, love."

Grimacing as cold water sluiced over her body, Alessandra said nothing but allowed the women to scrub the worst of the filth of the dungeon from her as she stood shivering in a washbasin in the middle of the bedchamber. The water ran nearly black. *If this is what I am like after only a few days in that squalid place, what must have become of others left there to rot?* She was thankful her mother's and grandfather's deaths had been swift.

Once a proper bath was drawn, Lucia dismissed her servants. "Thank you, but I'll see to Lady D'Allyon." She had changed into a new robe, a soft greyish blue to match her eyes.

The doors shut silently behind them as Alessandra smiled through chattering teeth. "Was that payback for Silver Cove?"

"No. My bath is my sacred space, and you were not about to get in it covered in whatever that was."

Lucia's eyes lit with mischievousness as she held out a hand. "Come on."

The bath chamber was warm, the air heavy and steam filled as they entered. A mosaic of hyacinths and the pink blossoms of the almond tree covered the floor. Alessandra's body was racked with chills and exhaustion as Lucia helped her lower her body into the near-scalding, milky water.

"There, how's that?" Lucia asked.

Alessandra smiled. "Delivering on your promise of a proper bath, I see." She sniffed the air. It was a light scent. There were notes of sandalwood and cognac, perhaps even rum. It smelled just right. "Perfume and all."

"I did tell you it was the first thing we were doing when we made it to the capital." Lucia's lips brushed over her bruised knuckles, her thumb skimming the dark purple framing one golden eye.

"Don't." Alessandra caught Lucia's hand in hers, holding it tight, wishing to hold the rest of her. *That moment will come soon.*

Lucia let Alessandra keep her hand in her grip, but her voice was still tinged with rage. "I should kill them for harming you."

Alessandra shook her head. "No. They didn't know. They thought I kidnapped their queen, and they were right. I'm safe now. We're together. Let that be enough," she said.

"Royce promised me you weren't hurt. He told me he saw to your safety," Lucia spoke through gritted teeth. "I'll flog him for lying to me."

"He did. All this," Alessandra said, indicating the scrapes and bruises, the black eye, and the cut lip, "happened before. No one touched me after he came to see me. They even brought a bowl of gruel, though I admit to not being able to keep it down."

There were tears in Lucia's eyes. "They didn't—no one. God," she said, blinking back the tears.

Alessandra took her meaning. Her captives had roughed her up a bit, but no worse than she'd been in the numerous tavern fights of her life. "No! No!" She shook her head, pressing kisses to Lucia's palms.

"I almost lost you! I don't know what I would have done if I'd woken to find you hanged."

"It didn't happen."

"But it almost did. Why would you risk yourself like that?"

Alessandra sighed. *After all this, does she still doubt my love for her?* "Don't you know why?" She searched Lucia's face. *You are my life.* "A lot of things have almost happened. They don't matter."

Lucia looked as though she were about to say something, then changed her mind. Her shoulders relaxed for a second before they tensed once more. "Royce came back while you were being scrubbed. Vetreon's navy has been spotted skirting our territory. There will be war now."

Alessandra was almost grateful for the topic change. She had promised herself she'd tell Lucia she loved her if they were ever reunited, but when the time came, she hesitated. *Hasn't my time in the dungeons proven we cannot be together?*

"There was always going to be a war. You said that."

"I did," Lucia said heavily. "The waste of lives for one man's ego makes me ill. War was never something I wanted. It's not Ramir's subject's fault he's a prick."

Alessandra placed her hand on top of Lucia's. "We'll fight him together."

"Ramir has a finer navy than mine."

"Do you know where my crew is? The Medusa? Are they safe?"

"I've already sent a ship after them with word of your pardon and their actual pardons themselves. I didn't want them to think it was a trap."

Alessandra chuckled. "They will. If I had to guess, Cyril won't have gone too far. He'll lie low close enough that word of my death or life will reach them. We'll need them if we mean to make an actual fight of it." The Medusa was a grand battleship with an expert crew, but they'd need more than one to win a war. *Defoe?*

Lucia groaned. "I can see those wheels turning." She took Alessandra's chin between her fingers, holding her attention. "Can we take one night for ourselves? Before the world goes to pieces again. I shouldn't have even brought it up tonight. You need your rest."

"So do you, I imagine."

Lucia smiled wickedly as she took a sponge. Dipping it in the warm water, she ran it up one of Alessandra's legs until her head tipped back. Alessandra bit into her bottom lip, wincing at the pleasure and pain as her thighs parted under Lucia's guidance.

"I love you," Alessandra breathed into the steamy air, her voice almost a whisper. She hadn't meant to say it so casually. She waited, breath held, chest tight, for Lucia's response.

Lucia's gray eyes softened as she bent her head, her lips pressing a tender kiss to Alessandra's. "I love you too."

She loves me.

Alessandra's near purrs vibrated in her throat as Lucia's tongue licked a slow trail along her slender neck while stroking swirls up her lean torso with the sponge. Steaming water ran in rivulets over her as Lucia's ministrations made her squirm and moan.

"That feels heavenly," she said as Lucia lay the sponge aside and plucked at an erect nipple.

"Not too heavenly, I hope." Her teeth skimmed an ear. "I wouldn't want you thinking this is the fulfillment of this night's pleasures."

Alessandra smirked. Tired as she was, Lucia's lips and fingers were playing her body with expert precision, arousing her just enough to keep her on the edge of an orgasm. She thrust her breast forward, fully into the queen's grasp, sighing as she heard a pleased laugh.

"I love it when I can get you to make that sound," Lucia acknowledged.

Water splashed outside the tub as Alessandra began to writhe in wild ecstasy. Any fight she usually had, the resistance of her imagined submission to pleasure, had been stripped away by the fear of death and bone-deep exhaustion. That, combined with her lover's dexterous virtuosity, made for a shortened sexual experience.

"I—I can't hold on," she breathed.

Lucia's words were stilted. "Don't, love. I want you to come for me. I want to please you."

Their eyes locked as Alessandra cried out, breaking around Lucia's fingers, the echoes of Lucia's orgasm ringing in her ears.

Alessandra felt Lucia kiss her matted, damp hair as she rested her head against the queen's rising chest, her heartbeat beginning to slow. Tilting her head, Alessandra looked up at the lazy smile spreading over Lucia's features. "You're going to have to get someone in here to help get me out. I don't think I can walk."

Lucia laughed. "I don't think I can either."

With the excitement of the day drained from them both, they lay like that for a time. Lucia on the cold stone floor. Alessandra in the cooling bath. Neither was eager to let go.

Epilogue

Alessandra awoke tangled amongst silk sheets, the aroma of coffee and warm bread in the air; it was a heavenly perfume. Lucia appeared before her, a heavy velvet robe tied around her, her hair loose, her eyes bright. Alessandra stretched, her joints popping with misuse, then sighed. Her arms circled Lucia as she mounted the bed to lay with her.

"Mmm," she nuzzled Lucia, "is this what you smell like clean?" Orange blossom and rose, with a smokiness beneath.

"Like it?" Lucia asked, her hands moving over Alessandra's breasts and rib cage, coming to rest at the indentation of hip and waist.

"I like it very much, indeed." Alessandra nipped at Lucia's throat, her hands grasping the queen's rear. "Too much," she said, giving Lucia a swat across her backside.

Lucia moaned, then pulled away, rolling up onto her heels. "Too much?"

Groaning while rolling her eyes, Alessandra said, "We don't have time for this, and you know it."

"I know this is what I've wanted all my life," Lucia rasped.

"To have a pirate in your bed?"

Lucia smiled, nestling into Alessandra's open arms. "To have someone I love and trust."

She swallowed the lump in her throat. "There's a war to plan for."

"A war that may be won or lost. It won't hinge on the next fifteen minutes."

THE END

About the Author

Riley West is an emerging author of women-loving-women romance. This is her second book.

facebook.com/RileyWestWriter
amazon.com/author/rileywestbooks
tiktok.com/@rileywestbooks

Also by Riley West

Love On The Westside

A WLW Age-Gap romance set in the fast-paced world of Contemporary Art.

Printed in Great Britain
by Amazon